BETRAYED

Stone turned his hand and gripped her fingers, his eyes solemn as he looked at Coady. "I'm not entirely who you think I am, lass. Actually, I've omitted to tell you because duty would not permit."

She furrowed her brows with curiosity. "Duty?"

"Duty. I am a member of the police."

"The police? A Mountie?"

He nodded his head. "I could not tell you because I was brought here under special assignment. But I will be going back. I wanted to talk with you before you saw me in uniform."

"Special assignment?" she whispered anxiously.

"I had to explain that when I ordered the investigation, it was a matter of duty, an automatic reflex, if you will. I had no thought—"

Coady pulled her hand from his, her fingers icy. "You? You ordered an investigation of ⋯

"I . . ."

Coady was on her feet, ⋯ he rose as well, standing a head ⋯ out," she whispered. "Get out ⋯

Marriage By Design

Jill Metcalf

LEISURE BOOKS NEW YORK CITY

A LEISURE BOOK®

July 1999

Published by

Dorchester Publishing Co., Inc.
276 Fifth Avenue
New York, NY 10001

ISBN 0-8439-4553-2

DEDICATED TO

AUDREY STANCIL

Because you sent me that first warm, wonderful letter,
I have gained a much-valued friend.

This one is for you, Audrey.

With Love,
Jill

Marriage By Design

Chapter One

"Your price is too high, little lady."

Coady Blake shrugged slender shoulders as her seemingly innocent brown eyes stared up at the grizzled man. "You could always go elsewhere."

The man's weathered complexion, bronzed by hours of working under a broiling sun, darkened to a deeper hue. "There is no 'elsewhere' and you know it!"

"That's true."

Her pink lips tilted upward but that sweet smile and those soft, doe-like brown eyes didn't fool him. Men up and down the Yukon and Klondike rivers, and all the gold creeks that took life from those larger bodies of water, talked about this particular woman. Some heard the story of how she crossed the mountains over the dangerous, snow-covered Chilkoot Pass in the company of thousands of rough and ready male stampeders and admired her grit. Many a man had claimed he'd like to match up with such a stalwart skirt.

Gullible saps.

9

Any man who had been in the territory any length of time knew the way she was. It did not take a genius to figure out the one thing that drove Coady Blake to do foolhardy, unthinkable things no other woman would consider.

She was greedy.

Purely in love with money.

Most folks figured the way Coady eagerly hugged every penny, she might never get enough. She was like a child who had been denied candy as a tot and a voracious appetite for the stuff had grown from the lack thereof.

Well, she was getting more than her fair share now. Of money, at least. Like it or not, there were times when even a man wise to her ways had to deal with Coady.

That did not mean he had to like it.

And it was more than a little galling to admit she was smarter then most men around. Every hare-brained scheme she came up with seemed to increase her wealth. Or so he had heard. And she certainly wasn't wading in cold creek water up to her knees summer and winter, battling the elements, suffering from backbreaking work, guarding against thieves and killers to get rich. She seemed to anticipate what would be in demand by the miners before the miners knew themselves. And, in a place where a hungry man would pay eighteen dollars in gold for a dozen eggs and twenty-five dollars for a bitsy can of oysters, that kind of cunning could make a girl rich real fast. And it purely irritated him that Coady was going to fleece him, one way or another.

Clive Olsen tipped forward, planting his bulbous nose very close to Coady's lovely face. "You're worse than them women in them bawdy houses down the street. You screw a man without givin' him any pleasure."

Coady resented his crudeness and felt anger well up inside her, hot and fluid. Planting fisted hands on her hips, she defied his charge. "If you feel that way, Clive what-ever-your-name-is, I think you should leave my establishment.''

He looked around scornfully at the conglomeration of goods in her so-called *establishment* before returning his glaring attention to the prettiest young woman in the territory. "You got what I need!"

Again, Coady seemed unmoved by the man's plight. "It's only June. You can survive without it for a few months."

"That's exactly what I plan to do!" he shot back before stomping toward the ill-fitting plank door.

Coady stared at his broad back and taunted, "I'll see you round about early September, Clive."

"What the devil is all that?"

Ben Keystone looked at the object of his companion's attention. "That? That's Coady's place."

Stone MacGregor stared curiously at the collection of hand-painted signs nailed willy-nilly to the board storefront:

BREAD! FRIDAY AND SATURDAY ONLY!

TENTS FOR RENT

STOVES FOR RENT

LETTERS TO YOUR SWEETHEART

MARRIAGE BY DESIGN!

His attention caught and held on the last sign. "Marriage by Design?"

Ben grinned at the newcomer. "All you have to do is supply the woman. Coady will look after the rest."

Stone's dark blue eyes focused on the younger man. "I don't think I want to hear another absurdity." The little he had seen of Dawson City so far had his mind reeling.

He was about to hear it, nonetheless.

"Coady will plan just about any kind of event a body could want, big or small. She arranges for the preacher, bakes the cake, sells some fancy doodads for brides and such; all for a fee, of course. But, with all the desperadoes here to mine the miners, I think Coady will be the least of your worries. She's just a young woman alone, trying to earn a living."

"An entrepreneur." In a territory where women were in short supply, Stone was somewhat doubtful of her financial success in the marriage business. Selling bread was probably another matter, however.

Ben nodded his head. "I think Coady does all right. Her prices are high but it costs her a fortune to have goods shipped in here from Alaska or British Columbia. And what she's doing is better than being an inmate of a house of ill fame. We have enough of those *ladies* to deal with."

Stone was staring curiously at the strange-looking edifice when a large man dressed in bib overalls and a red-checked shirt burst from inside the structure into the brilliant sunlight. The man's cheeks were weathered and wrinkled, his nose large and veined, and he immediately focused his dark beady eyes upon Stone and Ben.

"Take my advice and don't go in there. She'll fleece ya sure."

Stone merely stared at the man.

Ben stepped forward. "You're Olsen, aren't you? From down along the Bonanza?"

His small eyes narrowed. "That's me."

"I don't know that you've got call to talk that way, Olsen. Coady Blake has been running an honest business here for close to a year."

"Hah!" he barked. "Don't you think it's a little suspicious that my perfectly good tent comes up ripped and tattered and this Coady woman's got the only tents in town? For which she's chargin' a king's fortune in rents."

"Now see here—" Ben would have taken an angry step toward the man save for Stone's restraining hand on his arm.

12

"Do you have proof that this woman had a hand in ruining your tent?" Stone asked reasonably. "If your claim is down river, it doesn't seem logical for her to travel a ways out of town simply to ruin one man's tent."

The man's head swung in Stone's direction. "I don't need proof. Makes sense, if you think about it, mister. I'm not the only man to lose a tent. And she's got that old coot who does the marryin' up of folks around here workin' for her. He comes and goes over half the territory when he's sober enough to sit on a horse."

"Perhaps you should take the matter to the police."

"Huh! Those fancy-panted, Nancy-boys? They're too busy trying to keep their woodpile high to care about a man losin' a tent. They'd probably arrest *me* and have me choppin' wood for their winter fires."

"You apparently hold the Mounties in high regard," Stone said dryly. He could see the man's anger was blinding him to any suggestions that might make sense.

"The Northwest Mounted Police ain't worth nothing when it comes to dealin' with the high-takers in the territory and this woman is one o' them." He redirected his attention to Ben. "You've been around here awhile, ain't ya? You'd best fill your friend in on how things work."

Having vented only a small portion of his spleen, he stomped off toward the Dominion Saloon. There, presumably he could hand over his gold and get something reasonable for the price in exchange. And there would be no extra charge for the hangover.

Ben turned his attention toward Stone. "Inspector—"

"No rank, mister," Stone said quickly. "Use my given name."

Ben briefly closed his eyes in dismay over his blunder. "Yes, sir, uh, Stone." When he opened his eyes again, he found Stone MacGregor staring at him thoughtfully.

"You were quick to defend Coady Blake to that man, Keystone," he observed.

Ben suspected he was about to be on the receiving end of an interrogation. "The town is bustling with people,

13

with more coming every day. But Dawson's still a pretty small place in the scheme of things. Everybody gets to know everybody else pretty quick." He stared at the canvas and wood structure that was Coady's home in addition to being her place of business. "I know her about as well as anyone, considering Coady doesn't let any man get closer than a business deal."

"Does that mean you'd rather put business aside when it comes to this woman?"

Ben noted a sparkle of humor in Stone's blue eyes and laughed. "That's not likely! I earn a dollar a day, Insp— er . . . Stone. Coady Blake likes money too much to give a fellow like me a second look."

All hints of amusement were immediately erased from Stone's face. "Does she like money enough to cheat to get it?"

Ben blinked. "What?"

"Do you think there is any merit to that miner's accusation of Miss Blake slashing his tent?"

"I do not."

Stone was impressed with Ben's conviction. "You're that sure of her?"

Ben was instantly thrown back into the turmoil of being interrogated. "I . . . well . . . she . . . wait until you meet her!" he blurted at last.

MacGregor's attention again returned to the structure he now knew as "Coady's place." Like so many of its fellows, the building looked flimsy and incapable of providing much in the way of comfort. It was little more than a large tent with the lower half of the outer walls protected by wooden planks. He knew he would find a plank floor when he stepped inside. Coady's place had a two-story wooden facade in front, but the building would offer shelter from the elements and little else. On a winter's morning when the wood stove was lit, she would have to put up with *rain* inside, as heavy frost melted and dripped from the canvas. It was hard on a man, enduring the discomforts of living and working in such quarters. It would take a woman of remarkable fortitude to abide such conditions for any length of time.

Meeting such a woman could prove interesting. It would also be interesting to see if she could be as "honest" as Ben Keystone seemed to believe. Many a man older and wiser than Keystone had been blinded by a pretty smile. "I think I would like you to introduce me to this Coady Blake."

Ben was not certain why, but MacGregor's tone rang an ominous bell, giving him a sense of foreboding. "Certainly. But I thought you wanted to see the town."

"We'll see the town," said Stone, turning steely blue eyes upon the younger man. "After we spend a moment or two with Miss Blake." So saying, Stone stepped forward and opened the door that would lead him into Coady's world.

Ben followed him inside and the two men stood surrounded by a hodgepodge of wares. Stone's dark blue-eyed gaze slowly circled the room. On his right stood two pot-bellied stoves and, occupying wide shelves above were several large rolls of canvas; "Tents for Rent." Straight ahead, directly in front of a canvas sheet that apparently created a back room, stood a garish arbor, a wooden lattice structure liberally decorated with ribbons and silk flowers. The marriage bower, no doubt. To his left was a work table on which sat a tidy stack of paper, a pen and an inkwell. Behind the table stood a single, straight-backed chair. Beyond this were shelves laden with silk flowers and frilly bits of lace. Unable to resist, Stone stepped to the shelves and picked up one of the frillies—a ladies' garter. "For God's sake," he muttered. It seemed incongruous to see such feminine bits of civility in a rustic place like Dawson. Almost as outrageous as a prettily decorated arbor situated amongst the gray canvas tents and soot-blackened wood stoves. He did admit that the room was organized and neat. The place was austere at best, but more than that, it alerted one to the determination of the owner. Coady Blake was determined to earn her daily bread, all right.

"She makes them," Ben offered, nodding toward the garter.

Stone turned at the waist and cast his friend a comical look. "Resourceful."

"Quite."

The canvas sheet rustled. "A little something for your sweetheart?"

Stone turned to face the source of the mellow, feminine voice. And stared straight into the largest, warmest, brown eyes he had ever seen. Considering Stone MacGregor was an intelligent man, his first words to the beautiful young woman were particularly inane. His gaze dropped briefly to the frilly piece of frippery in his hand. "Do women here really wear these things?"

Coady laughed a note sweet and clear. "Depends on the woman."

The sound of her laughter, surprisingly, sparked a playful little ember within him and Stone grinned. "Do you?"

Coady would have taken offense at such a question from most men but, oddly, with this man, she did not. She returned his grin but slanted her eyes in mock disapproval. "That, sir, you will never know."

Stone threw the garter back on the shelf. "You end the game too soon, Miss."

Coady felt a quickening in her chest, a curious response to his appealing, masculine tones. The reaction briefly startled her. When a man walked through the door to her place she tried to judge the size of his purse and nothing else. But with this man she found herself staring into a ruggedly handsome face without a thought for business. "Were we playing?" she asked quietly.

Stone feigned a sigh of disappointment. "Apparently not."

Coady cast Stone a cocky smile and turned her attention on Keystone. "Hello, Ben."

Ben nodded his head. "Coady."

"I haven't any bread left today. You should have been here earlier."

"I don't know how you do it. Five dollars a loaf and still there's a run on this place every Friday and Saturday morning."

Stone blinked. "*Five* dollars?"

"I have what the miners want," she explained proudly. "Besides, I bake the best bread in the territory." Her gaze moved from one man to the other. "You're together?"

"Yes. Ah, this is Stone MacGregor," said Ben. "He's just arrived. I was showing him the town."

Stone bowed slightly at the waist. "Miss Blake." She was the most engaging creature he had seen in a long while. He would not go so far as to call her beautiful, but there was a radiance about her that seemed to seep through every fiber of her being. She was dressed in a plain brown, wide skirt that was belted at her slim waist. Her beige blouse was high-collared and tailored, accentuating prominent, ample breasts. There was not a single snip of lace to be seen, but her femininity was unquestionable. She was delicate and soft looking, with a wealth of auburn hair loosely pulled away from her face by a yellow ribbon and left to flow down her back. He didn't doubt that, given the incentive, Coady Blake would indeed wear feminine undergarb. And his vision included one of her very own frilly garters.

Possessed of more than a touch of arrogance, this one, Coady mused as she returned his regard. A big man, obviously muscular beneath his clothes, Stone MacGregor's courtly little bow had signaled a modicum of respect along with a goodly portion of cockiness. His hair was the color of rich wheat, neatly parted and curling softly over the collar of his navy coat. His blue eyes were dark and intense. His nose, centered in a rugged face that was as masculine as it was handsome, seemed just a little

17

crooked as if someone had broken it for him years ago. His upper lip sported a fair, neatly trimmed moustache.

His were aristocratic features, pleasing to look upon. The *ladies* of Dawson City would be eager to catch this man's attention. Besides, in the few words he had spoken, Coady had detected the rich burr of a Scotsman. She imagined those deep melodious tones could seduce almost any woman. Almost.

But he was probably a dreamer, just like every other man who had stampeded to the Yukon. All fancied instant riches, but few realized the goal. "Have you come to establish a business or are you here to make your fortune in the rivers, Mr. MacGregor? If you're seeking gold, you'll have to work harder at it than Ben, here. He spends more time in town than at his claim, I swear."

Stone took note of her comment for later consideration of Ben's next assignment. "I expect I'll try my hand at some of each," he said in response to Coady's question.

She had been right! He was a Scotsman. *"Some of each,"* she murmured, gracing him with a curious smile. "That is rather noncommittal of you, Mr. MacGregor."

Stone's blue eyes met hers directly. "I don't like to limit my options."

"Wise of you." Coady returned his stare with like intensity. She sensed no small bit of danger in him—danger for her. He was too beautiful by half. And the other half she credited to his smooth, Scottish tones. With just a look and a soft word from him, she felt feminine and pretty, putting her in mind of a fancy porcelain doll she had once seen years ago. The thought almost made her laugh because the image was as far from the truth of her *real* self as dry streets were to the mud-plagued Dawson.

What she was feeling was heady and eerie and she decided, in her next breath, to flee the only way she knew. "What can I do to help you today? You're in need of living quarters, perhaps?"

"How large are your tents?"

Ben frowned, curious over MacGregor's demeanor. And he knew damned well and good that the man had no need of a tent.

"Large enough," Coady responded.

"Seems a waste for me to occupy a large tent, all on my own."

Coady smiled, finally understanding. "I'm sorry, Mr. MacGregor, I don't supply companions."

"Oh? You have a sign outside . . . Marriage by Design.' "

"That's correct. I *design* the wedding ceremony and party to suit the desires of my customers but they have to come to me already paired."

"Ah."

"So," she said hopefully. "You will need a tent?"

Stone wrapped his hand around the opposite wrist behind his back. "What are your rates?"

"Thirty dollars a month, payable in advance."

"Thirty dollars!"

Coady had experienced this reaction on more than one occasion. "It's costs dearly to have goods shipped to me, Mr. MacGregor. The price of a tent is nothing compared to my other expenses. Believe me, when a man loses everything coming through Miles Canyon and the White Horse rapids, he's happy enough to still be in possession of his life. The rental of shelter is nothing to him."

"Put that way . . ."

"I will need the location of your claim."

Stone's right brow arched upward; this woman looked as delicate as a flower but she was all business. "My claim?"

"I must know where to find you, Mr. MacGregor, in order to collect my rents."

"You go out to the claims to personally collect the rents?"

"Certainly. It's all a part of the business."

Ben felt a now familiar sense of foreboding return.

Stone smiled knowingly. "I suppose that is also the

Jill Metcalf

only way to insure your property is not being abused by the renters.''

Coady nodded her head. "True."

He studied her for a moment, attempting to determine whether she was at all uneasy discussing such business with a man. In this day and age, women suffered apoplexy at the mere mention of something as humanly natural as a *lower limb*. If he were to raise the topic of male sleeping accommodations in a room of twenty women, Stone was certain the nearest doctor would be faced with reviving eighteen swooning females. Clearly Miss Blake ranked, admirably, as one of the two women left standing.

"Well," he drawled, knowing she was waiting for his answer. "The guarantee of meeting with a pretty, gracious woman, such as yourself, at least once a month is most tempting but I believe I will stay on at the hotel for a time. Until I get my bearings, you understand?"

Coady understood, all right. She had just wasted considerable precious time and a lot of breath. "Certainly," she said tightly. "Now, if I cannot be of service . . . ?"

Stone tipped his head a bit to the side, staring at her curiously. "I've upset you, Miss Blake?"

"Time is money, Mr. MacGregor," she informed him as she turned toward the canvas room divider. "If you'll excuse me, I have a great many things to do."

He stared at her slender back, appreciating the angry twitch of her skirts until the canvas dropped in place between them. "I understand," he said softly.

"Stone?"

Reluctantly tearing his attention away from the drop sheet which deprived him of further contact with the intriguing Miss Blake, Stone turned and walked toward the door. "Let's go."

Ben followed into the bright sunlight. "She's something, huh?"

"Is she really as hard-nosed as she lets on?"

20

Ben fell into step at Stone's right side. "Oh, Coady is all business, that's for sure."

"But is her business completely honest, my friend? That's the question."

Ben came to an abrupt stop. "Why must you assume the woman has to be dishonest to earn a living?"

Stone turned back briefly. "I simply take nothing for granted, Keystone."

"It's because of Olsen shooting off his mouth," Ben was quick to counter as he fell into step again, striving to keep up with Stone's long strides. "He made you suspicious."

"I was born suspicious."

"Well, that doesn't mean . . ."

Stone waited for Ben's next comment in defense of the pretty Miss Blake. "You were about to say?"

"You'll find out for yourself in time," he finished lamely. He had complete faith in Coady's honesty. But he could not afford to be seen as her champion, not in Stone MacGregor's eyes, if there should be the most remote chance it was not so.

"Are you really going to stay at the hotel?"

"For a week or two, at least. Superintendent Simmons agrees I should live there for now." Stone turned his head and cast Ben a wry smile. "I wasn't lying to your Miss Blake when I said I want to get my bearings before moving out of the hotel."

"She isn't *my* anything," Ben muttered. "God knows I sometimes wish she were."

Stone had heard many such wistful comments from many other men. "It gets lonely, doesn't it, Keystone?"

"Yes, sir."

Stone let the small error of Ben's respectful address pass and walked on. "Tell me about some of these other establishments."

Normally a quiet man, Ben Keystone could talk his way into next week when the situation demanded he do so. Now was one of those times.

As the two men strolled along Dawson's wide, bustling Front Street, Ben carried on a detailed briefing of every business, saloon, cafe, music hall and theater they passed. He had long known almost every owner, proprietor, card sharp, bartender and barber who worked and lived in the tent city. He had learned a good deal about many of the long-term residents of the town in the past year. That was about as far back as Dawson's history went: a year.

But new and unfamiliar faces continued to appear in droves almost daily since the outside world had heard the news that gold had been found in the Yukon Territory. Many of the new faces were flushed with the glow of excitement and eagerness, warmed by the dream of easy riches.

Other faces blushed with greed of another kind.

These were the faces that had brought Ben and Stone and their companions to the Yukon in 1898. These were the faces of thieves, murderers and claim jumpers. Faces of slick gamblers ready to fleece an unsuspecting miner of every speck of gold dust, every rough and brilliant nugget. There were those who talked tall tales of impossible schemes, smoothly hooking in the listener. There were those who conducted simple games for money; games that were not simple at all.

If an honest man was not alert and wary, he could go home far poorer than the day he arrived.

Ben had been around Dawson long enough to have seen it all.

Stone had seen it all, too, but in other places.

While seeming to center on little of interest, Stone's blue eyes took in details of passers-by as well as his surroundings. Dawson's Front Street appeared three times as wide as the streets of most cities and, sporting banners and gaudy signage from every post and building, presented a carnival-like atmosphere. There was a decided excitement amongst the pedestrians they passed, as if this was a world of complete wonder, a land of promise. A man could feel it in his gut. It was like the rushing of blood, the pounding of one's heart, the heady excitement that only a warm, hot seductress could generate. The lure of unimagined wealth went a step further than even that for most men. And Dawson had it all. It was a place that brought out the worst and the best of men and women alike.

Stone and Ben ambled by the open doors of the Dominion Saloon and were assaulted by the harsh notes of a piano being badly abused, the screech of a female's forced laughter, and a din of male voices all wafting toward the street and hanging on the warm June air.

"Who is the preacher working with her?"

"You really are focused on Coady," Ben said flatly.

Stone shot the younger man a quick glare. "And *you* are very defensive of her, mister."

As with all well-trained men, Ben reacted when a superior chastised him. "Yes, sir," he returned respectfully.

"And stop calling me *sir*."

"Yes, s—Stone."

"Well, do you know the preacher or not?"

Ben studiously stepped around a steaming pile of horse leavings. "His name is Zachary Bloodstone."

"Good God!"

Ben looked sharply at his companion. "You know him?"

"No. I was making reference to the name."

He grinned wryly. "It is rather strange."

Stone nodded and continued his surreptitious inspection of the places and persons around him. "Does he have a parish here?"

"No."

"I suppose that was a stupid question," Stone muttered. "I imagine few would cease trying to find their fortune even on the Lord's day."

"That's true. You'll find the creeks full of men panning for gold every day of the week. But we have a small

23

church and an Anglican minister who manages to draw a piddling crowd come Sunday.''

"Rev. White," Stone added. "The archbishop's man. I'm aware of him. But why would a minister come here and not attempt to gather a flock?'' he questioned more of himself then of Ben.

"Bloodstone doesn't seem to have any interest in that. He does some panning now and again,'' Ben said. "But I think he spends most of his time getting drunk.''

"A man of the cloth publicly indulging in one of the devil's vices?'' Stone questioned wryly. "He *is* an ordained minister?''

Ben had taken several steps before he realized Stone was not at his side. Frowning thoughtfully, he turned and faced his companion. "Bloodstone calls himself a preacher.''

Stone did not like the care with which Ben had obviously chosen his words. "In other words, you don't know if the man is legitimate?''

"I don't know that anyone ever thought to check his credentials. Coady found him and added 'Marriage by Design' to her list of businesses shortly afterward. She would have verified whether or not Zachary was what he claimed to be.''

Stone's face registered doubt as he crossed the street, moving toward his hotel. "Supposing Miss Blake did not think to question Bloodstone's authenticity?''

"Damn,'' Ben breathed thoughtfully.

"That's what I thought,'' he returned dryly. "How many couples have this darling duo married up?''

"Only a few as far as I know.''

Stone stopped at the open doors of the hotel and looked back toward Coady Blake's establishment. "Have someone check out Zachary Bloodstone and let me know the results,'' he said before disappearing into the cool, dark lobby of the hotel.

Chapter Two

Coady handed the paper-wrapped bundle to the small, broad-faced boy who stood at the only door her home possessed. "Now don't be dropping this package in the dirt, Little Joe." In truth, the boy's name was Joe Little but Coady affectionately reversed the names, making the child smile.

"No, ma'am. I won't drop 'em."

Joe, like hundreds of his people, worked for the new-comers to the Yukon. Many acted as guides and aides to the Royal Northwest Mounted Police; prized positions, for the policemen respected the knowledge and experience of the First Nations people and paid as well as budgets would permit. Others, like Joe, worked for civilians, performing many chores. The one task that Joe always enjoyed was running to the "Coady Lady" twice a week to fetch parcels he would then take to Mr. Trelaine. Coady always gave him a peppermint treat and Mr. Trelaine paid him a penny for each trip; a whole *penny!* And that was in addition to the nickel he received each week

25

for keeping Mr. Trelaine's storeroom floor well swept. It was not such hard work but Joe Little hated sweeping out the remainders of the rat carcasses the cat did not totally devour. That was one fat cat! For this he felt he earned his weekly nickel.

Coady fished in the pocket of her skirt and brought out a small paper-wrapped peppermint stick. The costly candy, with which she treated the loveable little boy twice per week, was her one and only extravagance. Joe's smile of appreciation always made her overlook the expense. "What would you do if I ever forgot your candy?" she asked, smiling as she gave the peppermint to the boy.

Joe's brilliant smile disappeared from his bronzed face. "I would understand, Miss Coady. You are very busy. You cannot always be thinking of Joe."

In spite of the ten-year-olds' hesitation, Coady admired his brave front. The child possessed many qualities she admired and was the only person in her present-day world for whom she held any affection. She touched the top of his head. "I was teasing you, sweetheart," she said softly. "I would never forget."

Joe's smile returned as his fingers tightened around the peppermint, even as his arms tightened around the large bundle. "I will run now to Mr. Trelaine."

Coady's smile remained in place as she watched the boy run along the rutted street. They had been blessed with just enough sun to dry up most the of mud through which pedestrians were forced to slog. The hour was late but the light of day remained. During June, Dawson was bathed in almost twenty-four hours of daylight, and in only a few hours less each day during July.

The land of the midnight sun.

Coady had thought the prolonged daylight wonderful in the beginning. Think of the savings in candles and lamp oil! But the constant daylight had its drawbacks, too. Sleep was sometimes difficult to achieve and she often missed the comfort of looking up at a darkened sky, sparkling with brilliant, far-off stars. A romantic notion, but there it was. The lack of a proper night as she knew it left her strangely yearning and unsettled at times.

In truth it was a wonder Coady had any difficulty sleeping at all. She was dogged tired by the end of most of her days. In addition to the "advertised" services she performed for the community, she secretly carried out laundry chores for some of the more prosperous men of Dawson; if the men were clean of themselves, that is. Coady had no liking for people who would not devote time to the care of their person. She was plain sour on touching any clothes that had come off an unwashed body.

Harrison Trelaine, owner of the large Golden Slipper Saloon, was one customer for whom she harbored no such fears. Harrison was almost fanatical about his grooming and his appearance. He paid Coady well to tend to his clothes and starch his shirt collars and he never spoke of the secret agreement between them. Harrison understood Coady's need to be seen as one of the respectable business personages of Dawson and "washerwoman" did not fit with her image of herself. His understanding was one reason why they got on so well. Another was the fact that Coady's heart beat a little faster each and every time she was near the gracious, elegant and dapper Trelaine.

She watched Joe climb the wooden steps that led to the Golden Slipper Saloon before turning back toward her storefront door. It was in turning that she saw first the black leather encasing a man's well-shaped lower leg. Looking upward, Coady was surprised to find Stone MacGregor a few feet away, leaning comfortably against *her* wall. "How long have you been standing there?"

Defensive, he mused. "Good evening, Miss Blake." His gaze flickered briefly in the direction the boy had run. "Could it be you like children?"

27

Coady could not see what possible interests her likes and dislikes could hold for him, but she answered reasonably. "I like that particular child. There are others I've known who were not at all likeable."

"None of your own, I hope?"

Coady had drawn herself up, armed to fling a heated reply, before she noticed the glint in his eye. "Are you well known as a tease, Mr. MacGregor?"

"In some circles, I suppose."

Her clear, brown-eyed gaze bathed him with humor. "As I suspected."

"Is the boy an employee of one, or more, of your many businesses?"

"Joe runs errands for Harrison Trelaine. I have no employees, Mr. MacGregor."

"Ah," he drawled, nodding his head. "With the exception of Mr. Bloodstone."

Coady was not certain why she felt the need to respond to his comments, humorous or otherwise. It was, however, disconcerting the way Stone MacGregor could turn a new phrase and in a single breath make her feel as if she had to justify her very existence, let alone her affairs. He was harrying, to say the least. "Zachary Bloodstone is hardly an employee. We have an arrangement."

That should satisfy that, she thought. Whether he was satisfied or not, she had answered enough questions.

Coady placed her hand on the doorknob but, before she could step inside, Stone moved a step closer.

"It appears I have made you angry again, Miss Blake."

She fought the urge to look up into those dark blue eyes of his. Examining the fist she had locked around the doorknob, she said, "Not at all, Mr. MacGregor."

Stone crossed his arms over his wide chest and leaned a shoulder against the doorframe. "But I sense a change in you. Could it perhaps have something to do with this "arrangement" between yourself and Mr. Bloodstone?"

Coady's head turned and her brown eyes shot him a

warning. "It is because you ask entirely too many questions."

"Ah. You have something to hide, lass?"

"I have nothing to hide," she said shortly. "I simply find your probing annoying. Now, good evening, Mr.—"

"Wait." Stone lightly gripped her wrist. "I'm sorry. What you say is probably true. I do ask too many questions. Drove my parents quite mad as a lad, asking what about this and about that? I fear I'm no different as a man, curious about everything and everyone. I have an insatiable appetite for knowledge."

"Or are you merely a *curious* man?" She smiled sweetly. "Curious as in *odd*, perhaps?"

Stone accepted her insult with grace. "I apologize for annoying you."

She feigned a weighty sigh. "It's difficult to remain angry with one who admits his own shortcomings."

Stone's expression immediately registered his surprise. "I admit to nothing," he said. "I don't believe a thirst for knowledge is a fault."

Ah, but there were many other failings a man might possess and his "prodding" manner was one of them.

"I am, admittedly, exacting at times. Being a single man, I converse more frequently with other men who tend to be as demanding as I am. I fear I suffer deplorably from the lack of a woman's softer influence."

As reluctant as Coady was to feed his ego, she recklessly blurted a skeptical, "You expect me to believe *that*?"

And hit her mark.

Stone's grin was immodest as he shrugged his shoulders. "I tried."

Coady shook her head in mock disgust. "I don't think you intended to apologize for your behavior at all, Mr. MacGregor."

"I did, lass. Truly."

She stared into the deep blue depths of his eyes, uncertain he was genuinely contrite. "Does that mean you will cease harassing me with probing questions?"

His smile turned genuinely regretful. "Alas, most likely not."

There was a moment of silence between them as a stunned Coady stared at Stone MacGregor, disbelieving of his audacity. Although she would have had it otherwise, a brief, choking laugh overtook her. "Well, you are disarming, if nothing else, Mr. MacGregor."

"I can be quite charming, given the opportunity."

Oh, she did not doubt that! "And never conceited, I'm sure."

"Why don't you sell the tents?"

Coady blinked, amazed by his gall. Perhaps, once considered, it was more a matter of reckless abandon on his part. "There you go again!"

"Well, why don't you? It seems to me that selling the tents would be profitable and less of a nuisance. You wouldn't have to worry about collecting rents."

If there was one thing Coady hated, it was green stampeders nosing into her business. She knew exactly what she was doing every single moment of every single day. "It is more profitable to rent them out, Mr. MacGregor," she said shortly.

He ignored her obvious anger. "I should think most men would be willing to purchase what they need to survive, no matter the cost."

"The men who come here are more willing to pay rents for what they feel will be only a month or two. They all foolishly seem to think they will be millionaires within that time."

Stone straightened and jammed his fists into his jacket pockets. "I've angered you again."

"You certainly have! My affairs are none of your business and I . . ."

He tipped his head to the side and waited. "Yes?"

Coady took a deep breath and shook her head. "I don't

know why I'm standing out here talking with you. Good night.''

He was not certain why he was talking with her, either. Except for the fact he was patently curious about the boldness of a young woman who had the aplomb and the incentive to engage in not one, but several businesses. And the one question that was beginning to nag him was that of the legality of *all* those businesses. That aside, however, it was rather refreshing to engage in a little harmless sparring with an obviously perceptive, quick-witted woman who had the smile of an angel and the drive of a money-grubber. "I was on my way to the cafe to have some supper," he said. "Join me."

Striving for a civil tone, Coady shook her head. "Thank you, no. I've had a very long day. *Good night*, Mr. MacGregor."

"The name is Stone," he said softly, but the ill-fitting wooden door closed upon his words. He stared at the feeble portal for a moment, thinking of how easily she could be irked. Such a temper could lead the lass to do and say foolish things, if she did not take care.

Stone turned away from the curious place that was Coady Blake's residence and place of business and strode toward the Dominion Saloon. It was just as well that she had refused his impulsive offer of supper. There were weightier matters, beyond his curiosity and suspicion of Coady's various trades, needing his attention. Matters that he *should* not put off.

As Stone opened the door to the saloon he nodded briefly to the shadowed figure of Ben Keystone, who stood beneath the overhang of an adjoining building, before stepping inside.

Someone was plunking out "A Hot Time In The Old Town" on a piano in the corner. The tune could barely be heard above the din of male voices and the occasional shrill, high-pitched laughter of a woman of doubtful virtue. The air was blue with low-slung clouds created by a variety of tobaccos favored amongst males and females, alike. Bodies pressed against bodies in an attempt to get from one place to another. Clearly it was safer to garner an area near the end of the bar and remain there. Unfortunately, several men had already claimed that prime bit of space.

Stone pushed his way to a likely spot where the barkeep might notice his arrival. As his attention focused on those men in his immediate vicinity, he ordered a beer. Turning, once his order had been filled, he held the full mug high and began to push against the wave of humanity that was intent upon slaking its thirst for the first or eighth time.

"Heads up!" he bellowed. "Let me through!"

Because he was more than a head taller then most in the saloon, a gap was reluctantly provided. He managed to squeeze through the crowd only to have it close in behind him. Arriving at a corner table, feeling he had just been mashed beneath a millstone, Stone was relieved to see there was one vacant chair.

"May I?" he asked, eyeing each of the five seated men in turn.

"Sure."

"I got no claim."

"Go ahead," came the simultaneous responses.

Those who did not voice an objection were deemed in agreement as far as Stone was concerned: He sat. "Damn," he murmured swiping a little spilled beer from his trousers. "You'd think this was the only saloon in town."

"Oh, the others is just as bad," offered an elderly man who appeared to possess only one lonely front tooth. "Maybe worse. It's Saturday night, young fella. Ya got to fight for yer space. Or anything *else* ya got yer heart set on." This last seemed to be of particular interest as several of the other men laughed.

Stone looked around at his unlikely companions. "Well, all I want is to ease my thirst."

"Sure!"

"Ha! Ha! Ha!"

"Tell us another windy!"

The same three who had spoken when he approached mocked him in unison.

"Maybe he got it froze in the creek the past winter!" another offered.

Stone glared at the giver of that insinuative comment.

The old man with the long, snowy white beard gripped Stone's arm and leaned toward him. "It'll cost ya to get it from one of the girls here, boy. Some says it cost them their whole poke for just one night. If ya want a night's worth, go see the girls on the west side."

Stone looked in the man's tired blue eyes and nodded. "Thanks. I'll remember that."

The old man sat back, chuckling. "Then again, if ya was as old as me, ya wouldn't worry 'bout none of it. I'm too weary to do more than dream."

"Ha! Ha! Ha!" boomed another. "Dreams? That's why I hear ya moanin' in yer tent!"

Stone turned his attention from the arrant elderly men and gazed around the room. There were few enough women, to be sure. He spotted a pert little strawberry blonde walking down the steps from the second story, followed by a burly man. But the girl's attention had already switched from her previous companion. She was obviously looking for her next client as her gaze roamed the room.

An older girl, a young *woman*, was suddenly bearing down upon the corner table. She looked from one man to the next, gauging their interest. Her pasted smile became one of invitation when her dark eyes collided with Stone's. "Hi, honey," she said smoothly as she sidled close. "You looking for company?"

Stone raised his glass off the table. "Got it."

"Ah, now, sugar," she purred, stroking her hand across the breadth of his shoulders. "All that's going to do is send you runnin' out back to pee." She bent close and whispered her next words in his ear. "I can send you to heaven, sugar."

Stone threw back his head and laughed.

The girl did not take kindly to his laughter. Straightening, she smacked him a good one on his upper arm. "Don't you laugh at me!"

Stone felt the pressure of her small fist smartly warming his flesh and turned his head, frowning up at her. "You're a bit quick-tempered, aren't you?"

Chelsea Manor saw the potential loss of a virile client, one pleasing to the eye, and instantly changed her ways. "Ah, sugar," she crooned. "I'm more a lover than a fighter."

Stone arched a brow, clearly dubious. "Really?"

Chelsea nodded her fair head. "Let me prove it to you, darlin'. I can make all your dreams come true."

"She's givin' *me* somethin' to dream about!" shouted the near toothless man with the beard.

Chelsea ignored the others. "You've had a hard week, haven't you, darlin'? Don't you want to relax a little?"

Stone shook his head. "I can relax in a hot bath," he returned, before swallowing the last of his beer. "I think I'll head back to the hotel and . . ."

Looking again at the fine cut of his clothes, Chelsea presented one last valiant effort. "I can arrange for a bath for you, sugar. Nice and hot," she whispered against his ear. "And little ol' me to scrub your back for you."

From the corner of his eye, Stone noticed Ben standing in a near corner of the saloon. The young man gave a barely discernible nod. The motion was no more than a drop of the chin but Stone caught the intended meaning, and his manner toward the girl changed abruptly. "You make it tempting, lass," he said softly.

Stone's table companions directed their undivided attention toward Chelsea.

The old man with the white beard snorted. "Don't say I didn't warn ya, boy."

But Stone had taken heed.

Despite the old man's warning, Chelsea could smell victory. "You just follow me, lover," she whispered, taking Stone's hand and tugging him to his feet before he could change his mind—or have it changed for him. She shot the old man a malicious glare before turning away.

Stone allowed the girl to continue holding his hand as they worked their way through the crowded room. She was an appealing little thing. He could not deny that. But his long abstinence from the pleasures of women would not make him foolhardy. She would bear watching. He had already been briefed on the activities of the Dominion girls. Activities that caused a man to lose more than he gained for the price of a whore.

Stone's newest companion stopped at the end of the bar where she talked briefly to a man of slender build who possessed the hard, dark eyes of a scavenger. Stone heard her order a hot bath to be brought to her room, all the while noting that the man's intense interest was directed *his* way.

"There we go, sugar," she purred as she led her mark toward the stairs. "You'll be comfy in no time."

"And *clean*," he suggested dryly.

The girl smiled over her shoulder as she led the way up. "I'm Chelsea. What's your name, sugar?"

"Stone."

"Stone? Is that your last name or your given name?"

"That's my *only* name for now," he muttered.

Chelsea stopped in front of a closed door and turned to him. "You don't have to be nervous of me, darlin'. I'm not about to tell your wife what you do when she's not around. Besides," she added with a grin, "I bet she's not even in the territory." A safe enough wager, considering most of the men currently in the Yukon had left wives or sweethearts behind. "Well, here we are!" she declared happily before closing the door behind him.

Stone looked around the small room that housed nothing more than a wide, brass bed, a single, roughly made chest of drawers and a commode. Sheer curtains fluttered at the open window.

"I like fresh air, don't you?" Chelsea asked, noting the direction of the attention. "The breeze is so nice this time of year."

But there was no breeze God ever created that could rid the room of the stench of sex.

He eyed the drab bed linens with distaste.

With little ceremony, Chelsea unhooked the bodice of her knee-length dress and allowed the garment to flutter to the floor. "Let's just get you comfortable, shall we?" she murmured as she moved toward him and reached for the button front of Stone's trousers.

His hands shot out from his sides and captured her wrists. "Don't we have business to discuss first?"

Chelsea looked up, noting the severity of his gaze. The strength in the hands that gripped her wrists like iron bands gave her pause. "Well, sure, honey," she murmured, her smile once again pasted in place. "Why don't we do that over a little drink," she said, as she turned her wrists in an attempt to be free. "You seem tense, sugar."

He released her.

"That's better." Chelsea turned toward the single chest of drawers and reached for the bottle she kept there. There was only one glass sitting atop a yellowed linen cloth but the glass was relatively clean; as clean as any, Teddy, the bartender would provide her, at least. "Why don't you just sit down and pull off those boots? Your bath will be here any minute."

Stone continued to stand.

He stared at her red-corseted back, ignoring the fine curves of the woman as he concentrated on the movements of her arms. He could not see her hands but it was taking a good long time to pour one little shot of whiskey.

Thus reminded of his reason for being there, and the risk he knew he was taking, Stone's elbow automatically pressed against his side; the reassuring rigidity of the revolver beneath his coat dug into his waist. Reassuring, yes, but useless to him if he were too drugged to raise a hand in his own defense.

And he had every reason to believe this little assignation was going to go that way.

Chelsea turned and walked seductively across the room to stand before him. Smiling, she offered a shot-glass half filled with dark liquid. "Here you are, sugar. This will warm you up a little."

He did not doubt that.

Staring down into feminine eyes that had quite obviously seen too much for one of such tender years, Stone arched a brow. "You think I need *warming up*?"

"Well, at the rate you're moving, sugar, you're going to stretch this little meeting of ours into next Tuesday. That will cost you, you know?"

"I understand," he said dryly.

"Aren't you going to drink?"

Stone extended the glass. "Why don't you share with me?"

Chelsea whirled away playfully toward the bed. "Oh, I don't use hard liquor."

He chose that moment to upend the tumbler, dumping the contents into the large pitcher on the commode. The next person to use that wash water was going to come up smelling of whiskey instead of roses.

"Nothin' finer than hard liquor to warm a man," he muttered, ceremoniously wiping his mouth with the back of his hand as he went to stand beside the bed.

Chelsea had artfully draped herself across the thing. He had to give her one credit, at least; she had long, beautiful legs. Black garters graced her thighs, holding sheer, black stockings smoothly in place. Her generous breasts and rounded hips, accentuated by the trim waist encased tightly in the red, black-trimmed corset, could tempt even him.

Much to Stone's chagrin.

He wondered how quickly the drug was supposed to work.

Allowing his eyelids to droop wearily, he smiled. "How about moving over, *sugar*, and letting a man rest his weary bones?"

Chelsea giggled and shimmied back across the mattress toward the wall. "You're not going to sleep on me now, are you, honey? We haven't started our party yet."

Stone stretched out beside her on his back, closing his eyes as his head hit the pillow. "Where the devil is that bath?" he muttered thickly.

Chelsea's smile disappeared as she propped herself up, staring hard at his face. "Why don't I help you off with your coat?"

Stone's hands locked together over his middle and his head drifted to the side.

There was a knock at the door that startled her, even though she was expecting it. "Damn," she breathed taking a last look at the large man on the bed before easing herself across his prone body. The instant her feet hit the floor, she was running to the door.

Jon Charles was standing in the hallway, grinning, when she opened the portal to him. "You ordered a bath, ma'am?"

"Oh, shut up and get in here."

Jon eyed her severely as he entered. "Lost your sense of humor with this one?" He took only two steps into the room before his frown deepened. "Shit, you haven't even managed to get him out of his coat? What kind of a whore are you?"

Chelsea closed the door and rushed past him toward the bed. "He fell asleep faster than I thought. We'll have to search his pockets carefully. If he wakes up, we're—"

"Dead," Jon finished for her. "How much of that stuff did you give him?" he asked as he bent over the sleeping man. He immediately set to work, searching Stone's coat pockets.

"He's big, so I used—"

A second, unexpected, knock on the door had them both jumping back from the bed.

"Who the hell is that?" Jon whispered

Chelsea cast him a dark look. "How the *hell* should I know?" Moving lightly, she rushed across the room and eased the door open a crack. "Yes?"

Ben Keystone grinned as he insinuated his booted foot into the narrow opening. "Is this a private party?" he asked as he raised his gun to waist level. "Or can anyone join in?"

At the sound of the male voice, Jon stepped forward.

He did not get far, however, as Stone rose up off the bed, revolver in hand. "Join us, Mr. Keystone," he said as he pushed the barrel end of the gun into Jon's ribs. "I'm glad you've come."

Momentarily stunned, Chelsea released her hold on the doorknob.

When Ben stepped into the room, two uniformed Royal Northwest Mounted Police officers materialized from either side of the door and fell into place behind him.

"You set us up!" Chelsea screeched, rounding on Stone.

Stone smiled innocently. "I?" he drawled. "I'm merely fortunate enough to have a very good friend in Mr. Keystone. He's vowed to protect my hide, you see."

"From what?" she demanded. "From a poor little female half your size?"

"I'm sorry you didn't find any gold in my pockets, Chelsea. You're acting abilities deserve some kind of a reward." To the uniformed officers he said, "They are all yours, gentlemen."

Chapter Three

"I'm starving and in need of some lively companionship to accompany a good meal."

Coady crossed her arms beneath her breasts and smiled, her large brown eyes sparkling with delight. "Oh, you are, are you?"

Harrison Trelaine leaned toward her and whispered. "Two choice steaks are being cooked for us, right this very minute. What do you say?"

"At the Dawson Cafe?"

Which he owned in addition to a number of other enterprises.

"Where else? Best food in town," he said easily.

"I don't know how *lively* a companion I will be tonight, Harrison. I'm very tired. It's been a long day." Her tone sounded a little more wistful than she had intended; it rarely took much for him to talk her into joining him for a late supper. Harrison was delightful company, always the gentleman. Coady knew they had given more than one gossip fodder to munch on over the

40

past year, but she did not care. They were friends and nothing more. There had been times when she thought it might be nice to engage in a more complex relationship with him but she had given up those thoughts long ago. So, friends they remained.

Harrison reached for her hand and folded her slender fingers around the crook of his elbow. "Every day is a long day for you, my dear. You work too hard. Will you come if I promise to have you home before dark?"

"Very funny," she said, laughing as she turned with him toward the door of her shop. "Do you ever miss the darkness?" she asked as Harrison firmly closed the door behind them.

"Key?"

She reached into the pocket of her plain skirt and produced the iron key. Locking her door was such a farce. Anyone who had a mind to could cut the back of her tent and steal whatever he liked.

Once the door was locked and the key had been returned to her pocket, Harrison tucked Coady's hand in the crook of his elbow as they started off in the direction of the Dawson Cafe.

It felt good being escorted by him. Harrison was such a fine-looking man. Coady guessed him to be six feet tall. He was slender but not emaciated, and his black hair and equally black moustache had a way of making him appear quite sinister when his anger was aroused. Fortunately, she had not often seen him in that state. He was always very sweet with her. He made her laugh.

"You didn't answer my question."

He frowned and looked down at her briefly. "What question was that?"

"Do you miss the darkness during the summer months?"

"No. I simply avoid planning midnight seductions during the month of June."

She sighed, as if pained. "I should have known."

"Well, in July we get about four hours of darkness. That's time enough for any man."

"Harrison!"

She was laughing. He loved to hear her laugh. She needed to do more of it.

"What did you mean, you *should have known*?"

"That I wouldn't get a straight answer from you."

"Yes, I, too, occasionally tire of constant daylight. How is that?"

She turned her head and smiled up at him. "Better."

They walked on in silence for several moments with Harrison acutely aware of the proud stride of the lovely woman on his arm. He cared for her, it was true. He cared quite deeply, in fact. As he would a sister.

He would like to buy her lovely gowns—rich colors that would complement her own natural beauty, unlike the drab, serviceable clothing she usually chose to wear. He would like to see her as impeccably clothed as he was himself; wrapped in only the finest of materials with nary a wrinkle to be seen, fashioned in the latest style by the best of tailors. She deserved the finest the entire continent had to offer simply because Coady was . . . well, Coady.

"You're quiet all of a sudden."

Harrison returned from his musings and turned his head to smile at her. "Forgive me. I wasn't purposely ignoring you."

"I should hope not," she teased.

He lightly squeezed her fingers. "In fact, I was thinking of you."

"You were?"

"Hmm. I have a proposition for you. A business proposition, Coady."

She responded quickly. "Of course." she chirped. "What else is there?"

Harrison directed his attention to the street in front of them. "I've been thinking of opening a bakery."

Coady felt a quick twinge of resentment. "In direct competition to me?"

He shook his head. "I was thinking more along the lines of a partnership with you. Dawson is growing every day. I think it time we help her *grow up*. It's time a few refinements were added to the town. Certainly there are enough unattached males hungry for bread and any other treats their gold will buy. What do you say?"

"I have my own business to consider, Harrison. I can't run a bakery and still have time for my work."

Again, he shook his head. "I've considered that. I've already sent for one of the best pastry chefs in the West. He's on his way here from San Francisco now. He will manage the shop for us and bake whatever pies and cakes prove viable and profitable here. But I believe the success of the place will depend upon you baking the bread. Too many men have acquired a taste for what only you can do."

She tipped her head to the side. "Are you sure there isn't a bit of the Irish in you, my friend? That sounds suspiciously like blarney to me."

He laughed.

"It's a bit like rowing the boat."

Harrison graced her with a puzzled frown. "What?"

"When my mother was a girl, her father sometimes took her fishing with him. She was always eager for his approval you see, because he was stingy with his praise. As soon as she was big enough to handle the oars, my grandfather taught her how to row the boat. From that point on he would frequently tell her how good she was with the oars. She would row all the faster for the glory, while her father sat back and enjoyed the ride. Mother often tried to trick me into working harder using the same tactic. 'Keep on rowin' that boat, Coady!' she'd say."

"A fine story, but you *do* happen to bake the best bread in town!"

"I bake the *only* bread in town!" she shot back with a laugh. Suddenly, Coady found herself pulled up short. "Harrison?"

"Get back," he ordered brusquely, pushing her against

43

the wooden facade of the Dominion Saloon. Hurriedly, he then stepped in front of her.

Coady placed her hands in the center of his chest and pushed. "What are you doing?"

"Saving you from something unpleasant."

She heard the screeching then; a woman's shrill voice consigning some poor devil to a place worse than hell. Looking around Harrison's arm, Coady saw a young woman struggling desperately in the arms of a policeman. Her hair was waving madly around her face, her arms were flying in all directions, her feet flailing the air. But the man held fast, tightening his arms around the girl's waist as she cursed every hair on the Mountie's head, in addition to his ancestry.

Harrison moved, pressing Coady's face against his shirtfront. "You don't need to be seeing that."

"She's a whore, Harrison," Coady muttered. "I've seen one or two before."

A deep male voice, uttering threats, captured Coady's attention then. Pushing forcefully against Harrison's upper body she managed to free herself. "Really, I thank you for being my protector but I am not a child," she muttered as she smoothed her skirts. It was during that moment she saw him. A young man she had never seen before, manacled to still another policeman, was threatening Stone MacGregor with some future vengeance. Stone and Ben Keystone were standing near the entrance to the Dominion Saloon as the male prisoner vented his fury.

Curious, Coady squeezed Harrison's forearm reassuringly as she stepped away from him.

"Coady, don't."

"I will be fine, Harrison," she said over her shoulder as she ventured closer.

It was then Stone saw her. "Take this man away," he ordered softly.

The young policeman obeyed immediately.

"I'll see your mangy carcass rot!" Jon Charles bel-

44

lowed as he was led away. "Chelsea and me didn't do nothin' to you! It don't matter where they send me, I'll come back and I'll see you rot!"

Coady's complete attention was focused on Stone MacGregor's face. "My, my," she said softly. "You seem to have earned that man's resentment. Have you been asking questions again, Mr. MacGregor?"

"You might say that, Miss Blake."

Stone's eyes briefly focused on something behind her and Coady sensed Harrison had moved close. He was being particularly protective tonight and she was not certain she liked that. On one count, it warmed her somehow to know he was there, that he was possessed of genuine concern for her. On the other, such watchfulness could be stifling. After all, she had been on her own for a very long time. A girl learned to look after herself. It was one thing when a woman enjoyed the care and devotion of her dearest love. But it was something else again when a friend behaved in a manner more akin to a doting father.

While her mother had been alive, they had struggled and scrimped and had barely survived their very humble existence in Boston. They had faced starvation more times than Coady cared to count. The tent she called home now was a palace compared to places she and her mother had lived. Her mother had died in one such place; died of overwork, lack of food and the consumption caused by constant cold and damp. Coady had sworn over her mother's lifeless body *she* would not succumb to such a death. Yes, a woman learned to look after herself.

Ignoring Harrison's closeness, Coady slanted Stone MacGregor a curious frown. "Do I understand you have just denied that young woman the opportunity to earn a living by having her arrested?"

Stone and Ben looked equally stunned by the question.

"Coady, she's a *whore*," said Ben.

Her attention focused briefly him. "She's a woman

45

trying to earn a living the only way she knows how.''

Stone now appeared more thoughtful. "You feel you must defend this woman, lass?"

"I am not defending her actions but neither can I judge her. I don't know her circumstances. Sometimes desperate situations call for desperate measures, if one is to survive.''

Stone's surprise diminished as he considered her words.

"Might you be speaking from experience, Miss Blake?"

She nodded her head stiffly. "I suppose I am."

"But you did not prostitute yourself."

She felt the warmth of a blush heating her skin. "True."

"And you did not turn to stealing or cheating others," he said, actually inviting comment.

"I suppose I've been fortunate enough to earn a reasonable living in other ways."

He nodded his head. "Is that fortune or cunning, lass?"

Coady experienced a sense of foreboding as she continued to peer up at him. He was the strangest man, always questioning, always probing. She wondered what there was about her humdrum life that so intrigued him. Not that it really mattered what he thought. But she was beginning to find him annoying. "It is called intelligence, Mr. MacGregor," she returned smartly. "I'm just a huckleberry above a persimmon, and that is all there is to it."

"Intelligent and modest, too," he noted with wry humor.

Stone did not know why he felt he had to press her. He should be admiring of a young woman who had the skills and fortitude to go out in a man's world and fend for herself. But the women in his past had always been in need of him. He was more familiar with women who were soft and vulnerable and there was apparently nothing vulnerable about Coady Blake. Apparently. Stone sensed a hidden vulnerability about her—suspected her last comment was one of sheer bravado. Coady put on a brave front but she was a young woman and she was alone. And everyone, including most of the men he knew, needed someone, sometime.

He was also dealing with a niggling suspicion that Coady was not the innocent she appeared to be.

Harrison stood by and watched the exchange between Coady and the stranger with great interest. He had never seen her quite so cocky. It was curious to him that she even got involved in a discourse over the arrest of a prostitute. There were arrests taking place on the streets of Dawson every day. It was only the presence of the Mounties that kept the city from complete and utter chaos, not to mention bloodshed. It was curious, too, the way Coady looked at the tall, blond stranger, as if she were challenging him. But challenging him to what? Whatever was going on between these two was making Harrison mighty curious. And Coady was so involved in addressing the other man, she had forgotten to make any introductions. He also suspected she had completely forgotten *he* was there.

Stone's attention was again drawn to the man standing so close to Coady's back. He had seen this man attempting to shield his companion from the unsavory performance of the whore. He had also witnessed Coady's failure to accept such protection. "I don't believe we've met."

Harrison stepped to Coady's left. "Harrison Trelaine."

Stone accepted the man's hand. "Stone MacGregor."

"You know Coady, obviously."

Stone's gaze focused briefly on her lovely face. "Indeed. We met earlier today when I happened by the, ah . . . her establishment."

Ben admired Stone's choice of words; he just *happened* by?

Stone was busy trying to determine the relationship between Coady and Trelaine. Certainly Harrison seemed attentive. Coady, on the other hand, appeared more distant, leaving him to assume the two were merely friends. And, if he should be wrong, well . . . the relationship between them was really none of his business.

But he tended to feel that Coady's naiveté was his business. "Getting back to the topic at hand," he started, returning his complete attention to the young brunette, "I agree with your belief that a young woman should be able to earn a living. In theory, that is. I would not agree if 'earning a living' entails causing harm to others."

"Are you suggesting that woman tried to harm you?" Coady asked lightly. "You're considerably larger than she, Mr. MacGregor."

Stone was not moved to smile by her teasing tone. "Chelsea and her partner attempted to drug me and rob me."

"Chelsea?" she murmured as she stared up at him knowingly. "I see. Certainly her *partner*, as you say, is not overly fond of you."

"All they got for their efforts was a trip to jail." He shrugged casually. "They may possibly be deported."

"How did you manage that?"

Stone blinked. "Manage what?"

"To have them arrested?" she probed. "I mean, one must assume you were alone with, ah, *Chelsea*. Whatever were you doing there, Mr. MacGregor?"

Stone eyed her severely. "I believe you know the answer to that, lass," he said quietly.

Coady ignored the soft chill that ran down her spine as he uttered the word *lass*. He used it almost as an endearment. Which, of course, he had no right to do. It was just another biff that spurred her into prodding him. "And you did not succumb to the drug? Should we admire your cunning? Or is it your nature to be as suspicious as you are curious?"

"Suspicious," he agreed.

"How then did you know they were about to rob you? Surely if you were awake, they would not have been so bold? I find this curious. You must have felt threatened somehow? And how did you manage to extricate yourself from such a terrible situation? Did you merely call out for the police?"

Stone did not consider turn-about was fair play. Having mocking questions thrust in his direction, at his expense, was not something he would normally tolerate. And, as much as she was having a very good time of it, he could not allow her to delve too deeply. Slanting Ben a surreptitious, cautioning frown, he said, "Suffice it to say, Mr. Keystone, being the good friend, came to my rescue."

"Ah, good ol' Ben. That's what some say."

A teasing smile from Coady made Ben feel his shirt collar had suddenly become too tight.

He laughed. "Please don't tell me what the *others* say, Coady!"

"*I* say you should keep your friend out of a place where he could get into trouble, Ben. You'll have less rescuing to do."

"I wouldn't call it a *rescue*."

Coady's laughing expression turned on Stone. "What would you call it, Mr. MacGregor?"

He was stuck; what the hell could he call it without giving away too much?

"Very well," she continued, "I suggest, Ben, you keep your friend away from females he's not capable of handling."

"Now just a damned minute . . ." sputtered MacGregor.

Harrison frowned at her, demanding softly, "What the devil are you doing?"

Coady realized then that she had gone too far. There was just something about Stone MacGregor that turned out the worst in her. He roused in her a need to spar, a need to prod and plague, as a method of protecting herself. It was beyond her why she felt this way. Perhaps because he had unsettled her when he had appeared at the door of her shop earlier. She had not liked the fact that he had been watching her. And she certainly did not like his terrible habit of constantly questioning. Then again, why should she worry about his questions? She had a past, true. But what could a man like MacGregor do to her? He was more of a nuisance than a threat; after all, the man could not visit a whore without getting himself into trouble. Still, she was possessed of a distinct notion she should avoid him at all costs.

Her apprehensions over MacGregor did not, however, negate the fact Coady was somewhat disturbed by her behavior toward him. Looping her arm around Harrison's, she said quietly, "I think you had best take me to supper."

Not usually a man of great conscience, Trelaine, nevertheless, felt he should attempt to somehow right the moment. Besides, he had an almost licentious desire to see Coady and Stone MacGregor engage in further verbal pugilism. "We are on our way to the Dawson Cafe for a late supper, Mr. MacGregor. You are welcome, if you would care to join us."

Stone's curious attention was directed completely toward the young woman at Harrison's side. "I suspect *welcome* is a poor choice of words," he said. "But thank you for offering."

Coady's steady gaze locked with his for a moment, mirroring equal measures of confusion and contrition.

Harrison nodded his head, bade both men good evening, and turned away with Coady on his arm.

Ben frowned as he and his companion watched the couple move along the busy street. "I've seen Coady conduct business with men. I've watched her barter, I have witnessed her at play. I once observed her consoling a man who missed his loved ones. I've even seen her quietly order a man to leave her shop. But I've never seen her quite like that.''

"It appears Miss Blake has taken a distinct dislike to me."

"I wouldn't say that."

Stone turned a frown upon the younger man. "You wouldn't?"

"I would say her behavior bordered on flirtation."

Stone's head jerked in reaction. "Flirtation!"

"She's not very good at it, though," Ben said thoughtfully as he watched Trelaine and Coady move farther away. "Perhaps she's never had an opportunity to practice."

"With all the men in this town?" he asked skeptically.

Ben turned his head and smiled at his companion. "Maybe she's never had *reason* to practice before now."

"Keystone, you are close to giving me reason to question your sanity. Not to mention your powers of reasoning."

Ben shook his head. "I do have to wonder what you've done to her."

"*Done to her*? Nothing other than engage in conversation."

"Must have been quite a chat," he offered dryly.

"I ask too many questions, according to her. Don't you find that curious?"

"Not really."

"Why would she resent a few friendly inquiries, unless she has something to hide?"

Ben seemed to find that humorous. "I suggest you didn't get where you are today by making *friendly* inquiries."

The corners of Stone's mouth curved upward. "Perhaps you have something there."

"Are you concerned over what we may find out about Bloodstone? Is that why you're so suspicious of her?"

He wasn't certain how to respond to Ben's question. For the first time in recent memory, he was completely uncertain of his motives. "Possibly." Stone looked again in the direction in which Trelaine had escorted Coady. The couple had disappeared amongst the throngs of people who milled about Dawson's Front Street.

Coady Blake's mysterious behavior lingered in his mind.

"If Zachary isn't legitimate, I'm quite certain Coady is not aware of the fact."

Stone snorted. "You keep jumping to that woman's defense. I find that curious, too. You must remember ignorance is not an excuse for partaking in any sort of illegalities. There could be a number of couples living in sin, quite unknowingly. How do you think they are going to feel?"

"They might feel any number of things, I suppose. The least of which could be anger. But that is not to say Coady knowingly led anyone astray."

"I don't recall saying that she has. Or *would*, for that matter."

"Will you tell her? Coady, I mean. If Bloodstone should prove to be a fraud."

Stone gave the matter a moment's thought. "I won't be the one to tell her." Considering the mayhem going on inside his head, this, his first day in Dawson, he would not be in any hurry to reveal his true colors to the lovely Miss Blake.

They walked the remainder of the way to the Dawson Cafe in silence. The only thing that captured Coady's attention along the way was a wolf who boldly dared to scavenge in the refuse strewn between two hastily constructed places of business. Such scenes were the plague of Dawson. There was no shortage of discarded food scraps and other leavings thrown about the alleys without a care. Open ditches ran appallingly with filth. During the warm summer months, the stench could only be described as revolting. It was rarely a pretty sight when a mix of humanity converged by the thousands upon a place. Dawson was no different. It was the early throngs who had made Dawson and they would have been responsible for bringing it down if not for the arrival of the Royal Northwest Mounted Police, their medical officers and appointed clergy. These men, new to the territory, were likely the ones who would save the town. The legitimate residents of Dawson, of whom Coady considered herself one, gave their support to the Mounties.

Harrison held the cafe door for Coady and, with the palm of his hand riding the small of her back, directed her toward his favorite corner table. The cafe was somewhat quiet at this hour; only two other couples and a pair of miners occupied the spacious room.

"You think I was rude," Coady stated as Harrison held a chair while she sat.

He eased her chair forward before taking his place opposite. Smoothing his spotless black suit coat over his thighs, he replied, "I must admit your behavior surprised me."

Coady smiled, chagrined. "How diplomatic of you, Harrison. Thank you."

"You seem to harbor considerable dislike for Mr. MacGregor. Why?"

Failing to meet his eyes, she shook her head. "I don't know. There's just something about him."

"Has he offended you somehow?"

"His presence seems to be offense enough. He is constantly probing. Each time we have met, questions have rolled off his tongue with the speed of a professional interrogator. I find it annoying."

"You don't have anything to hide, my dear."

Thank you for that, too, she mused. His faith in her was touching, if a little misguided.

"I shouldn't think a few questions would bother you. Perhaps MacGregor is just a healthy male wanting to know more about a beautiful woman?"

Coady doubted that very much and the look she sent Harrison told him so.

He laughed. "Don't look so disbelieving. There is that possibility. You are a very lovely woman, Coady."

She smiled at him as she propped her elbow on the table, her fist supporting her chin. "Do you really think so?"

"I do."

"Would it bother you if Stone MacGregor was 'a healthy male wanting to know more' about me?"

"It would bother me if you were not desirous of his attentions."

Chapter Four

They were coming in droves. Thousands of poverty-weary people plodded along the hazardous journey north to the Yukon through the Chilkoot and White Pass trails. Six hundred miles of grueling mountain passes and treacherous waterways tested the strength of the youngest and most fit. Some lost their battle against the elements even though the Mounties did an admirable job of safeguarding the stampeders along the trail.

The police had only twenty men in the territory when it all began.

It had taken time for word to spread beyond the territory to the outside world. George Carmack and his First Nations companions, Skookum Jim and Tagish Charlie, had struck a bonanza on Rabbit Creek, a tributary of the Klondike River, in 1896. Now the whole world seemed to know.

The Mounties had their small contingent at Fort Constantine when the cry of "gold!" rent the air. That news sent a chill through Inspector Charles Constantine that moved him to desperate measures. His men would be helpless against a concerted public uproar, should one occur. And, when the smell of quick riches was in the air, anything could happen. Levelheaded men became unbalanced. The most honest of citizens resorted to cunning behavior and adopted trickery and deceit as their means of gleaning wealth. Constantine begged his superiors in Regina to send reinforcements and a Maxim machine gun.

Help arrived.

The machine gun did not.

No one really took Inspector Constantine seriously back then.

Stone MacGregor had been among the first to arrive. Assigned to oversee customs operations at Chilkoot Pass, Stone had directed his men in the care of the newcomers, in addition to the unit's other functions of collecting duties and inspecting the supplies being brought into the territory by the stampeders. The aim was to ensure the safety and survival of everyone who crossed the Canadian border—although no one knew the exact location of the boundary between Alaska and Canada—at a place where staples were in short supply and communication with the outside world was slow, at best.

The Mounties passed on the best of their hard-earned knowledge of survival to those who cared to learn. Mossy spruce swamps up and down the major waterways were sites to be avoided. In addition to battling ferocious insects, a man could not even pitch his tent.

Stripping ground cover down to the rock-hard permafrost in an attempt to build a cabin was also a big mistake. The exposed permafrost tended to melt in summer and buildings would tilt and sink in the muddy ground.

Men had to sometimes travel thirty miles to find construction-quality timber. But structures built from the wood provided little in the way of comfort for the inhabitants, as it was the nature of the green wood to sweat. With experience, and the help of the First Nations people, the Mounties learned all these lessons and more.

By the time Stone had been ordered to report to Dawson City, he had watched a sea of faces, male and female, cross the border via his customs post. There were few people he had met at the Chilkoot Pass who remained in his memory, but now and again he would see a man on the streets of Dawson and swear he had seen the face before. The women did tend to stand out more as they were fewer in number, but at no time could he say for certain he had met specific people before.

Coady Blake was one such suspicious shadow from another place and time.

Stone would see her on the street and something in the way she smiled, or the way she frowned, would tweak his memory. By the time he had spent a month in Dawson City, however, Stone had decided his sense of having met Coady before was mere wishful thinking on his part. A prior meeting, after all, would give him reason to talk with her at length, to discover just when and where they had met.

When he caught himself looking for excuses to converse with her, Stone became angry. He had shared no more then a few brief greetings with Coady since the night of the whore's arrest and that was probably for the best. As long as his orders were to remain undercover, he could not afford to get too close to anyone; particularly not a curious little brunette.

In spite of the fact that his good sense told him to keep away, Stone possessed a healthy interest in the woman whose business partner he had ordered investigated. Like many men, he often found himself wishing for the companionship of someone softer than the rowdy gold miners and the task-oriented policemen who occupied his divided, clandestine world.

But, aside from the ladies of the evening, Coady Blake was one of only a few unattached females around. None of the other single women he had met was as ardent, as impetuous, or as intriguing as Coady. And, certainly, none could match her in beauty. Coady alone made it difficult for a man who admired beautiful and intelligent women to resist pursuing her with decidedly male intentions; good or otherwise.

Resist he should and he would.

Coady would not be in the best of spirits for a good while, at any rate, and Stone suspected he would be better off to avoid her. Actually, he probably should have warned the entire town to avoid her for a day or two.

The woman who was frequently the object of his thoughts lately was meeting with Superintendent Simmons at the Dawson headquarters of the Royal Northwest Mounted Police. There, Coady would be informed that her partner in business—her partner in *crime*, as it were—was not an ordained minister. The man was nothing more than a self-appointed preacher who had fleeced a dozen miners of their gold. Between sobriety, performing weddings and the numerous occasions he was too drunk to lift his head, his days were filled with schemes and scams.

Unfortunately, not only had Coady hooked up with a cheat, a drunkard and a liar, she had been party to several illegal marriages.

Stone and Ben had managed to convince their superintendent that Coady was as much a victim of Zachary Bloodstone's deceptions as anyone else. Their tactics had worked, with the result no charges would be brought against her. But Simmons would likely not go easy with her. "How else is the young woman to learn a valuable lesson," he had asked, "if an indelible impression of the wrong done here is not stamped into her memory?"

Stone had witnessed Simmons' brand of discipline on more than one occasion. The superintendent could make seasoned policemen quiver over the possible ramifications of the smallest misdeed. He shuddered to think what Simmons could do to the tender side of a naive young woman. And he believed Coady to be *naive*. Despite the fact she was clever, ambitious and possessed of a good head for business, he was convinced she was an ingenue in other respects.

Stone pushed away from the building façade against which he had been leaning as the front door of the rough cabin across the street opened. For the past ninety minutes he had been watching the structure in which the Dawson detachment of the police made their headquarters.

Finally his patience was rewarded.

Coady emerged into the unbearable heat of the late July day. Torrential rains had plagued them with little respite for the past three weeks, bringing heat so excessive it was not unusual to see grown men collapse on the streets. And, if the heat were not enough, this summer of 1898 seemed to have spawned mosquitoes as big as horse flies.

But, clearly, there was more than heat and rain and mosquitoes pestering Coady Blake today.

When she walked to the edge of the boardwalk and raised her skirts, Stone called out to get her attention.

Coady lifted her head as the male voice called for her to wait.

"I'll help you!"

She watched Stone MacGregor make his way gingerly through the ankle-deep mud of Front Street and could barely suppress an audible groan; of all the people she did not want to see right now, he had to top the list!

"I can manage just fine, thank you!" she called, even though she was facing mire that resembled a bog more than the main street of town.

Stone was not about to be put off.

"I'm sure you can," he agreed as he stepped in front of her, steadying the position of his booted feet in the slick mud. "But you're wearing a particularly fetching gown today. I would hate to see it caked with muck."

"So would I," she muttered ruefully.

He smiled and made a showy bow. "Then allow me to assist, Miss Blake."

"Mr. MacGregor, I am really not in the best of humor and not at all in the mood to play. If you'll excuse me?"

Stone's hand snaked out and he grasped her wrist. "What's wrong?" he asked quietly as his gaze searched her eyes. "What's happened? You're as white as—"

Coady held up one hand. "Please don't say it."

"Are you ill?"

For a moment he thought she would laugh, but the smile she offered up as she shook her head was ghostly.

"Ill? Yes, I suppose I am. Quite ill, really. If you'll let go of my arm, I'll—"

"Be on your way back to work?" he suggested. "I think not, lass," he added with genuine concern. He was a little taken aback with this show of humility from her. As a hard-nosed businesswoman, he had not thought Coady would be so shaken by what she had just learned from his superior. Apparently he had been wrong. She appeared completely distraught and, seeing her like this, made Stone feel somewhat guilty—much to his surprise. "Come with me."

Coady stepped back as he mounted the decrepit excuse for a boardwalk. His hand slipped upward from her wrist to support her elbow.

"I have a lot to think about, Stone. Please, just let me go."

He did not miss the fact she had addressed him in the familiar. He simply chose not to comment; now was not the time to tease her. "Come to the cafe. You look as if you need a good strong cup of coffee."

"I don't think coffee will help," she suggested in a small voice.

He studied her pale complexion, the dark pools of her eyes which looked as if they might flood the banks of her auburn lashes if she blinked. "I think you're right. Come along," he said firmly and, turning, pulled her along at his side.

"Where do you think you are taking me?"

"The Dominion Saloon. You need something stronger

than coffee.'' It was in that instant that he felt a stronger resistance.

''I can't go there!'' she squawked as she firmly planted her feet.

When he turned his gaze upon her, Stone could see Coady was teetering on panic at the mere thought of entering the place. ''Would you feel better if we went to the Golden Slipper?'' he asked easily. ''Your friend, Trelaine, will find us a quiet corner where we can talk unobserved.''

Coady tipped her head to the side. ''Why are you being so nice to me?''

He was genuinely surprised by the question. ''Have I ever *not* been *nice* to you?''

She had to think about that one, but after fleeting consideration she had to acknowledge the truth in his question. While he was a pest with all his questions, he had never been rude to her. Whereas she had probably earned his contempt, at least once or twice. ''No,'' she admitted.

''Good,'' he said cheerfully. ''For a moment I thought perhaps all my mother's teachings had been in vain.''

It suddenly occurred to Coady that he was not asking questions of her. She liked him far better this way; attentive and concerned. Somehow she felt as if he could be a genuine friend if she put forth a little effort in return. Lord knew she needed someone to talk with at this very moment. She had committed a terrible wrong and, while she knew what must be done, she also needed confirmation that there was not more she should be doing. Harrison would listen and he would be honest with her. But he would also be protective. He would be so concerned that she not punish herself when she was not wholly to blame that he would not give his entire attention to the needs of the people she had harmed.

Coady had an instinctive feeling it would be different with Stone. ''All right,'' she said quietly. ''I'll go with you.''

Stone nodded his head as she stepped up to his side.

He immediately released her hand. It was not his place to give comfort. *His* objective was to ensure Coady notified the victims of her "Marriage by Design" scheme that they were, indeed, casualties of a money-making venture gone wrong. "Am I to assume you've received bad news?" he asked as they walked along.

"Bad news is rather an understatement."

He took her elbow briefly, steadying her as Coady lifted her skirts and picked her way through a minor bog. As they progressed, Stone helped her through more sections of mud where feeble attempts to protect the boots of pedestrians had failed. His hand was warm, his grip sure and Coady found herself wishing she could just lean against him, if only for a moment. No matter how they had responded to each other in the past, Coady knew instinctively—as she knew herself—that Stone MacGregor was a man who could shelter a woman tenderly if that was what she needed.

With his next breath, Stone scattered her thoughts of tenderness on the hot July breeze, like so many dusty gray ashes.

"If I understated the situation, how would you describe this news you've received?"

Here we go with the questions, she mused. She should have known it would only be a matter of time before he reverted back to his usual medium of conversing. "The news I received is quite devastating, Mr. MacGregor." She stopped walking, forcing him to do the same. When he turned to look at her, Coady raised a face that projected her misery. "You're looking at a ruined woman."

Her dramatics forced Stone to jam his hands into his jeans pockets as a means of forestalling additional guilt on his part. "Oh, surely nothing as drastic as that?"

She graced him with a brisk nod of her head before marching on toward the Golden Slipper. "Well, possibly not *ruined*," she muttered as he matched her determined gait. "But I've done a terrible thing I cannot right. I can only try to make amends."

Contrary to everything he had heard and thought about her, Coady's tone was suggestive of the concern of a softhearted woman and not the cool-headed logic of a huckster. He felt his own heart begin to soften toward her a little. "What is this terrible wrong you cannot right, lass?"

Before Coady fully realized the distance they had traveled, they arrived at the swinging half-doors of the Golden Slipper.

She stood before the portal, hesitant to enter. Odd, in all the time she had known Harrison Trelaine, for all the evening suppers she had shared with him, she had never set foot inside this particular establishment. Saloons were out of her realm and she knew it. There was a side of life beyond those doors she knew little about and did not want to experience firsthand. In her mind a saloon represented a man's world where liquor was sorely misused, companions cheated and women abused. In spite of the words she had thrown out by way of challenge to Stone MacGregor, she did feel that prostitutes were victims of men's base behavior. The women would be forced to earn their living in a more respectable fashion, if not for the demands of men.

During her early days in Dawson, Coady had avoided Harrison because he owned such a wicked place. But his charm had eventually worn away her reluctance. And, as of today, who was she to judge a body right or wrong?

"We don't have to go in if you would rather not."

Stone's quietly spoken words came from close behind her.

She shook her head. "I'm here and I'm going in," she said quietly. "Who knows? Perhaps this is where I belong."

Stone's face crinkled in a confused frown. "What do you mean by that?"

Coady looked over her shoulder as her hand reached out to push one of the doors. "It doesn't matter."

As she entered the relatively cool, dark interior of the

Golden Slipper, Coady acknowledged that perhaps she had patterned her own life closer to the seamy side than she had realized. In her quest for survival and a modicum of wealth she had, without conscience, pushed the legal edge of the law a time or two. Even during a time in her life when desperation had dictated her actions, Coady had crossed over that nebulous legal line but once. This situation, however, was very different. It was one thing to act under one's own initiative and be solely responsible for any consequences. Being responsible for the actions of another was quite a different matter.

A scoundrel had duped her and, completely fooled, she had unwittingly deceived others.

"Let's find a table in the back, shall we?"

Coady had almost forgotten her escort. Now, having been pulled from her musings by Stone's softly spoken words, she could feel his hand riding ever so lightly on the small of her back, guiding her through the maze of tables, gambling and otherwise.

Very few people frequented the Golden Slipper at this time of day. It was early yet. Within hours the large room with its overhead oil lamps and high beams would be bursting at the seams with rowdy men drowning their sorrows over the day's failure to produce wealth while others celebrated the find of a mother lode. Women dressed in gaudy, tight-waisted gowns that liberally displayed not only their bosom but a wealth of leg as well, would be there to soothe the forlorn and revel with the victorious. Coady had seen and heard it all a hundred times while passing the doors of a dozen such places in town.

Stone pulled a chair back from a round wooden table set in a dark corner of the room. "Sit. I'll fetch us something to drink."

Coady smoothed her skirts beneath her legs and sat. "I don't drink spirits."

Stone looked down at her pale face and frowned. "You do today."

"Coady?"

Her head turned at the sound of the deep, familiar male voice. "Harrison," she said warmly as he approached.

Harrison cast her a curious glance before frowning at MacGregor. "Why would you bring her in here?"

Stone did not care to be taken to task by any man, least of all a saloon owner. "I thought you were her friend."

"Of course I'm her friend."

"Well, look at her, man."

He did. Harrison forgot his original concern and focused his attention on Coady's white face and dark eyes. "What is it, Coady?" he asked softly as he sat in a chair at her side and reached for her hand across the tabletop. "You look like death."

"Ohhh," she moaned with disgust. "It isn't that dire, for heaven's sake. I've just got a terrible mess to sort out."

"A mess?"

"I'll get some drinks," Stone offered.

Continuing to stare at Coady, Harrison shook his head. "No. Leave that to me." He squeezed her hand and got to his feet. "I'll be right back, sweetheart."

Stone pulled out a chair on Coady's left and sat. "Sweetheart?" he questioned.

Coady shot him a unappreciative frown. "Well, we *are* friends."

"The last time I called a lady *sweetheart*, we were not friends, lass."

"I can imagine."

Stone eyed her speculatively as he slumped back in his chair and locked his long fingers together across his middle. "Can you now?"

Much to her chagrin, Coady experienced a decided warming of her complexion. "In a manner of speaking, of course."

"Of course."

"Oh, stop that," she admonished even as relief light-

Jill Metcalf

ened her large brown eyes at Harrison's return.

"From my own private stock," he told them as he set three glasses and a bottle in the center of the scarred wooden table.

Without ceremony, Stone reached for the bottle, withdrew the cork, and began pouring amber liquid into each of the shot glasses. The first he placed in front of Coady's hands. "Go easy on it," he said quietly.

Coady eyed the drink speculatively. "I don't think so," she muttered.

Stone filled the remaining glasses.

Harrison reached for her hand again and lightly squeezed her fingers. "Go ahead. Just take a sip. You'll feel better."

"I feel all right now," she admitted sardonically. "Aside from the fact that I am angry, disgusted, humiliated and apprehensive."

Harrison flashed Stone a curious frown before returning his attention to Coady. "Drink. And then you can tell me your troubles."

Coady placed her fingers around the glass and slowly raised it toward her lips.

"Where did you find her?" Harrison asked of Stone.

"I saw her come out of police headquarters and she looked a little pale . . ." He allowed a casual shrug to complete his statement.

"Police? What did they want with her?"

Stone shook his head. "She hasn't told me yet."

"Stop talking as if I weren't here," Coady ordered as she continued to hold the glass beneath her nose.

Harrison pressed his forefinger beneath the bottom of her glass. "Drink." He smiled as her nose wrinkled before the liquid had even touched her lips. "Good!" he added as she shuddered over the taste of the fiery brew. "Now talk."

Coady released her hold on the glass and sat back with a weary sigh. "Zachary Bloodstone is a fraud."

"A fraud? In what respect?" Harrison's brow furrowed in curiosity.

Stone's gaze wandered lazily but intently from one companion to the other.

Coady was busy inspecting the back of her hand. "He's not a preacher."

"What?"

She responded to Harrison's question by locking her gaze with his. "He is not ordained," she said with increased emphasis. "For some reason the police decided to examine Zachary's credentials. Whatever possessed them, I'll probably never know. And why now? He's been working with me for months, after all. Zachary has been the very marrow of 'Marriage by Design.' And now I'm informed he doesn't have any," she added wearily. "*Credentials*, that is."

"Oh, Lord," Harrison breathed as he, too, slumped back in his chair.

"Precisely."

Harrison raised his hand, his forefinger covering a wicked grin that threatened to change the entire course of the conversation. "You're saying all those people he married aren't married at all?"

She sighed. "That's what I'm saying."

He couldn't help it. He threw back his head and laughed.

Coady's brown eyes darkened and flashed him a warning. "It isn't funny, Harrison Trelaine! You're laughing at other peoples' expense."

Harrison nodded his head at her as he attempted to control his mirth. "I know. I'm sorry. It's just that . . ."

Coady linked her fingers together on top of the table. "I'm responsible for this mess," she said quietly.

That comment abruptly sobered Harrison. "Not entirely, sweetheart," he said in her defense. "You were tricked by Bloodstone, after all."

She bent her elbows and pressed the tips of her thumbs against her forehead. "But 'Marriage by Design' was my

67

idea. I'm the one who hired Zachary. I never thought to check whether or not he was legitimate."

Harrison looked at Stone. "Too trusting."

Stone nodded his head. "Apparently."

"I simply took him at his word," she added unhappily. "More fool I."

Harrison squeezed her hand. "Don't punish yourself, my pet. You are not the first to be taken in by a scoundrel. And at his age, Bloodstone has had a number of years to perfect his craft."

Coady suddenly envisioned every person in Dawson having a good laugh at her expense. The money-grubbing Blake woman getting set back on her heels. Oh, she knew what they called her. It was jealousy, pure and simple. She had the brains and the wherewithal to earn a very good living and people, mostly men, found that hard to swallow. But she had not, frankly, given a damn.

Until today.

So, you've made a mistake, she silently reflected. *Let them laugh. I'm not the first person in the history of the human race to have made a mistake. Look at the whopper Adam pulled and he got himself kicked out of a beautiful garden. A place that had to have been a whole lot better than Dawson.* That settled, Coady determined she would walk the streets of Dawson with her head held high, as she had in the past. Still . . . "I have to make amends."

Both men directed their attention to the source of the small voice.

"I have to find those couples and pay back the money they paid for their weddings." A shadow of a smile, an unhappy expression, moved across her face as she looked at each man in turn. "First I have to tell them they are *not* husband and wife."

"That should stir up some unpleasant reactions," Stone muttered, staring into the half empty glass that rested between his hands.

"MacGregor's right," Harrison said thoughtfully. "It

could be dangerous for you. Lord knows how some of
the people might take the news.''

She nodded her head and stared at him earnestly.
''How would you react?''

''I'm, ah, not in a position to answer that, now, am
I?'' he said quickly. ''I'm going to send someone with
you, Coady,'' he added thoughtfully. ''I'll find a good
man I can trust to protect you and—''

''I'll escort the lady.''

Stunned expressions turned his way.

Stone shrugged. ''I'm fairly capable.''

''Of what?'' Coady asked ruefully.

Stone scowled. ''Of protecting you.''

Harrison pushed himself up straight in his chair. ''No
offense, MacGregor, but we know very little about you.''

Stone shrugged and drained his glass. ''Ask away.
Anything you want.''

''Why would you offer?'' Coady asked in complete
wonder. ''The few occasions we've been together I seem
to annoy you as much as you irritate me.''

Stone's dark blue gaze met her look of utter puzzlement. ''I wouldn't say that.''

''You wouldn't? You mean you would be prepared to
spend several days gallivanting around the countryside
with me?''

He grinned lasciviously. ''Sounds like fun.''

Coady felt her complexion warm again and balled her
fists on the tabletop. ''No, absolutely not. I will not have
you.''

''I'm not offering marriage, lass,'' he returned dryly.

His jocular thrust merely earned him a murderous
glare.

However, having little choice and, knowing he had
truly angered her, Stone relented. ''All right. I'll stop
teasing,'' he promised as he sat forward, resting his forearms on the table. ''Such a trip could be of benefit to us
both. I will agree to protect you and, while we're searching out your former . . . ah, clients, you will provide me

with suggestions of a likely place to stake a claim.''

One auburn brow, as silky as sable, arched high on her forehead. ''Oh, I will?''

Their gazes locked, Stone nodded his head sharply.

''And what if I give you advice on a claim that brings you millions?''

He smiled. ''I shall be a very happy man.''

''That is not what I had in mind.''

He stared at her a moment and then raised his chin in a knowing gesture. ''Ahhh! Of course! You would want a share!''

Coady smiled prettily.

''Are you willing to share in the work?''

''I have plenty of work of my own.''

''And if I should suffer a loss? Would you be partners with me then, lass? Would you finance me a second chance?''

Coady turned to Harrison as she raised one hand. ''You see?'' Her delicate palm slapped the table. ''He converses only through questions.''

Harrison *saw*, all right. He saw something far more interesting than two people sparring. He wondered if Coady realized that MacGregor quite possibly had more on his mind than panning for gold? Intriguing possibilities flashed through his mind. Of course, Harrison wanted Coady to have a good man; the best. He wanted her well cared for and happy.

He ignored the indignant Coady for the moment and directed his comments to Stone. ''I'm not in any way Coady's keeper, Mr. MacGregor, but I cannot bring myself to send her off with a man neither she nor I have known well. Would you be opposed to our giving you an answer to your kind offer in a day or two?''

Coady's eyes almost crossed in vexation. ''What are you saying?''

Harrison shot her a brief warning glance. ''We'll discuss the matter, pet.''

Stone's curiosity over the relationship between these

two had been piqued, that was for certain. But he thought he had best let them get on with their discussion. One way or another, however, he would be taking that trip with Coady. He had his orders.

Getting to his feet, Stone extended his hand to Harrison. "I'll leave you to it," he said. "I'll stop round in a day or two."

Harrison rose and accepted MacGregor's hand, holding on just long enough to test the man's strength. "Tomorrow should do just fine, Mr. MacGregor. Stop by after the noon hour and I will buy you a drink."

Stone nodded his head, gave Coady a brief farewell glance, and turned away.

"I'm not going anywhere with that man," she muttered, as Harrison lowered himself into his chair.

"If MacGregor proves to be the best man for the job, my pet, I just might have to persuade you."

When next we have a frosty Sunday in July, she mused.

Chapter Five

She could not have forgotten how to saddle her own
horse.

But she had, apparently. The cinch knot had Coady
baffled this morning for some strange reason. "Not
enough sleep," she muttered, her eyes glaring as her nervous fingers refused to obey a simple mental command.

"Here. Let me do that."

Coady stepped away from the roan she had rented and
let Harrison take over.

"Be gentle with her," she admonished softly. "There
are few enough horses as it is."

She was not telling him anything he, and everyone in
the territory, did not know, but he let the comment pass.
"You didn't sleep well, I take it?"

She smiled ruefully. "It is that obvious?"

Harrison turned his head briefly and grinned. "I know
you." A simple statement and a matter of fact.

"Yes, you do."

"I don't envy you your mission."

"Neither do I."

Stepping back to his side, keeping her back to the horse and her gaze on Stone MacGregor, Coady muttered, "I can't believe I let you talk me into this."

Harrison stuck his knee against the horse's belly, forcing the animal to draw in. The moment her belly was no longer distended, he pulled up, tightening the saddle cinch. "Are we going through this again?"

Coady's arms uncrossed from beneath her breasts and fell to her sides. "Harrison, I would rather go alone."

Reaching up, gripping the saddle horn, he half turned toward her. "You are not going alone. I know," he added, holding a hand palm forward to halt her protest, "you know your way around. You've been out to the creeks a dozen times. But you haven't been out there under these circumstances. You're not collecting rents this trip. You might well receive greater protests than the grumbles that you usually get from the men who hand over their hard-earned gold to you."

Even though his initial reaction had been to laugh over all those married folk not being married at all, Harrison knew the toll the situation was taking on her. Coady was truly in anguish. God alone knew the sort of reception her news would bring. If all the couples were content in their relationships, then the return of their money and a few harsh words might suffice. They would simply seek a legal marriage the next time they were in town. However, should a man not be happy with the relationship, while the woman lived in a state of loving bliss, or vice versa, he did not want to think of the repercussions.

"These people you are looking for on this trip may not be overjoyed with the message you're bringing them. And, sweetheart," he added, *sotto voce,* "I am not convinced, as the saying goes, that no one ever shot the messenger."

Her head tipped in Stone's direction. "Who's to say that *he* won't shoot me?"

"Every bit of information I could dig up about this

man indicates he's honest and capable, as he said. He shoots straight, is an expert with a knife, and has the survival instincts of a native. Besides, I brought you this." Reaching inside his coat to a breast pocket, Harrison pulled out a derringer. "It's small but very effective, I assure you."

Coady stared at the gun nestled in the palm of his hand. And then she looked up, small worry lines creasing her brow. "This is so ridiculous. If you insist someone go with me, why could it not be you?"

He had thought about that. As her friend, he should be going with her. But Harrison's instincts told him this arrangement might be far better in the long run. He felt he was amply providing for her protection and, as much as she protested against MacGregor, he suspected a friendship between them would develop into a stronger tie. He often wished that for her. She was a young and vibrant woman who needed a good man. To her he said only, "Who will mind our respective businesses if we are both away for a week or two?"

There was that, of course. There was no one else Coady would trust with her affairs while she was out of town. Staring down at Harrison's shiny boots, she said, "Well you have me there, I suppose."

He reached out and placed a forefinger beneath her chin. "Look at me." When she did, their gazes locked, each staring at the other with open honesty. "You're not afraid of him, are you, pet?" he whispered.

Coady shook her head. "Of course not."

Of course not, he parroted silently. She did not think she was afraid of anything. "Then be good and don't make me worry. You be nice to him and he'll be nice to you," he teased, lightly squeezing her chin between his thumb and forefinger. "You help him and he'll help you."

"Very funny."

"That's how it works."

"I'll probably die of a severe case of *questioning*."

*   *   *

Stone checked the knots in the thick rope that held their supplies in place on the back of the pack mule. He could not hear the conversation taking place only a few feet away.

Coady looked damned enticing this morning. He could hardly believe trousers could look so good or be rounded out so nicely. The belt around her slim waist accentuated the fact there was a very womanly figure above and below the thing. The early morning heat had already forced her to undo the top button of her high-collared blouse and roll the narrow sleeves back to reveal slim, fine-boned wrists. Coady had twisted her abundant auburn hair and pinned it loosely high atop her head. The style looked elegant, yet simple and cool. She *looked* cool. She *looked* delightful.

God help him.

Stone was still amazed he had been so readily invited to participate in this little venture. It seemed more logical for Trelaine to be Coady's escort. Particularly given the depth of their relationship. The fact Harrison was entrusting Coady to *him* spoke volumes.

True, Stone had a few fellows place some well-designed information about town; facts to share which would prove him worthy of being an able escort. But why trust her to the hands of another man unless Harrison either did not feel himself capable of the task or he was not as *involved* with Coady as Stone had first suspected. And Stone did not believe Trelaine would be afraid of the confrontations that were inevitable as Coady shared her news with her victims. That left him ruminating on the relationship, or lack thereof.

Walking around the mule, Stone was reaching for the reins of his rented mount when Harrison approached his side.

"I'm placing something very precious into your care, MacGregor," he said in a low voice. "I expect you to guard her well and treat her with respect."

Stone's gaze collided with Trelaine's dark, fixed look. "Understood."

"If you don't," he added quietly, pressing a finger into Stone's chest for emphasis, "I'll have more than your head. Whether you come back or not, I'll find you."

Nope. Fear of confrontation was not keeping Trelaine in Dawson.

Stone grinned wryly. "I'll take your concerns to heart."

Harrison nodded shortly and turned away, giving Coady a tender smile and a wave before sauntering off toward the Golden Slipper.

"I'm ready."

Stone looked over his shoulder to find Coady mounted and waiting a few feet behind. "Do us both a favor," he muttered as he returned his attention to Trelaine's back. "Don't do anything foolish on this trip."

Coady took instant exception to his remark. "I'm not in the habit of doing 'foolish' things at any time, Mr. MacGregor."

Stone shook his head as he placed his left foot in the stirrup and heaved himself into the saddle. "I'm asking only that we return here with your lovely self as fit and as well as you are at this moment."

Now she felt guilty for having misjudged his motive. "How touching, Mr. MacGregor," she said softly. "Thank you for your concern."

Chapter Six

Dawson City was situated in the valley where the Yukon and Klondike rivers met. Although the town rested on a swamp, the place flourished as the territory's major supply and transport center. In 1897, Dawson had consisted of a handful of cabins. By the summer of 1898, 20,000 souls had landed there. Steamships lined the docks, their tall smokestacks spewing clouds of gray toward the clear blue sky. Banners waved boldly above the townfolk, advertising everything from a ten-day voyage to Seattle or Vancouver, to eggs at eighteen dollars for the dozen. Ships' captains barked out orders as precious goods were unloaded and hawkers peddled their wares. It was a carnival-like atmosphere. But the stakes of any games played in Dawson City were far higher, and oft times more dangerous, than those to be found in any exposition midway.

Around the more prosperous mining sites, smaller settlements quickly grew. It did not take much to create a town; the establishment of a store or a roadhouse was encouragement enough for further construction. Soon, rough-hewn cabins and commercial buildings would spring up. The results of raising structures in a hasty, haphazard fashion were often experienced within months as the underground search for gold undermined many a building. It was not unusual to see cabins, hotels and stores condemned as unsafe for habitation or the operation of business.

Coady loved it all; the small settlements, the more established towns and everything in between.

"Pretty country."

Coady nodded her head as her gaze roamed the horizon. "I've seen plenty of it," she said appreciatively. "I've crossed grasslands of sedges, sagewort and blue grass. I've traipsed through rainforests and over alpine meadows. The meadows are best. I love the wildflowers. In springtime there are hills covered with millions of them, hundreds of colors, too, I'd bet."

Riding at her side, Stone smiled. "Sounds like love to me, lass."

The soft tone he used in which to stress the word *love* caused a pleasant shiver to ripple along Coady's spine. After his rather harsh parting remark as they left Dawson, Stone had softened his manner considerably. In fact, he was being quite solicitous, asking if she would like to stop and stretch her legs one minute, or if she was in need of food the next. She was not sure she liked him this way. When he spoke harshly, demanding that she "not do anything foolish," she felt quite at ease shooting back an equally harsh reply. But when he was considerate and pleasant, Coady felt quite out of her element. In fact, for some strange reason, he made her feel very nervous; *nervous*, as in goosey or unstrung. In her mind, she wanted to continue viewing him as a nuisance, an annoyance. But her heart seemed to be sending her an entirely different message. It was a silly thought—this matter of her heart—and it left her filled with confusion. She wondered why he had been harsh at all. If he had not really wanted to accompany her on this journey, then why was he there? Then again, she considered that the few private words Stone had shared with Harrison had not been favorable at all to the newcomer. She sighed, staring sightlessly across the pretty meadow through which they were travelling. Worrying about Stone MacGregor's changes in temperament was too wearying a load for her to cope with on top of all her other concerns. She decided talking about the land she loved was the safest topic to pursue. "The Yukon is better than any place I've ever been," she said softly after a long silence.

She had been quiet so long Stone had begun to think his captive audience was not so captive after all. He thought it rather bizarre that her silence unsettled him. He liked the sound of her voice. He liked her smile. In fact, he *liked* Miss Coady Blake, which was probably foolhardy on his part. The policeman in him warned that Coady could be more than she seemed; not necessarily the honest, upstanding citizen she portrayed. Though he increasingly doubted it. The *man* in him made him desire to view her as a soft, sweet innocent. Either way, he knew he had to be cautious. If Coady were to discover it was by his order that she was in her current predicament, she would, no doubt, have his hide. His softer side demanded that he tell her of his artifice. But Stone MacGregor, the policeman, knew he could not reveal his true identity. He could not trust her not to give him away and the work he was doing was important to the future peace and prosperity of the Yukon. He reckoned an entanglement with Coady could be dangerous. It was best that he kept his distance, professionally speaking. And so, he merely posed a seemingly innocent question generated by her last comment. "You've been a lot of places?"

"Some."

"Like where? Where did you call home before this, for a start?"

Questions, she thought. Well, she had prepared herself

this time. "I was in Seattle for a while and then Vancouver. But I was raised in Boston."

"A long way from home."

"There is nothing in Boston for me," she said flatly. Realizing she had just broken the essential sequence of her account, Coady's heart slammed against her chest, hard. "Actually, I came from Seattle to the Yukon to live," she said quickly. "I went back south, to Vancouver, just for a short time, visiting a friend." She stole a glance at him to see if her tale was drawing any unusual interest; she saw none. "Nice place, though, Vancouver."

Coady did not, however, understand that often when her traveling companion appeared disinterested, he was frequently very interested . . . and most curious.

Stone was busy inspecting their surroundings. "So, you've been here a good long time?"

"Oh, years."

He looked at her and grinned. "Coady, you are not that old."

"I was young, true, but I've been here for several years. Excluding my short visit to my friend in Vancouver."

She had turned her head away as she spoke and that made him suspicious. Stone never trusted a man, or a woman, who would not look him in the eye when they talked. "Of course," he said dryly. "But you have no family here, do you? Weren't you very young to be making such a trip on your own?"

Mention of family always hit a bruised spot deep within her. "I've been on my own since I was fourteen. Traveling alone is usual for me."

Her tone warned Stone away from this particular subject and he reached for the first thing that came to mind. "There must be something about this country you don't like. Nothing is perfect."

"Well, the Yukon is close to perfection. The snow-covered mountains look better from down here, though, believe me.''

Having spent many months living up in those ''snow-covered mountains'' he could understand her sentiments. ''Which route did you take in here?''

''The Chilkoot Pass.''

He could not prevent a curious frown from creasing his brow. ''Both times?''

Coady's mind had wandered back to the grueling, treacherous walk that still had the power to haunt her dreams. ''What?''

''Both times? Did you cross over the Chilkoot on both trips into the Yukon?''

''Oh!'' she grinned sheepishly. ''I was wool-gathering. Sorry.''

She failed to answer his question but it did not matter. He searched the sea of faces in his memory, the faces of those hundreds of people he had watched tramp through his post at the Chilkoot Pass. He suspected she had, indeed, arrived via the pass at least once, as she said. If he needed to know for certain, he could easily find out. He had more important things to consider—such as if the people they were seeking would be easily dealt with.

He reckoned not.

The first couple was not at all difficult.

In fact, Gladys Phipps, former prostitute—turned respectable, or so she had thought, laughed at Coady's news. And John Phipps? He was just as happy to see his gold returned. The couple decided they had no problem going on as they had been. Gladys cooked meals, was a lively companion, and an ardent lover. She also worked John's claim almost as hard as he did. If she was happy to stay, he was delighted.

''She's a keeper!'' John announced jovially. ''Warms my bed, cooks my meals and stands in that damned cold creek right next to me. If she don't mind livin' in sin, I sure as a feather is to a goose don't. Maybe we'll get

81

hitched for real next time we're in town. Maybe." With that he grinned and gave Gladys a playful swat on the bottom.

When Coady and Stone found Vernon and Isobel Shield farther along the Eldorado Creek, the news was not as easily accepted.

"What?!" screeched Isobel.

The pretty blonde woman, although slender, stood a head above Coady.

Stone moved to stand protectively next to his charge.

"I know this is a shock, Mrs. . . . ah, Isobel," Coady said quickly. "I had no idea the man was a fraud. I've come to make amends as best I can." She reached into the canvas pouch she had carried at her waist since leaving Dawson and pulled out a small, cloth bag. "The gold you paid me for your wedding arrangements is all here. I've also included the price of a real preacher to wed you."

"You don't understand," Isobel said harshly. "I don't care about the gold. I'm supposed to be this man's wife," she shook a finger in Vernon's direction, "and you're telling me I'm not!"

"I'm sorry."

"Sorry! We've been living in sin for months!"

"I don't know that anyone can look upon it as sin, under the circumstances," Stone said quietly. "And it's a simple matter of standing before an ordained minister as soon as the opportunity presents itself."

Isobel's mind seemed eased by the simple thought he had put there. "You're right, of course," she said more reasonably. "I can't be happy about the past but we can correct the problem by going up to Dawson."

"No."

Three sets of eyes turned toward the man who was standing in the flowing waters of Eldorado Creek.

"What?" asked Isobel after a moment's stunned silence.

"I don't want to go to Dawson," said Vernon.

Isobel smiled and wiped her palms down the front of her apron. "But, Mr. Shield, we have to have the words said—"

"No, we don't."

Coady's heart sank, her attention shifting between Isobel and Vernon. She had never heard a wife refer to her husband as *Mr.* It seemed a tad formal. And there appeared to be more distance between them than the narrow span of geography that physically separated the couple. She was curious as to what kind of arrangement this man and woman could possibly have. And she was sick that she might have inadvertently given Vernon a way out. Isobel would be completely on her own. What could Coady do about that?

Stone frowned at Vernon.

Coady looked frantically at Isobel whose blue eyes appeared ready to roll back, as if she might swoon.

"I don't want to be married," Vernon added.

Stone quickly squeezed Coady's arm before he walked to the bank of the river. "Let's talk, Vernon," he said. "Come out of the water."

Vernon shook his head and Isobel moaned.

"Oh, now, Isobel," Coady whispered fiercely as she gripped the woman's forearms. "Don't you faint on me."

"Vernon," Stone said quietly. "I think we *must* talk."

Vernon refused to budge.

Isobel turned and walked a few steps away from the men with Coady continuing to hold onto one arm. "You don't understand," she whispered. "This is the sorriest day of my life. He's got to marry me."

"Isobel, maybe he's not right for you. I mean, if you haven't been happy—think of this as a second chance!" she chirped. "A blessing in disguise!"

"It is not a *blessing*, you fool!" Isobel snapped. "I'm . . . I'm in the family way."

83

Coady's chin dropped fairly close to her chest. "Oh, Lord," she breathed.

"I haven't even told Mr. Shield the happy news," she whispered miserably. "There hasn't been the right moment."

Coady thought this might be *just* the right moment.

"And now the father of my child has decided he doesn't like being married," Isobel cried softly.

"Oh, well, now . . ." Coady looked toward the river and made an instinctive decision. Rushing from Isobel's side she ran to Stone and gripped his arm, pulling. "Come with me. I need to talk to you."

Stone broke the standoff glare he was sharing with Vernon. "What?"

"Come over here," she insisted.

They moved several feet along the riverbank.

"You've got to talk to him," she insisted.

He frowned down at her. "*I've* got to talk to him? Why don't you try? Or would you prefer not to go wading to get to the man?"

"No!" she returned with quiet determination. "You've got to talk, man-to-man."

"Doesn't it take *woman*-talk to get a man to the altar?"

"Oh, don't be flip," she said with disgust. "This is serious."

"Coady, we cannot force a man to marry a woman he doesn't want to marry."

She felt her face turn brilliant red before the words were even out of her mouth. "Even if the woman is expecting his child?"

Stone's blue eyes grew larger than she had ever seen them. "Oh, shi—shoot."

"Precisely," she said dryly. "And he doesn't know there's a baby. Should we tell him, do you think? Perhaps a child will make a difference to him."

Stone glanced back at the anxious woman standing alone and the stubborn man clinging to the insignificant barrier of midriver. "Coerce Vernon into marriage?" he muttered softly, as if to himself. "That could leave them both miserable for the rest of their lives." He shook his head. "This could take some thought."

Coady crossed her arms and stared at him hopefully. "This could take a major, easily executable plan. You don't happen to have one, do you?"

"Perhaps we had better camp here instead of going on. We'll trying talking with them again a bit later. Even if that fails, once everyone has slept on the problem, cooler heads should prevail."

"Something had better *prevail*," she whispered fiercely, "or my conscience will drive me crazy."

He stared at her, amazed again that the hard-headed, tough-bargaining, Coady had apparently departed, leaving a softer, caring, concerned woman behind.

He had never allowed his personal life to encroach upon his professional duty. He was a dedicated officer. He believed that what he did made some small difference to humanity at large. But he no longer thought his growing fondness for Coady could lead to a shadowing of judgement. There were times when things she said seemed almost contradictory to other comments she had made, but he no longer felt that she was anything more than she appeared to be: a beautiful, young woman who was merely earning her way by the only means available to her.

Now he was actually feeling guilty that his professional standards had forced him to look at her with a suspicious and jaundiced eye. He should have been admiring her grit and determination all this time.

He had admired her, but for other reasons.

Coady seemed to touch something within him like no one ever had before. At times he wanted to take her in his arms and protect her from the cold, cruel world. At other times he just wanted to sit back and admire her ability to strike a deal with a man who was, most likely, resentful of having to bargain with a woman.

Her business acumen fascinated him.

But her sweet, vulnerable side fascinated him more.

Isobel invited Stone and Coady to join in the evening meal but, even though the food was fine, the atmosphere outside the tent the Shields called home was not.

Sitting beside Coady on a large rock near the river, Stone's attention was repeatedly captured by the couple who sat, stone-faced, in roughly made wooden chairs on the far side of the fire Isobel had made to cook their meal.

Vernon Shield had not looked up from his plate of food once since sitting down.

Isobel seemed as if she could be at her wit's end, well along the road to hell.

For several uncomfortable moments, Stone wondered what the devil he was doing. He was a leader of men. What did he know of affairs of the heart? Except with the Shields it appeared *hearts* were not involved. And Coady expected him to help her get this couple back together. How did one put together something that had apparently been apart all along? *What God has brought together let no man put asunder.* Well, Vernon and Isobel, it appeared, had been well and truly sundered.

Whether the break was due to their own misjudgment or the fault of "Marriage By Design" Stone was not certain. Not that it mattered. What mattered was two lives had been deeply affected by an act of a fraud: by Coady's partner, Zachary Bloodstone.

Stone jerked to his left as he felt Coady's elbow dig into his right side.

"Are you going to talk with Vernon or not?" she whispered.

Stone cast her a doubtful frown.

But Coady was not looking at him; she was looking across the fire at the other couple, as innocently as if she had not spoken.

"I suppose you would like me to take my shotgun along?" he asked dryly.

Her lips barely moved as she responded with, "This is serious."

"You're damned right it's serious."

Turning to look at him, Coady returned his frown. "If you prefer not to help, I'll speak with him myself."

"And what little pearls of wisdom do you think you'll share with the man?" he asked hurriedly. "If we interfere with these people further, we just might totally ruin their lives."

"Well, Vernon has to accept some responsibility in this mess."

"Does he?"

"Isobel didn't make her baby by herself," she pointed out softly.

Stone shot the morose looking Vernon another curious look. "I suppose she didn't," he admitted. "All right. I'll see if he'll talk." He handed Coady his empty plate and utensils before pushing to his feet. "Vernon? I wonder if I might have a word or two with you?"

Failing to raise his head, Vernon lowered his plate to the ground near his feet, stood up, and walked away, his long legs quickly covering a good distance along the riverbank.

Stunned, Stone stared at the man's broad back. "I don't know if that's an outright rejection or an invitation to talk in private."

"Take it as an invitation," Coady said quickly.

One corner of his mouth creased. "I might have known you'd say that." But, without a backward glance, Stone started walking in the direction Vernon Shield had taken.

Vernon stopped near a large outcropping of rocks far away from the women. "There's nothing you can say to change my mind," he said as he lowered his large frame to a boulder. "This situation is actually a blessing in disguise for that woman. Isobel just doesn't realize good fortune has fallen at her feet."

Stone jammed his fists into the pockets of his denims. "I don't think Isobel is seeing this thing in just that light, Vernon."

"She will."

"How old are you?"

Vernon raised his head and their gazes met for the first time in hours. "What does age have to do with this?"

Stone shrugged. "I don't know. I just thought . . ."

"I'm thirty-six and feel a hundred," Vernon said flatly.

Stone insisted on trying to make his point. Mainly because he did not know where else to start. "I just thought, if you've never been married before . . . well, a man can get set in his ways. Finding yourself playing the role of husband can be a huge adjustment."

"I was married before," Vernon said sharply, once again staring at the ground. "Not that it's any business of yours. I lost a good woman and a baby boy to childbirth. I *missed* being married. There was no *adjustment* as you say. At least not for me."

One of Stone's hands slipped from his pocket and brushed the night air. "Then why this refusal to marry? Or *remarry*, I suppose is more correct. Don't you like Isobel?"

"Isobel is one of the finest women I've ever known."

Stone shook his head. "Vernon, this is not making a whole helluva lot of sense to me."

"Then leave it alone."

Stone sighed, turned at the waist and looked out across Eldorado Creek, hoping for instant inspiration. "I can't leave it," he muttered, turning to face the older man again. "Don't you think there is a modicum of honor called for under the circumstances? You've lived with this woman as husband and wife."

Vernon barked a haunted guffaw.

"Honor?" Vernon taunted. "I'm doing the honorable thing by letting that woman go."

"Isobel appears to feel you are deserting her," Stone pointed out. "She's hurt and—"

Suddenly Vernon sprang to his feet, looming a half-head taller than Stone. "Don't you tell me what Isobel is feeling," he said harshly. "I just want your promise you'll see her safely to Dawson and put her on the next steamship heading south." He dug into his pants pocket and pulled out a small, cloth sack. "I'll give you plenty of gold to see to her comfort and her passage."

Stone stared at Vernon's dark eyes. "She won't want your gold, man. Isobel seems to want you."

Palming several gold nuggets, Vernon let his hands fall to his sides. "She wanted me to marry her so that she could get away from her family," he said flatly. "That is the only reason we're together. I owe Isobel a lot." He shook his head and eased himself back down onto the rock. His forearms resting on his bent knees, Vernon stared morosely across the swift running creek. "It was Isobel who got me here. Her money, not mine. I was trying to get to the Yukon when I met her. I was running short on coin and I wouldn't touch the money I needed to get into the country. I was mucking out horse stalls trying to earn steamboat passage up the West Coast." He grinned sadly at Stone. "It was her daddy's horse stalls I was mucking out, you see."

Stone nodded his head and sat down on nearby rock, waiting patiently for the man to continue.

"Isobel already considered herself a spinster. I guess everybody else did, too." Vernon shrugged. "I don't know for certain. She's only twenty-four now, for God's sake. I guess that's old for a woman of her station to be unwed. She complained to one of the maids that her mother seemed to hate the men who came calling and Isobel figured she would never find herself a husband as long as she continued to live under her parents' roof.

"One day she heard me telling one of the other workers that I was bound for the Yukon. I was sick of farming. I was lonely, even with my brother and his family living

Jill Metcalf

nearby. So, I left the farm in the care of my brother. I
wanted adventure. I wanted a bit of that Yukon gold for
myself. Isobel caught me alone the very next day and
offered more than enough money for the journey here if
I brought her with me and married her. I thought we
should do it proper and marry before we left San Francisco, but she wouldn't hear of it. Feared her mother
would find out and put a stop to us. Funny, a grown
woman so in fear of her mother. But I guess if the old
hag wanted to ruin Isobel's life, she'd find a way to do
it. So we came here and, as soon as we arrived in Dawson, we hired Coady to set us up a simple wedding.
That's it."

"It doesn't sound like such a bad beginning," Stone
pointed out. "You obviously think highly of the woman.
Love is bound to come along later."

Vernon turned an expression on Stone that halted the
younger man's next words. "You don't understand," he
said shortly, as if Stone were too completely stupid to
fathom the simplest concept. "I can't keep her here, living this life. Our house is no house at all, but a bloody
tent, summer and winter. Isobel is used to a fine mansion,
MacGregor. She's used to a soft bed and hot baths and
someone cooking her up more than the occasional cari-
bou steak. Her hands blistered our first day here from the
work she did trying to set us up as comfortably as she
could. She still works like that; too hard. Life here is
drudgery for a lady like Isobel. Hell, it's a struggle for
any woman. I can't keep her here."

But he would like to keep her. Stone finally understood
that. "I see your point."

"I can't talk to her like this," Vernon continued. "She
thinks she *owes* me, just because I got her away from her
stifling family. Isobel would never acknowledge that
she's going to die a young woman if she keeps working
the way she does. She deserves so much more from life.
She deserves to be with fine people, to live in a big
house, and to be pampered and petted by a man of her

90

own station. But Isobel would never understand my motives if I tried to explain. And she would never agree to leave.''

''I understand your motives,'' Stone said quietly. ''You love her.''

Vernon's head rotated in Stone's direction, displaying just how devastating love could be. ''That's why I can't talk to her about this. It's better if you just take her away.''

''And if she won't go?''

Vernon's jaws clenched. ''She'll go. I'll make sure she never wants to lay eyes on me again.''

The two men fell silent with only the rushing of water and the burble caused by rocks breaking the creek's swift flow to befriend them.

The night had cooled considerably compared to the extreme heat of the day.

Somewhere in the distance, a wolf howled.

Back at the campsite, two unhappy women sat with their heads close together while they talked.

Stone thought about telling Vernon he was soon to be a father, but quickly rejected the idea. That news was Isobel's alone to give, if she chose to give it. It was not for him, nor for Coady, to use coercive tactics in trying to resolve the present dilemma in which Isobel now found herself. He would like to think things could be different for Vernon and Isobel, but it would never be if she were to go away. And Vernon seemed to have firmly made up his mind on that score. Stone could respect the man's feelings; Vernon's concerns over the woman he loved. But he thought Shield was dead wrong in thinking he was not good enough for Isobel, or for anyone else, for that matter. Stone had already formed an opinion on that score. He was sitting next to one hell of a fine man. ''I'll do as you ask,'' he said reluctantly. ''If you're sure it's what you want.''

"It isn't what I want, MacGregor. It's the way it's got to be."

Stone nodded his head and stood. "We'll take Isobel with us in the morning."

Vernon got to his feet and faced Stone squarely. "I don't want you telling the Blake woman all the things I've told you. I don't want everybody knowing my business."

Stone wondered briefly if Vernon's comment was intended as a slur against Coady. But he supposed not. *He* wouldn't want the whole world knowing something like this either. He held out his right hand. "You have my word."

Stone spread his bedroll on the side of the fire closest to the creek; if Vernon and Isobel were going to engage in conversation that might become heated, he did not want to hear it. "I'm ready for some sleep," he groaned as he sat on the blankets and began to tug at his boot.

"Sleep," Coady hissed as she marched around to his side of the fire. "You haven't told me a single thing that man said."

Knee bent, his boot half off, Stone looked up at her curiously. "What has that got to do with my being tired?"

"You can't go to sleep and not tell me," she said insistently as she plopped down on the blankets beside him.

"I can't?"

"No. *I* would never sleep."

"Ah." He nodded his head and grunted as his foot pulled free of his tall boot. "Well, there isn't much to tell," he said as he began tugging at his remaining boot. "Vernon just plain does not want to marry Isobel, and that's that."

Coady's pretty mouth tightened into a severe line. "You were talking with him for at least an hour and that is all you managed to get?"

"That's the gist of it," he said, pulling off the second boot.

Coady huffed and stared at the tent that stood only a few feet away. "I can hear them talking," she said softly. "That's a good sign."

Stone positioned his boots side by side at the end of his bedroll. "Don't get your hopes up, lass."

"He's got to marry her. He's got to."

She looked tired and bedraggled and hopeless, sitting there with her knees bent and her arms wrapped around her legs. Seeing she was genuinely distressed, Stone placed a reassuring hand on her shoulder. "They've got to work this out for themselves, Coady," he said gently. "We can't help them."

"I was quick enough to 'help them' get into this mess," she pointed out.

Once again her conscience had come to prick her and he was still just a little surprised to realize just how deep-seated her concern for others could be. "You didn't know there was a problem at the time, as I recall."

"I don't think I would feel quite as bad if Isobel wasn't carrying a child. Oh, it would be bad enough, seeing her hurt," she added quickly, "but it's worse this way. I don't think I'll ever forget the look on that woman's face this afternoon when Vernon said he would not marry her."

He smiled. "That's quite a conscience you've got there."

She turned her head and glared at him. "You're mocking me."

"No."

"It amazes you that I *have* a conscience?"

He shrugged his shoulders. "Oh, I think I've known all along."

The warmth of his tone sent a shimmering shiver down her spine. Surprised again at her reaction to his silver tones, her own tone, her oft-used defense, became overly harsh. "Well you need not be thinking my conscience gets in my way. It only functions when I see women abused by men."

In the act of pulling his shirt from the waist of his pants, Stone dropped his hands to his bent knees. "Have you seen a lot of that?"

Coady, quite suddenly, did not know where to look. "Some."

Stone turned to face her, moving close so that their bent knees were almost touching. "Who?" he asked softly.

Failing to look into his eyes, she shook her head.

"Who, lass? Someone close to you?"

A deep, pain-filled sigh had the effect of lifting her shoulders. Straightening her spine, Coady did look up then, trying desperately not to display the crumpling emotions the subject never failed to drive through her heart like a stake. "My father beat my mother terribly when I was very young. When he wasn't beating her with his fists, he was bellowing drunken insults her way."

Unconsciously, Stone reached out and placed a consoling hand briefly on her leg. "I can't imagine anything more terrifying for a child."

"It wasn't any picnic for my mother, either," she said, striving for humor and failing miserably. After a long pause, during which she sat thoughtfully plucking lint off the blanket, she added "I don't know why I told you that."

"Perhaps you needed to tell someone. Perhaps you trust me more than you realize."

She shot him a wry glance. "I don't think so, MacGregor."

"Oh? You've told other people?"

Her eyes narrowed. "You know darn well what I meant."

A ghost of a grin teased his lips. "I still think you trust me. Otherwise I would not be here with you."

"That is Harrison's doing, not mine."

"Ah, yes, Mr. Trelaine. Does he have such an influence over you that you would agree to travel with a man you distrust?''

''I occasionally bow to to his judgment.''

''That doesn't sound like a woman who hangs on a man's every word and breath.''

She frowned at him confused. ''What do you mean by that?''

Stone shrugged his shoulders. ''It seems to me that most women frequently bow to the judgment of the men they love.''

''Love?'' she blinked in surprise as the word blurted off her tongue. ''Do you mean *in love*?''

''I suppose . . .''

''I am not *in love* with Harrison. I love him as my dearest friend. Well, perhaps at one time I fancied myself in love with him, but he's entirely too neat for me.''

He laughed. ''Neat?''

''Neat,'' she nodded her head. ''Methodical, meticulous, he's almost fanatical about tidiness and cleanliness. Living with him would drive me mad. Besides, he doesn't *move* me that way.''

''Move you? I'm finding this conversation very hard to follow. Can you define *move*?''

She shot him another skeptical look. ''You know darn well what I mean.''

He did. And he was inordinately pleased by her revelation. But he was still curious about their previous conversation. ''What happened to your mother?''

Feeling the sting of old pain as if it were new, Coady frowned. ''Eventually she could not take anymore from him and we left. I was only ten or so. She had scrimped together some pennies over the years so at first we were able to live in modest lodgings. She found work but fell ill soon after. I swept floors in shops, ran errands, anything that would bring in a little money, but we were eventually forced to live on the streets. We slept in public shelters a time or two but after we woke up one morning to discover my mother's shoes had been stolen during the night, I could never convince her to go there again. She said the streets were friendlier than any shelter. So, we slept on the streets. Boston can be very cold in winter,'' she added in a whisper.

Stone felt her anguish as if he, too, had lived that terrible existence. He tipped his head to the side to see her face more clearly and was almost shattered by the hint of moisture gathering in her eyes. He quickly moved to her side and tucked her beneath his arm. "I'm so very sorry, lass," he breathed.

"We were hungry most of the time. Sometimes I could beg a crust or steal an apple but it was never enough. Without proper food, and exposed to the cold and damp, my mother's illness became much worse. She died curled up in a doorway in a filthy alley."

A fat tear rose up over the edge of her lashes and ran down her cheek and Stone turned her within the consoling comfort of his arms. "Oh, sweet one," he breathed.

Coady hid her shameful tears against his shirtfront. The warmth of his arms around her made her feel it was all right to be vulnerable just this once. The power of his muscles beneath her fingertips seemed to encourage her to take shelter in this strength. She had not meant to cry. She never cried! But the agony, the grief, the pain of calling up memories of those early years proved just too much. "I'm so afraid of being cold and hungry again," she whispered as her fingers curled into the folds of his shirt. "I'm so afraid of dying that way."

"But you won't, lass," he said quietly. "You are intelligent and resourceful and not afraid of work."

She sighed and pulled away from him until she could see his face. "But it haunts me, Stone. It follows me like an unwanted shadow. No matter how well I do, it never seems to be enough. It could all fall apart, you know? Look what happened with 'Marriage by Design.' "

"That is hardly an example of—"

"My other businesses could fail or the gold rush could end, which it undoubtedly will one day. I have to think about my future and how I can earn my way. I can't bear the thought of ever reliving my childhood.''

"Have you no thoughts about a husband and children?''

Coady wiped agitated fingertips at the moisture on her cheeks and pulled away form him. "That is not likely to happen."

"Why not? You surely do not believe you are not lovable?''

She allowed the sweet embrace of defensiveness to shield her as she said coolly, "It's due to my distrust of men, MacGregor. Witness my father's treatment of my mother. Witness Vernon's treatment of Isobel."

"Not all men are abusive, lass."

She would like to believe that. With *him* she could almost believe. With him, she wanted to believe. Those strange sensations that rippled through various parts of her body so often most definitely had to do with special powers. A touch from him sent her into spells of confusion. Her heart played little tricks sometimes, racing with strange rhythms that made her wonder if it might be ailing. And, now that she knew the force his embrace could inflame, it was worse.

Unable to reckon with feelings she did not fully understand, Coady removed herself from his blanket and sought her own bed for the night. "I'm exhausted," she said quietly. "Good night."

Looking thoughtful, Stone's attention remained on her even though Coady had rolled onto her side away from him. "Good night, lass," he murmured.

He was not feeling as tired as he had just moments ago. Reaching into the pocket of his shirt, be extracted a pipe and small pouch. As he prepared his smoke, Stone reflected on the things that she had told him. He understood her drive now and her need for security. The horror of a child watching her mother die in a cold, dirty street made his heart ache for her. But holding her, comforting her, had created another ache for which he knew he could not find release.

So, she was not in love with Harrison. That knowledge made him smile softly.

And thoughts of Coady kept him awake until near dawn.

Chapter Seven

Dawn came.

Coady rolled onto her side, pulling the blanket high over her shoulder in one single, lithe movement.

Stone watched from across the cold pit where their fire had been. She had looked like an inexperienced seductress just then, awaking slowly, reluctantly, rolling and stretching gracefully. There was something undeniably sensual about a woman being drawn from sleep. The words warm and soft came to mind. Which he was not! Oh, he felt *warm*, but the other . . . ? No. He smiled as he lay on his side and just stared at her. He could not remember when he had last experienced such a painful morning erection: He had not had a woman since coming to the Yukon almost a year and one-half ago. Even his *memories* of lovemaking had grown vague in that length of time.

A fat raindrop landed on her cheek.

She stirred again, moaning, until others joined the single drop of water.

The sky opened up and Stone's pleasant idle was instantly over. He plunked his hat on his head and reached for his oilskin.

"I hate July," Coady muttered as she scrambled from beneath her blanket and into her slicker.

Water was already rolling off the back of Stone's Stetson before Coady could roll up her bed.

Isobel was standing in the opening of the tent, looking for all the world as if she had lost her entire family as well as her best friend. Coady ignored any attention she needed to pay to herself and went to speak with the older woman.

"Something terrible must have happened between them last night," Coady said as she followed Stone to their horses several moments later. "Isobel wants to come with us and she didn't even shed a tear over leaving him. She's in there packing up right now."

"We'll double up. Isobel can ride your mare."

Incredulous, Coady stared at him. "That's all you've got to say? Aren't you at all surprised she wants to leave him this morning? Yesterday I thought she would do anything to stay with Vernon."

He took her bedroll from under her arm and began tying it on the mare's saddle. "Like I said, it's their affair and none of ours."

"Don't you think that's just a little cold-hearted of you?" she said grimly.

He sighed and half-turned to face her. "Obviously you have already passed judgment on the condition of my heart so I will not bother to rebut. As for Isobel and Vernon . . . these are their decisions, lass, and not ours."

"But I feel responsible," she said in a small voice.

She *was* partially responsible but accepting blame was not going to change anything. "Even if they had been legally married, perhaps the marriage would not have lasted. Have you considered that?"

She shook her head.

"You can't be blamed for other people's feelings and

100

emotions, Coady,'' he said more gently. ''What comes between a man and his woman can seldom be the fault of another. Things happen.''

With a quick, worried glance toward the tent, she whispered. ''But she won't tell him about the child. And she made me promise not to tell him, either.''

''It *is* her child.''

''It doesn't seem right that Vernon doesn't know. It's his baby, too.''

Stone found his heart touched more by her unhappiness than Isobel's plight. Coady was taking this all upon her own shoulders; and delicate shoulders they were, too. He was feeling a little helpless, having no way to give ease. He could not help Isobel either, for that matter. He rationalized that a man had no place toying with the tender hearts of women. But, surprisingly, Coady's heart seemed more tender than most and that's what spurred him into action. Taking her hand in his, he tugged gently. ''Come with me,'' he said quietly. ''Let's walk a little.''

She followed without resistance.

The rain had gentled and the dark patch shadowing the Yukon sky was slowly drifting to the east. Behind it, a large patch of blue was materializing and the first rays of sunshine were appearing behind a misty haze. Soon the bleakness of early morning would just be a memory.

''Perhaps Isobel has good reason for not telling Vernon about their child,'' Stone said as they walked slowly along the riverbank.

''Particularly now,'' she allowed. ''I don't suppose she could stay with him, knowing he doesn't want her. I guess telling him about the baby would only complicate matters.''

He looked at her briefly, smiling. ''Do you think there is anything you can do about how Vernon feels?''

Coady looked briefly at his profile. ''No.''

''Do you think there is anything you can do about the way Isobel feels?''

She shook her head.

"Do you remember the whore, Coady?"

She frowned at him when he turned his head to look at her.

"The one who was arrested for trying to rob me that night?"

Ah. Yes. She remembered.

"You jumped to that young woman's defense, too. Now do you remember?"

Her complexion darkened as she remembered how righteous she had been. "That was before I knew the girl was a thief."

The mustiness of damp grass and earth surrounded them, and the gentle, lazy sounds of water coursing past, flowing to a new place which neither of them might ever see: These were the scents and sounds that seemed to set the rhythm for the couple's own ambling, fluid motions.

"It's a fine thing to be a rescuer of those less fortunate," he said. "But if you turn it into a crusade, you'll find your own heart broken."

She thought of the time when *she* had been less fortunate, when she would have given anything to know there was someone who wanted to rescue her. She never did meet that someone. Only her own strength and determination had saved her. But there were women who could not do the things she did to survive. To Stone she said only, "My heart is strong."

"But there is something called self-preservation. You have to know your limitations."

"I don't have limitations."

He laughed at her undiluted frankness as he interrupted their walk and turned to face her. "So it would seem."

"I don't see that caring for other people is a limitation," she added.

"Indeed not, lass," he returned with a smile.

"Why do I feel that you are laughing at me?"

He shook his head. "I'm not laughing, Coady. I simply find it quite encouraging that you are more than what you want the world to see."

Her eyes narrowed. "Meaning?"

He tipped toward her, smiling again. "Meaning, you have a woman's heart."

Startled, she moved back from him "That isn't a disease, MacGregor. And, may I remind you, I am a woman."

"Oh, I don't need reminding."

She blinked. "You don't?"

"I held you in my arms last night, remember?"

Red-faced, Coady started marching back toward Vernon and Isobel's tent. "I wish last night had never happened!" she hollered over her shoulder.

Stone raced after her and caught her by the arm, turning her to face him. "Why not? What is so very terrible?"

Coady tore her arm free and glared at him. "Now that you know my weakness you can use it against me?"

"Why would I do that?" he questioned softly.

"Because . . ." For the first time in recent memory, Coady was at a loss for words.

"Last night only made you more human to me, lass, more feminine. Is that such a bad thing?"

"I don't want your pity."

"Trust me, I don't pity you."

She raised sheepish eyes to his. "You don't?"

"What is there to pity?"

Her shoulders sagged and a look of remorse stole across her lovely face. "I'm never very nice to you, am I? I don't know why. I just always seem to be short on temper when you're around."

He grinned ruefully. "Is that your way of apologizing?"

She matched his expression and held out her right hand. "Friends?"

Stone took her offering and held on longer than the gesture required. "Friends."

His hand was so large, so strong, so warm. This was not a firm handshake sealing a business pact. This was a

103

handshake she did not want to end. But there was dire business to which they must attend.

Coady eased her hand free as her weary mind gave way to confusion of another kind. "This situation between Isobel and Vernon has left me feeling a little bruised," she admitted.

Their smiles slipped into something more serious.

"I understand."

"I suppose we should be getting back. Isobel will surely have gathered whatever she needs and be ready to leave."

Stone fell into step beside her.

"She'll be all right, you know," he said after a moment's silence between them. "We'll settle Isobel at one of the hotels and visit with her often until she can get passage on one of the steamers."

"She won't be boarding a steamer," Coady told him. "Isobel will be living with me."

Stone stopped dead in his tracks. "What?"

Coady stopped walking and faced him. "I said, Isobel will be living with me. At least until after the baby is born. That will be in February. After that, she'll decide what she's going to do."

"Don't you think you're taking on a heap of responsibility?"

"I don't think so. Isobel needs a place to live until she can get her life back in order. Somehow," she added with a shake of her head. "It seemed the least I could do."

And that, was that. She turned and started toward Vernon's tent.

Well, he had to respect Coady for the strength of her convictions. And as rigid, as mercenary as she tried to appear at times, the woman was neither of these. Being in her company day and night, seeing Coady in situations entirely different from her business dealings, was unraveling a myriad of preconceived notions he had been lugging around. She was a woman hungry for money, true, but Coady Blake was also a lover of children, a woman who could reach out when others were in pain. In the past few days he had watched her conduct herself with maturity and considerable wisdom for one so young.

Stone was impressed with her.

He was also half in love.

He suffered a nagging curiosity far beyond a man's subtle attempt to identify the sort of elusive intrigue some women wore like a shroud. That thing which could drive a man mad, wondering if his attraction had been triggered by something as simple as the glint of her hair when the sun shone upon it a certain way.

He shrugged mentally as he walked along. Only time, time and familiarity, would solve it all, he supposed.

Vernon. Stone was not certain how Vernon was going to take to this relocation of Isobel in Dawson. He wanted Isobel sent home to her family. But then perhaps the man had not taken time to think it through. Isobel had gone to great lengths to get away from her parents. Why would she want to return to them?

As he followed Coady, Stone deliberated the wisdom of informing Vernon Shield that Isobel would not be leaving the Yukon.

He made his decision only moments before they left.

They found the last of Coady's former clients at Sulphur Creek.

Flora Gardner had been all of sixteen when twenty-year-old Johnny Flint had first paid to bed her. He asked her to marry him before leaving her room that night. She was too young to be in *the business* and he needed a woman. That was exactly what he had told her.

He had awakened Coady before dawn, declaring that he needed arrangements made, and fast. She remembered.

Coady thought he had wanted to get the ceremony over and done before the young lady could change her mind. They had made a cute couple. She recalled that, too.

Flora was not a pretty girl; her red hair had a tendency to escape any sort of control and her face was broad, decidedly lacking in any feminine display of cheek bones. But she had a way about her, a beaming smile and a curvaceous body that many an older woman would kill to possess. Coady remembered thinking Flora had a lot to recommend her as a wife when they had first met.

They remained a "cute couple" after months of being together as husband and wife. In fact, as they rode up to the small cabin Johnny had built for his bride, Coady thought they looked very settled, as much as any long-married couple in love. She hated having to destroy any part of that.

Continually protective and on guard, Johnny hurried from the middle of the creek, snatching up the ever-present rifle he left propped against a rock on shore. He stood, his weapon resting with apparent casualness in the crook of his elbow as he watched the two women and lone man approach.

Flora was out in front of their small cabin, bent over a washtub and scrub board.

Such normal scenes. Lives filled with daily chores which were not made easy in these rustic settings. Wood for building and for fires was difficult to find, often having to be hauled from miles away. Water had to be toted. The isolation alone was sometimes more than many women could bear. Coady had long ago decided that the women who fared best in the Yukon were those who admired the awesome beauty of the country and fell in love with nature. Often nature and her man were the only company a woman was to find for weeks, even months, on end.

"Ho! Miss Blake!" Johnny called in recognition as he stepped to Flora's side.

Flora dried her hands on her apron as the two horses were brought to a halt several feet away.

Stone reached behind and took hold of Coady's arm, easing her down from the horse's rump. She looked up at him as soon as her feet hit the ground, casting Stone a look of concern and remorse he had seen each time that she forced herself to relay her news.

He smiled, reassuring her, and dismounted. "I'm right behind you," he said softly as she turned toward the Flints.

Coady pasted a smile on her face and walked slowly forward. At least Johnny had built a proper cabin for his bride. The wooden structure was small, a single room no doubt, but it had a door and a window. Flora should be thankful she was not still living in a tent like hundreds of other women.

Standing side by side the way they were, shoulder to shoulder, they looked so happy, as if they had the world on a string with one end tied around their respective hearts.

"Hello," Coady said as she stopped with the tub between herself and the Flints.

"What brings you out here?" Flora asked. But she was smiling, delighted to have company.

"I, uh . . ." Coady pointed over her shoulder as her smile began to falter. "This is my friend, Stone Mac-Gregor."

The two men reached in front of the women, across the tub filled with water and laundry, and shook hands.

"We are here to bring you news," Coady said after the greetings. "It isn't good news, I'm afraid, but it isn't anything dire, either." She looked at the puzzled young faces, her own solemn gaze pleading. "I mean, it isn't something that cannot be remedied."

Johnny, with his handsome dark looks, cast her an uncertain grin. "What news could you have for us?"

"Well, you'll recall that I arranged for you to take your vows . . ."

"And a good job you did, too," said Flora. "It was a real nice wedding." She looked quickly at Johnny before returning her attention to the visitors. "It's something we'll always remember."

That made Coady flinch. "Yes, I suspect you will." She cast a quick glance at Isobel, who had remained seated on the mare, and found herself praying there would not be a repeat performance of the Vernon and Isobel saga. "It's about the ceremony that I've come," she continued, steeling herself as she again faced the young couple. "I've discovered that the man who said the words for you is a fraud."

The silence that fell between the two couples was as heavy as the winter snows.

Johnny propped his rifle against the cabin wall and jammed his hands into the pockets of his jeans. "What does that mean?"

"It means Zachary Bloodstone had no right to marry you or anyone else."

Flora was frowning in confusion. "You're sayin' we're not married?"

Coady looked sad as her gaze locked with that of the younger woman. "That is precisely what I am saying."

Again there was a moment of silence.

Suddenly Flora began to laugh.

Johnny frowned at her, not seeing anything funny at all.

Coady cast a worried frown over her shoulder at Stone. He placed a reassuring hand on her shoulder and squeezed gently.

Flora continued to laugh, falling against Johnny's side.

The young man became worried and put his arm around her. "Flora?" he said softly. "Honey?"

"Isn't it funny, Johnny?" she howled.

He shook his head. "I don't think so."

Her head was bobbing, her eyes watering. "Yes, it is. You thought you were saving me from a life of doin' bad and here we've been doin' bad all along!"

"We haven't been bad," he said solemnly.

Flora began to sober. "You don't think so?"

He shook his head.

108

"You don't care that we've been livin' in sin? Some people would call it sin."

"I don't see that we've been sinning."

Her brow furrowed and she turned to face him. "Why is that?"

He looked momentarily helpless. "Where is the sin?"

"You don't care we aren't really married?"

" 'Course I care . . ."

Coady took a deep breath and held it. Flora's tone was becoming a bit strained and there was a gleam in her eyes that had not been there a moment ago. She suddenly planted the palms of her small hands in the center of Johnny's chest and shoved. "You don't care!"

Johnny recovered his balance but not his wits. "What are you going on about?"

"You didn't want to marry me," Flora accused. "I bet you lined up with this woman to trick me."

"I didn't do any tricking," he shot back.

Coady held out a beseeching hand. "Just a moment . . ."

"You just wanted to get me down here, keepin' you warm at night," Flora went on. "You didn't really want a wife, you just wanted to be humpin' regular."

"That is not so!" he bellowed. "I love you."

"If you don't have a wife all legal like, you can up and leave as soon as you strike it rich," she babbled on heatedly.

"I don't want to leave here without you!" He turned on Coady. "Tell her!"

Coady moved around the tub toward the young woman. "Flora, listen, please."

Flora was not in the mood for listening. This woman had just brought her world to ruination. "He musta paid you plenty for them fancy vows that don't mean nothin.' "

"He paid me, yes, but—"

"To trick me!"

Coady reached for Flora's hand but the girl quickly

stepped back. "It wasn't a trick, Flora. Johnny thought he was doing the right thing. He wanted your wedding to be nice. *I* thought I was doing the right thing. We were *all* tricked. Can't you see that?"

Tears of anger turned to tears of disappointment as Flora stared at Coady. "I thought something nice had happened to me for once in my life," she said softly. "I thought things would be different from now on. And now you're telling me it's all a lie."

Johnny stepped between the two women, facing his Flora. "It isn't a lie, sweetheart," he whispered. "I love you. You know that isn't a lie."

Flora looked up at him, staring through a sea of water.

"We'll go to Dawson right away," he said hurriedly, reaching for her hands. "We'll find us a proper preacher to say the words."

She hiccuped. "We will?"

Coady breathed a sigh of relief and rubbed the tips of her fingers wearily across her forehead.

Stone began to smile as he, too, watched the young couple work their way back to the right track. The only regret he had in that moment was the pain he knew Coady had managed to keep hidden from everyone's eyes. And while he had only done what his duty required him to do in having Bloodstone checked out, he acknowledged himself as the cause of her grief.

And knowing that was beginning to sour his gut.

"Course we will," Johnny continued speaking to Flora, pulling her into his arms. "I'm not letting you go," he whispered.

Coady reached into the pouch she wore on her belt and retrieved the last of the small sacks of carefully measured gold. "I'm returning the price of the wedding to you plus a little more," she said.

Flora and Johnny turned their heads to look at her.

"I'm sorry for this, really," she added as she dropped

the gold into Johnny's palm. "I wish the best for you."

Behind them, silently watching from the mare's back, Isobel was crying for the happiness of the Flints and the loss of her own.

Chapter Eight

The gold-fevered residents of Dawson paid little attention to the warnings of the police surgeon general over the matter of the abhorrent sanitary conditions in the town. By early August typhoid had struck the community.

Superintendent Raymond Simmons immediately issued orders having to do with the disposal of garbage, the guarding of drinking water and other sanitary requirements, thereby keeping the situation from getting worse. But by the time Stone, Coady and Isobel returned, three hospitals, including that of the Royal Northwest Mounted Police, were crowded with victims of the fever.

The trio had been told of the sickness in Dawson upon their arrival in Grand Forks, but try as they might, Stone and Coady could not convince Isobel to remain there where they felt she would be safe from the disease. Coady, too, rejected outright Stone's request that she remain. And so it was, after having notified all those affected by the "Marriage By Design" Design disaster, they rode into a town ravaged by fever and deluged with fear.

The first priority to which Coady addressed herself was Isobel's welfare. Taking one of her previously rented tents, she and Stone scrubbed the canvas with chloride of lime and rinsed it thoroughly with a mixture of water and vinegar. The tent was then raised directly behind Coady's own storefront with Isobel instructed to remain inside or take fresh air by walking in the fields behind her new home, well away from the town. The woman agreed, for the sake of her child, to avoid the general populace as well as those places that could possibly expose her to unsanitary conditions.

Which only added to Isobel's misery.

Being rejected by Vernon had taken its toll. She had admitted to Coady one evening during the journey to Dawson, theirs had not been one of the great historical love affairs one could read about in books. Her relationship with Vernon had been far more tentative. They had started with a mutual need for each other. Needs that had been more material and far more elusive than any definition of love. But Isobel had come to believe a bond had formed between them, a friendship, a kind of caring that would one day bring upon her the realization she had fallen in love with him along the way. But Vernon had destroyed the possibility of that ever happening.

Isobel was miserable and Coady did not know how to help her.

Somehow Coady did manage to unwittingly make Stone feel he was at least partially responsible for Isobel's welfare; and, of course, he had promised Vernon he would see to the woman's safety. To that end, he volunteered to procure daily rations of food and clean water drawn from a spring well outside the town. Along with these he offered one or two feeble reasons why Isobel might want to return to her family, under the circumstances.

Jill Metcalf

Isobel laughed until tears threatened to spill over her lashes. She did manage, however, to inform him, albeit in a broken voice, that she no intentions of leaving and certainly *not* merely to return to her family.

Coady did take Stone's concerns enough to heart to allow for some precautions with respect to her own health. Since Harrison and Stone were bent upon nagging her to death, she agreed she would not venture out to collect her rents for the month of August. But she could not, would not, close down her businesses completely. It seemed senseless to diminish her monthly profits over such minimal risk. If customers entered her establishment, Coady saw to their needs. If one or two of the bodies who pressed gold into her hand were not the most immaculate, there was little she could do other than to immediately scrub her hands with harsh lye soap and hope for the best.

They had been back in Dawson only four days when Coady awoke with a headache so severe her stomach heaved a time or two in protest of the blinding pain.

Fighting the nausea the pain in her head seemed to be parenting, she managed to dress and cautiously pull a brush through the thick cascades of her hair before her first customer arrived.

"Anybody t'home?"

Coady gave herself a mental shake and moved quickly toward the canvas partition. "Coming!"

When she entered the storefront, Coady came face to face with tall, slim, Joseph Evans who was gleefully brandishing a piece of paper.

"Mornin', Miss Blake." His smile was all toothy and broad.

"Morning, Joseph."

"I finally got some writin' back from my missus. 'Member, you wrote to her for me 'bout a year ago now."

She did not remember. Coady did not remember much

114

of anything this morning. But to Joseph she said only, "Of course, Joe."

"I was wonderin' if you might read her words to me, Miss Blake? I hate to ask but . . ."

Coady started to nod her head but thought better of it and plopped down on the chair behind her desk. "It's all part of the service," she said, extending her hand and receiving the single sheet of paper.

Joe stood eagerly before her, watching with childlike anticipation as Coady unfolded the paper and smoothed out the creases. "What's she say?"

Coady was still trying to focus uncooperative eyes. The letter opened with *'Joseph Evans!'* Hardly a warm, wifely greeting and it gave Coady some niggling doubts about continuing. But, when she looked up at the eager man, she knew she could not stop now. She did, however, improvise a little in the beginning.

"Joseph, I know you can't write your own name and here you are after a year or more, sending me some letter some female has writ. I can tell by the letterin' and I don't guess you been missing me while I been sitting here waiting for you."

"Oh, dear," Coady murmured. She looked up. Joe was frowning now. "Perhaps I had better not . . ."

He shook his head. "Read."

Coady's attention returned to the letter.

"I trusted you to go up there to those gold fields and pick us some gold but I shoulda guessed a man ain't likely to stay on his own for long. I guess they got floozies running around there all over and you just natural, like a man, ran into one of them. One who writes flowery words too. Well, the kids and me been keeping this sorry farm going, waiting for the day you come back and we could buy us a cash crop of young oinkers to better our state some. We ain't waiting no longer, Joseph Evans!"

Solemnly, Coady folded the note.

Joseph remained still, standing in front of Coady's

desk with his hands fisted. "Guess she's pretty mad. She don't sign her name."

What did it matter whether the woman signed her name or not? The context of the letter was fairly clear. "I suppose there's little doubt who wrote this letter?" she questioned lamely.

"That's one fine woman, Miss Blake," Joe said through gritted teeth. "She works hard and gave me five younguns, to boot."

Coady looked up, meeting his dark angry eyes. "I'm sorry, Joe."

He leaned forward and planted white knuckles on the top of the table. "I want to know what you put in that writin' to her!"

Stunned, and pained by his bellow, Coady blinked. "I wrote what you asked me to write."

"You said somethin' about some woman. Says so right on that paper." He took a stab at the offending page with a blunt finger. "I didn't tell you nothin' about no woman!"

Coady jumped to her feet and wished she hadn't as pain shot from the back of her neck up to the front of her head. "I am quite certain I did not write anything about a woman, Joseph. Susan has wrongly surmised the woman who wrote the letter must be . . ." She raised her fingertips to her temples and tried to massage the pain away. "Look, we'll write back to her and explain that you hired me to—"

"Oh! *Payin'* for it will make things a lot better!"

Her eyes narrowed as her patience grew thin. "Will you let me finish, please."

Joe stared at her as he stood to his full height and waited.

"We'll write back to Susan and explain that you came to me because I offer a service of letter-writing. I'm just a woman who gets paid to put down the words men want to send home. It's as simple as that."

"Nothin's simple," he muttered. "Writin' ain't going

to do no good. When Susan gets her anger up, I gotta be there to soothe her.''

Coady suddenly felt defeated in yet another venture. She had not counted on the world of romance being quite this complicated. ''I'm sorry, Joe. The only thing I know to make it right is—''

''Nothin's goin' to make it right,'' he grumbled as he glared at her. ''Ya ruined my life. I love that woman.''

''I didn't ruin your life. I mean . . .'' Her hand waved through the air in a hopeless gesture. ''Maybe I should have explained who was writing the letter for you. Perhaps then your wife would not have jumped to conclusions and—''

''Susan didn't jump at nothin'!'' he returned defensively.

Coady suddenly felt too ill to continue the useless conversation. ''Look, I'll return the gold you gave me to write the wretched letter. I'm sorry it went wrong, Joe. I don't know what else to do.''

''I know what to do,'' he barked. ''I gotta go home and try 'n' get my woman back!''

She nodded her head and walked away from him, entering her private room to fetch the chest where she kept small amounts of gold. Retrieving a cloth sack from within the confines of a false side of the chest, Coady tested the weight in the palm of her hand and returned to her unhappy customer.

She dropped the small sack in Joe's hand and watched him stride angrily from her place.

As bad as she felt about Joseph's predicament, handing back still more of her profits was a painful experience. Coady wondered how things that had been so right could suddenly go so wrong all at once! As if some evil curse had decided to pay her a visit. And the damned torments seemed bent on continuing! Unless, of course, she interfered with what seemed her newly imposed fate.

Resigned to the fact the love business was no business to be in at all, Coady followed the path Joseph Evans had taken only moments before. She went outside and took firm hold of one of the wooden signs, pulling and wrenching until the thing came free of the wallboard to which it had been nailed. She was dispatching "Letters to Your Sweetheart" to the same ignoble grave as "Marriage by Design." At this rate, her enterprises would be reduced to the selling of bread. And with her luck, somebody would choke on a damned crust and she would be charged with murder!

Caught up in dispiriting thoughts of dwindling businesses and, worse, shrinking profits, Coady did not take note of Stone's arrival.

"What are you doing?"

Startled by the words spoken so close behind her, she flinched and a sharp pain shot up the back of her neck again. She turned and faced Stone. He was standing so close she had to tip her face up in order to see his eyes.

"I'm giving up another business."

Stone looked at the hand-painted sign in her hands. "Now what?"

She told him about Joseph and Susan.

Stone would have thought the entire incident funny had Coady not told the story in so grave a fashion. "The woman must be madly jealous," he told her as he placed a consoling hand on her shoulder. "He'll get her back, lass. The man is doing the right thing by going home."

"Except he might arrive home to find an empty house," she muttered. "You know what the mails are like. It took months for that letter to get here and it's going to take weeks for Joe to get home. His wife could have another man by that time."

"With five children to her credit already," Stone said wryly, "she would be better off without a man at all."

Coady shot him a pained expression. She should have appreciated his attempt at humor but she was just too wretched to find anything amusing.

With a weary sigh, she closed her eyes, letting her head fall forward until Stone was supporting it with his chest. "Why do seemingly simple things have such serious consequences when they go wrong?"

Balancing a small box against his hip, Stone placed his free arm around her back. "Life isn't always easy."

"Another question," she muttered, "is *why* are things going so wrong?"

Ah. His primary reason for coming to her. Things were about to change and he wanted her to hear it all from him. Stone felt he owed her that much at least. He had not counted on her entire world falling apart when he had ordered the investigation of Bloodstone. Actually, he had not worried about the effect on Coady at all in the beginning. Duty first, as it were. But after spending several days with her, after seeing her genuinely distraught over the woes of others, after getting to know her better, duty was a taking a secondary role when it came to Coady.

She had become that important to him.

"Let's go inside, Coady," he said softly. "We're attracting attention."

With her forehead remaining pressed against his shirtfront, Coady turned her head just enough to see several passersby openly gaping. She did not want to pull away from the small comfort of Stone's nearness. She did not care what people thought; she was too sick to care. "Let them talk," she muttered.

Frowning, Stone placed his fingers beneath her chin and raised her head. He looked at her narrowed eyes, the paleness of her skin. "There's more wrong with you than another failing business," he said, convinced. Talking her elbow, he turned her toward the door. "Inside, miss."

Lacking the strength of will to contest his order, she lethargically walked into her tent.

Stone removed the wooden box from under his arm and lowered it to a shelf. "I've brought fresh food."

She grimaced.

"What is *really* wrong?"

Coady tried to shake her head, thought better of it, and said, "I have a little headache."

"Little," he muttered as he stepped in front of her. "Look at me," he ordered. Raising her chin with his forefinger he looked into her eyes, studying her more closely this time. "You have more than a *little* headache, my girl." The back of his fingers pressed against her forehead. "You are very warm."

"I tend to get that way when you're around," she quipped feebly. "We've had so many arguments, I save myself a lot of bother by getting heated up *before* the fight begins."

"Funny," he muttered. His palm touched her cheek.

Bracing herself with one hand on top of her worktable, she said, "This ache has obviously dulled my wit." Moving cautiously she worked her way around the desk and sat down.

"I will be fine," Cody muttered as she tipped her head up and shot Stone a silly lopsided grin. "I hate losing businesses, Stone. It ruins my whole day. Now that I have given up two, it might ruin my entire month."

Well, if *that* did not, what he was about to tell her probably would.

"Are you certain you are all right?"

She waved his concern away. "An ache, nothing more."

Stone sat, raising his right thigh to rest on the table so that he could more easily face her. "I have something to tell you."

Her gaze met his. The pain in her head aside, he had her complete attention.

Stone suddenly faltered. He had rehearsed this speech a dozen times but, having her look up at him so trustingly, he could no longer remember a single planned word. "You are not going to like what I have to say," he said with conviction. "I ask only that you consider my position at the time."

"Ah," she drawled, "this is something from the past.

That is good, Stone. I'm known for not possessing much in the way of foresight. Witness the reasons for my expired businesses.''

He normally appreciated her humor but self-deprecation was not something in which he wanted to see her indulge. Not today. Seeing her take aim at herself was too painful a reminder of the shot he had taken at her. "This is not a game, lass," he said quietly. "What I have to discuss is . . ."

The seriousness of his countenance suddenly caused Coady concern. Sitting forward, she reached for his hand as it rested on the table top not far from his knee. "What is it, Stone? What could be so terrible?"

He turned his hand and gripped her fingers, his eyes solemn as he looked at her. "I'm not entirely who you think I am, lass. Actually, I've omitted to tell you because duty would not permit."

Her brows furrowed in curiosity. "Duty?"

"Duty. I am a member of the police."

"The police? A Mountie?"

He nodded his head. "I could not tell you because I was brought here under special assignment. But I will be going back into uniform."

"Special assignment?" she whispered anxiously.

"I wanted to talk with you before you saw me in uniform," he continued, as if she had not spoken.

"Special assignment?"

"I had to explain that when I ordered the investigation of Bloodstone, it was a matter of duty, an automatic reflex, if you will. I had no thought . . ."

Coady pulled her hand from his, her fingers turning icy. "You? You ordered an investigation of me?"

"Of Bloodstone," he corrected. "I . . ."

Coady was on her feet, ignoring the fact that he rose as well, standing a head taller than she. "Get out," she whispered.

"Coady." Stone reached for her but she took a step back.

Jill Metcalf

"Please leave," she whispered brokenly. "And do not come back. I do not ever want to lay eyes on you again."

Her sudden paleness concerned him. "I asked you to see this from my perspective, Coady, from my position at the time."

"Forgive me," she returned stiffly. "I can't see much of anything with this blinding ache in my head." She turned away then, the picture of abstract misery, and walked behind the curtained wall.

Stone followed. "Please, let's talk about this."

She stood beside her bed and turned to face him. "Why? So you will feel better? As I recall, policeman, I asked you to leave."

Stone crossed his arms over his chest. "I'm staying."

"That's too bad," she muttered, her words curiously drawled, "because I'm—"

To Stone's utter amazement, Coady went down, folding as if she were melting before his eyes. "Jesus," he breathed, lunging forward to catch her before she hit the floor. In one swift, gentle motion, he laid her on the bed. "Coady?" He felt her hands, cold as mountain ice. He felt her forehead and the evidence here was just the opposite. "Fever. Damn." His stomach twisting, he looked around quickly, spying a water pitcher and wash bowl on the crudely constructed commode in a corner of the sparsely furnished room. Wetting a cloth, Stone hurried back to the bed and placed it on her forehead. He tried to rouse her again. "Coady."

But Coady was lost in the oblivion of unconsciousness. The pain in her head had been a symptom of something worse to come—typhoid.

Stone sprang into action.

He ran to her worktable and snatched two pieces of precious paper. The first note was to the attention of the surgeon of the Royal Northwest Mounted Police Hospital.

The other he wrote to Harrison Trelaine.

Folding both papers, he searched in his pocket for

122

coins as he rushed outside. Spying a young boy playing, Stone hailed the lad. "You want to earn a dime, boy?"

The young lad nodded his head.

"Take this one to the hospital and ask one of the policemen to give this note to the doctor. Then take this one to the Golden Slipper. You tell Mr. Trelaine, *Stone* said he was to give you a nickel when you hand this to him," he said. "He'll pay you again. Now, *run*, boy."

The lad ran for all he was worth.

Stone's next duty was to post a new sign on Coady's storefront. This one was hastily written on another piece of paper and warned of TYPHOID FEVER within.

That done, he returned to Coady's side, his mind racing with questions of what he could do for her until the doctor arrived. He refreshed the damp cloth for Coady's forehead before undoing the top buttons of her shirtwaist.

Helpless to do more, he sat on the bed and waited.

One thing was certain: He would not allow her to be taken to any of the hospitals. Aside from the fact they were already overflowing with the sick, Stone believed she could recover more quickly if Coady was tended in her own bed. He did not know why he believed that, he just did.

But waiting patiently, impotently, for anything was not something Stone did well. He wrote a third note to his superior, explaining his situation, his exposure to the fever, and requesting a few days leave. He knew his request would be granted.

Only moments had gone by since he had dispatched the boy but Stone paced to the door and stepped outside. He stood there no more than three minutes before Harrison came down the street at a run.

"What?" he called, still several feet from the tent. "What's wrong?"

Stone turned, holding a hand out to halt Trelaine. "Don't come too close."

Harrison stopped moving six paces away. "What the devil . . . ?"

"She's sick, Trelaine," Stone told him regretfully. "Coady has the fever."

Harrison quickly closed the distance between them. "I'm going in," he said. When Stone raised an arm to block his way, he added sternly. "I want to see her."

"There's little use in both of us being exposed."

"Then *you* stay out here," he returned sharply. "I'm going to Coady."

Stone refused to lower his arm as his gaze remained fixed on Harrison's dark eyes. "I've already been exposed to the sickness, Trelaine. I can care for her but I need you out here, and *well*, to help me."

Harrison's dark, worried gaze locked with Stone's. "Coady won't thank me for allowing you to be near her. If *you* become ill," he muttered ruefully, "you can imagine what she'll do to me."

Stone should have been happy with the implied message of Harrison's words. But things had changed. "Actually, it is more a matter of what Coady will do to *me* once she is well."

Harrison frowned. "What the devil does that mean?"

"It doesn't matter."

But Harrison heard in those words that it did matter. Confused and more worried then ever he gripped Stone's forearm. "Move aside."

Stone reacted quickly and sternly. He stepped back, putting a small distance between himself and the older man, but his threatening posture made it seem as if he had stepped forward and grown taller. "No! Think, man. There are many ways in which you can help her if you have the freedom to move about. Coady will have need of things I know you can procure. And there is Isobel to consider. I can't see to the woman now I've been exposed. I was hoping you would find some men and move Isobel's tent farther away from this one. And she'll need supplies and water daily."

"I'm not a damned nursemaid."

124

"If Coady were the one standing here asking, would you hesitate?"

Harrison knew he would not. He shook his head. "I don't like this."

"Look, Trelaine, I know how much you care for her, but—"

"Do you?"

"Yes. It's apparent," he added prudently.

"And how much do you love her, MacGregor? Enough to die for her perhaps?"

Stone was taken aback by the question. "I hate to see anyone suffer."

"That doesn't answer my question, MacGregor."

Stone jammed his fists into his pockets, demonstrating his discomfort. "What do you want me to say?"

"It doesn't matter," Harrison muttered. "I'll see to whatever supplies you need." The other information he craved would be revealed to him in time, one way or another.

"You say you love her . . ." Stone bit off his words, watching Trelaine, feeling there was more the man wanted to say.

Feelings of awkwardness forced Harrison to search the street in hopes of finding something that would capture his attention as he talked. "You have to understand, I would die for Coady, but that is the best I have to offer. In a way, I think Coady understands." He dared to look briefly at Stone's face and saw the man struggling to grasp his meaning.

Harrison spied the police doctor, Ted Early, rushing toward them. Now was not the time for further explanation. His gaze briefly landed on Stone's face. "I'll do as you ask. I'll have Isobel's tent moved and arrange for whatever supplies you need."

Stone nodded his head.

"I will also be here several times a day, MacGregor. Tend her well," he added softly just before he turned away.

"I'll need fresh water. A good deal of it, I suspect."

"You'll have an entire lake, if that's what Coady needs."

Stone was moved by Trelaine's obvious concern. "I'll do the best I can for her."

Harrison paused just long enough to look at Stone's eyes. "You had better," he warned and walked away.

Stone had no chance to reply as Ted Early approached his side. "The boy gave me your note, MacGregor. Where is she?"

Chapter Nine

The shivering sent bolts of pain flashing through her head, behind her eyes. If only she could stop quaking. "Concentrate," she whispered, willing her body to be still.

"What?"

"Cold."

The word came through clenched teeth but Stone understood clearly enough. "I have another blanket here," he said, as he spread the gray flannel on top of the two with which he had already covered her. "You'll soon be warm, lass." As soon as the blanket settled over her, Stone reached for the damp cloth he had placed on her head and replaced it with another, cooler one. Her face, when he looked at it, was ashen with pain. "There must be something Early can do about this pain," he muttered.

Coady could not even bring herself to speak. She just lay there, her eyes tightly closed, her body quivering.

Stone wondered if the hot whiskey would warm her. He had started a fire in the stove and was heating water in the enameled coffee pot he had scoured. Two large, flat rocks, scavenged that morning, were warming on top of the stove as well. Wrapped in flannel and placed near her feet, the hot stones would help drive off the cold. He could remember his mother doing that for him as a boy, when he was chilled from a day of running in the snow with his chums. The minor difference in providing for his comfort back then was his mother had benefit of using hot coals, placed inside a proper warming pan. But the rocks would do the job. He concentrated, willing himself to recall other things his mother had used to treat her children whenever they had been ill. Anything Mary MacGregor had done back then might serve him well now.

He replaced the folded cloth on her forehead again before wandering out to the other room. Protecting his hands with several layers of flannel, he gingerly wrapped the rocks and returned to Coady's bed with them. Leaving the warm cloth bundles on the trunk he had drawn up to the bedside, Stone pulled the sheets and blankets from the foot of the bed and revealed slender feet and trim ankles.

"What are you doing?" she muttered weakly.

His gaze darted to her face. Her eyes remained closed.

"I have something to help warm you."

"Don't be staring overly long at my ankles," she quipped.

He smiled wryly as he replaced the blankets. "Perhaps you're not as sick as I thought I you were."

She sighed, having expended her energy on that one little teasing gesture. Her head rotated slowly on the pillow as she tried to find some ease from the tension in her neck. "I've never felt so wretched," she whispered.

Sympathy struck at his heart as he sat on the old scarred trunk. "I know, lass," he murmured.

And then her stomach complained, rumbling like distant thunder as muscles tensed, forcing her to roll onto her side.

Jumping to his feet, Stone's hand landed gently on her upper arm as Coady pulled her knees toward her chest. "Easy."

"Oh, Lord."

"Are you going to be ill?" He already had one of the buckets in his free hand.

"Stone," she breathed. "Why are you here?"

"I should think that would be relatively obvious." He did not move from his ready position, poised to give whatever support she might need.

"I remember ordering you to leave."

That again! "You can be angry with me later, Coady."

"The way I'm feeling, there may not be a *later*," she said weakly. "I think I have got to do it now."

"You cannot even open your eyes. What kind of wrath do you think you can bring down upon me in your current condition?"

"You would be surprised, policeman," she whispered.

If her situation were not so dire, he would have laughed. "Can't you be like other normal women and concentrate on getting well instead of thinking of how next to admonish me?"

"I thought that's what normal women did," she muttered. "I think men call it nagging."

Admiring her not only for her spunk but also for her fortitude, he smiled fondly as he admitted to himself that she was, indeed, a very strong woman in many ways. Anyone this sick and still able to jest could never succumb to something as simple as disease.

Stone had second thoughts about Coady overcoming this "simple disease" at three in the morning, however, as her temperature soared and sweat beaded like raindrops on her body.

He was sitting in the chair behind her desk, his head resting on his folded arms on top of the polished table, when her movements roused him. Looking across the few feet that separated them, he could see through the meager lamplight that Coady had thrown off her bed coverings. "Judas," he breathed, jumping to his feet.

He fought off the dragging remains of what little sleep he had managed to catch and raced to her side. "Coady?" But she seemed suspended somewhere between consciousness and death. Staring at her as he scrambled to cover her with the cotton sheet, Stone knew her temperature had risen yet again. He had seen men in the throes of delirium and, as he battled her feeble protests against having the sheet draped over her, he knew he was seeing it yet again.

Moving quickly toward the one barrel of water he had rolled just inside the door, Stone took one of the buckets Harrison had brought and filled it with water. He closed the door and raised the wick of the lamp on the desk before returning to her bed. "Coady," he said softly as he sat on the edge of the bed.

She was moaning, her limbs thrashing.

"Easy," he crooned as he gripped her wrists in an attempt to calm her. With his free hand, Stone dipped a clean cloth in the water and wrung out the excess. "This will feel good," he said. He talked endlessly as he sponged her fevered body, dipping the cloth repeatedly to keep it cool. The heat from her body was so intense he could feel the warmth through the stuff of his own clothes as he sat beside her.

"Tired," Coady muttered through her fever-induced delirium.

Stone's gaze returned to her face. "I know."

"We walk . . . we walk . . . tired . . ."

His brow furrowed as he realized she was not speaking of *now* but had traveled back to some other place and time. "Walk where, Coady? Where?"

"Mountains."

He dreamed of the mountains, too. Of the horrors there, the incessant cold, the never-ending snow, the glare that could blind a man when the sun shone. But, more often, he remembered the beauty.

130

He dipped a clean cloth in water, leaving it very moist, pressing it against her lips. The smooth, pink skin had become fever-cracked and raw. He would have to ask Trelaine to find some salve, something with lanolin. His men had spread lanolin ointment into the chapped skin of their hands while at the summit.

"Blake . . . she was . . ."

Her words halted so abruptly Stone's heart raced with alarm. But then he realized she was merely asleep. Sleeping more peacefully than she had in hours. Moving as quietly as possible away from her bedside, Stone returned to his chair, his place of vigil.

"MacGregor!"

Startled, Stone's attention veered toward the door. Fearing Coady's sleep would be interrupted he raced to open the thing. "Quiet, Trelaine. She is finally sleeping peacefully."

Harrison shrugged, looking only somewhat sheepish. "How is she?"

Honestly, Stone was not certain. "We've been through fevers and chills and back to fevers. She has cried with pain and moaned with the sickness in her stomach. We have been up, down and around, Trelaine," he added wearily. "And I still cannot tell you that she will live. It does seem that she is better tonight. I'm expecting the surgeon to come by anytime. Hopefully we will know more then."

"I hadn't given much thought as to all you would have to do for her," he murmured. "There have probably been more intimacies shared between you than I can imagine."

"And that bothers you?"

Harrison smiled, understanding Stone's dilemma. "I'm not questioning your actions, man," he said. "Nor your intent."

"My concerns have been somewhat alleviated, MacGregor. I can't have Coady depending on me for the . . . affection she needs. I'm her friend and I will always be her friend. I would move heaven and earth and slay a thousand dragons for her. But she needs more than I can give.'' His gaze slowly roamed across the distance toward the bed, concentrating on her pale, lovely face. ''I've watched her mature in the past year. Coady may not be fully a woman yet but she is certainly no longer a girl.''

Stone frowned but remained silent, giving the man all the time he needed to get it out. After all, where was *he* going for the next day or two?

Harrison shook his head. ''I don't know for certain that you would be good for her, MacGregor. I don't know you well enough to make a judgment. But Coady has needs that I can't attend.''

Stone's frown only deepened as he attempted to decipher Harrison's meaning.

''Let's just say I'm not moved by the female form as are most men,'' Trelaine explained further. ''Now do you comprehend?''

He did. ''Oh,'' he breathed.

Harrison smiled wryly. ''You understand.''

''Does she know?''

''Our little innocent?'' Harrison laughed brusquely. ''How can I tell her? How do I explain something she doesn't know exists, something she can't possibly understand? She has an inkling of something different about me, that's about it.''

Stone was not certain even *he* could understand; not really. But he questioned only, ''*Our*?''

''Coady has relied almost solely on my friendship. I suspect you might, er ... broaden her horizons, at the very least.''

''Now, just a min—''

''You already care for her,'' Harrison interjected quickly. ''Even a man as indifferent to romantic notions as I can see that.'' He cast Stone a threatening look. ''But if this should not work out between you, if you should hurt her or dishonor her in any way, I just might have to shoot you.''

Stone was not sure he liked any of this.

Harrison nodded his head. "I am entrusting you with something very precious. Please do not abuse it."

"I think Coady has been lucky to have you as her friend."

Trelaine actually looked uncomfortable with the compliment. "It is I who have been lucky, MacGregor."

"What you envision for Coady might very well have to be sought from another, Trelaine. I doubt, once she has completely returned to her senses, that you will see me within a golden mile of herself or her establishment."

Harrison stared at Stone's eyes as if he might read something there he did not want to see. "There is trouble between you?"

"Not as far as I am concerned, but Coady will argue the point, little fear."

Harrison, as if tired of standing in the street, took a step up onto the boardwalk. His movement toward Stone was tentative, as if he was not certain as yet whether he should make a more threatening move. "Explain."

Stone proceeded to confess; his work, the Bloodstone fiasco, and the part he had yet to tell Coady, the confession he had wanted to make before she fell ill.

Harrison rested his back against the wall of Coady's place and stared across the street. "That doesn't necessarily put paid between you two, MacGregor," he said thoughtfully. "Once she gets over her initial huff you will be able to talk to her. Prior to that," he said, slanting a wry grin in Stone's direction, "you had better brace yourself, man."

A half smile tipped the corners of Stone's mouth. "Thanks."

Ted Early arrived, looking disheveled and exhausted, but he gave the two men who had stood vigil over Coady hope that she would survive. "She is a strong young woman," Early declared. "I think she will make it."

*   *   *

Stone could envision Coady trudging along the hazardous paths that had brought her to the Yukon. He had watched them come through the post where he had been stationed at the summit of the Chilkoot Pass. By the fall of 1897, tens of thousands of gold-seekers traversed the six hundred miles of grueling mountain passes and treacherous waterways. It was difficult to think of Coady making such a trek. A single, small, beautiful woman surrounded by eager, gold-fevered, male stampeders. It was harder still to understand how she could have survived. This doubt in Stone's mind over whether Coady had actually crossed the pass several times had forced him to order a search of the records kept in the customs house at the summit of the Chilkoot. He did not know what it would prove, had she done so, other than she had told the truth—that she had, in fact, been a longtime resident of the territory.

Curiosity, and the puzzlement of a continuing, haunting, vague recollection to which Stone could not find any substance, had forced him to issue those orders weeks ago. Now he was very sorry he had. Now he feared the facts that would be uncovered could be damning. And now he had to determine what he would do if they were.

His growing fondness for Coady during the past weeks had taken him by surprise. He had not known her long and yet it somehow seemed an eternity. And, as he sat not far from her bed Stone knew he had made the gravest mistake of his career: He had become emotionally involved.

For the first time since his induction into the ranks of the Royal Northwest Mounted Police, he cursed his well-honed instincts. They had seldom steered him wrong and had saved his life more than once. Now he suspected his intuition, his suspicious mind could very well lead him along a path that would cause him pain.

And what of Coady's pain?

In the weeks to come he might well be forced to examine whether he would go on with his career or give it up for a woman he loved. Provided Coady, when she was well, would speak to him. Provided, she did not take a gun and shoot him for his mendacity. Yes, Coady might very well resolve the issue in her own fashion.

As he stared across the room at the pretty woman sleeping peacefully in her bed, Stone wondered how he would ever convince her not to hate him forever.

Chapter Ten

Coady lived.

Stone had managed with very little sleep for almost three days and Harrison had not fared much better. When Coady at last awoke with the glint of lucidity in her eyes, the men were sporting great purple patches of weariness beneath their eyes.

But Stone was not there.

He had suggested to Harrison that *his* was not the first countenance Coady should look upon when she awoke. In fact, he felt he should stay away until Coady had regained much of her strength. Their first meeting would, no doubt, be the most colossal upheaval Dawson City had ever witnessed.

Harrison hoped MacGregor was wrong.

''Welcome back, my pet,'' Harrison murmured, as he sat on the side of her bed, holding her hand.

Coady smiled for him; that special smile that was for

Harrison Trelaine alone. But her gaze was scanning the room even before she spoke.

"He is isn't here, love."

She turned innocent eyes toward her friend. "Who?"

He smiled. "The man you are looking for . . . Mac-Gregor."

"I was certainly *not* looking for Stone MacGregor," she said, frowning to add at least a modicum of conviction to her words. "You have no idea what that man has done to me."

"Do I not? I know he has remained at your side for the past three days. I know that he alone has cared for you. I know that he was worried for you."

"That was guilt, Harrison. He was purely trying to relieve his guilt for what he has done."

"And he put himself in harm's way to do that?"

She shrugged her shoulders against her pillows. "Why not? People have done stranger things."

"I think you are wrong, Coady."

Her large brown eyes displayed as much anger as Harrison had ever seen in her. Standing, he turned his back and walked toward the slit in the tent that served as a window. Thrusting his hands into his trouser pockets, he absently watched the flow of humanity along Dawson's busy Front Street. "MacGregor was doing his job."

"So you know?" she questioned in a small voice.

Trelaine turned and faced her. "He told me."

"Now you are defending him," she accused.

"I am not defending anyone, sweetheart. I believe you simply need a little time to think. He has proven a very good friend to you, you know."

She could hardly argue *that* point. That did not mean she could not question Stone's motives. "He does not even have the gumption to face me."

Harrison laughed. "Oh, he will *face* you, my sweet. MacGregor felt, and rightly so, that you should be stronger before your first meeting. He fully expects you to publicly flail him with your tongue. He will be back to see you, never fear.'' He has more he must tell you, he mused.

The expression in her eyes changed to an emotion Harrison had never seen before.

"He hurt me. I have never felt that kind of pain before."

As much as he hated to see her hurt, Harrison thought the fact that she was could prove very promising. "The man was doing his job, Coady. He did not set out to *hurt* you. He has a responsibility to protect the citizens of the Yukon."

"Heavens, Harrison, perhaps you should sign up. You obviously hold those Mounties in very high esteem."

He laughed. In actual fact, he found the Mounties to be a pain in the butt and she knew that. They were always skulking around the Golden Slipper, watching to see that his games were on the up and up. "Perhaps I hold one Mountie in particular in high esteem. I feel I owe him a lot, even if you do not."

"I suppose I do," she sighed. She also had a great deal to think about. "I'm sorry, Harrison, but I really feel the need to sleep."

His expression immediately became concerned.

"I am all right," she assured him. "I simply must sleep for a time." So saying, Coady turned onto her side and faced the wall of her tent.

But it would be some time before sleep would come to bring her relief from her tortured thoughts about Stone MacGregor.

Coady tolerated almost constant coddling by Harrison and some of the women from the Golden Slipper as she slowly regained her strength. And, as soon as Dr. Early deemed it safe, Isobel was there for her, too.

A week passed between her triumph over the typhoid and her first step. It was another two days before Harrison would allow her to walk around her tent unaided.

And all the while she thought of Stone.

She could not explain why he haunted her dreams and tormented her days, but he seemed always to be with her. She experienced pangs of guilt each time she remembered having a go at him in anger or annoyance. She smiled when she thought of him standing by her side, protective and supportive, through the trials of facing people who had not been particularly appreciative of hearing the news she had to share with them. Warmth enveloped her like a shroud when she remembered the night he put his arms around her. She grew pensive when vague wisps of memories from the days of her illness convinced her Stone MacGregor was a very gentle man.

One day a question popped into her head and she could not shake it off. Could Stone have possibly uncovered her secret? If he had, would he, the policemen, be indignant over a tiny misdeed that had nothing at all to do with him? Unless he felt his own life was above reproach and was so judgmental he made a practice of disdaining those who would dare anything for the sake of survival. Why else had he not come to see her when Harrison assured he would?

Coady lived with these doubts so long, she finally convinced herself that Stone must have uncovered the little lie from her past. This conviction led her to fretting over possible plans he might have for the information he had in his possession. Actually, Coady had the answer: Stone would have little choice in what he must do.

At the very least, she would be ordered from the Yukon.

But Coady could not leave.

She had too much to lose.

Coady was continually looking over her shoulder in the days that followed. By the third day she had grown weary of anticipating that some disaster would befall her as her thoughts ranged over possible reasons for Stone MacGregor's distance. She had to rule out the possibility that he was too cowardly to face her. She would never believe he was a coward. She had not heard of anything dire befalling him and news of that sort would have reached her ears one way or another. And she had not seen him about town. Therefore, she cleverly deduced, duty must have called him elsewhere.

But why was there a constant feeling of dread dwelling deep in her midsection?

"You haven't seen him at all, have you?" Having made a whole pot of tea in her own tent, Isobel had taken the brew around to Coady's place to share a warm drink or two.

Coady raised her head and stared across the table she also used for a desk. Since "Letters to Your Sweetheart" had reached its demise, the table was used mainly for meals and sewing now. "No."

Isobel was just as puzzled over Stone's actions as were Coady and Harrison. "It's all very strange."

"No one has seen him in days."

Isobel frowned. "Perhaps something has happened to him. Why not inquire at the police headquarters?"

Coady was already shaking her head. "It strikes me Stone MacGregor is a bit flighty, wouldn't you say? Worse than any woman I've ever known. He fought for days to save my life, Isobel, and then he decides to have no further contact with me. I expect he could have been assigned elsewhere or sent on another of his special assignments but one would think he would at least say goodbye. How can he appear concerned for my welfare, spending days caring for me, and then just disappear?"

"More reason to inquire after him."

Again, Coady shook her head.

"Are you so afraid you might appear forward?"

Coady laughed. "People have thought me forward for years. Nothing will change that."

Isobel reached across the table and covered Coady's cold hand with her own. "You care for him a great deal, don't you? More than you want to admit to anyone, including yourself?''

Coady smiled weakly. ''That's ridiculous. Except for the fact I quite possibly owe him my life, the man is a toad.''

Isobel laughed. ''Coady! You do not believe that.''

''It just irks me he has disappeared and I don't even know the reason why. And he left before giving me a chance to level a curse upon his head over the downfall of 'Marriage by Design.' '' She sent Isobel a look. ''All right. So I have given it all considerable thought and I know Stone was simply doing what he gets paid to do. But, since he earns a whole dollar a day, you would think he could turn his attention to weightier matters.''

''You love him.''

''I do not. I barely know the man.''

Isobel shrugged slender shoulders.

Propping her elbow on the tabletop, Coady rested her chin in the palm of her hand. ''Do you sometimes get the urge to go back and talk with Vernon?''

''No, not *sometimes*. I have the *urge*, as you say, all the time. It's constant, like breathing.''

''Why don't you go back? I'd go with you for company.''

Isobel smiled at the younger woman. ''You're a good friend.''

''I think you should go.''

But Isobel knew she could not do that. ''He doesn't want me, Coady. Vernon made that very clear.''

There was that, of course. How did a woman get around the spoken facts? ''I think you should have told him about your condition.''

Isobel laughed caustically. ''What would that prove? That he is willing to take responsibility for this child he left inside me? If he married me out of a sense of obligation toward his child, where would that leave me? Wed to a man who doesn't love me and probably never will because I forced him to take me back, that's where. I don't want to live that way, Coady. I want more from life than that.''

"You want his love," she said quietly.

"Precisely." She graced Coady with a sly look. "Exactly what you want from Stone MacGregor."

Coady shot upright in her chair, her back stiff with indignation. "I do not!"

Isobel merely smiled and reached for the teapot. "More?"

Stone was forced to admit he did not know who Coady Blake *was*. He did know she was no longtime resident of the Yukon. Ben Keystone, the only man Stone would trust with the special assignment, had brought him a secret report only a few days before. Coady had lied about who she was and how long she had been a resident. And he did not know why.

Not *yet*.

In his heart, Stone believed in her. But his heart was reacting in a different fashion than his superiors' would once they had their hands on the information. And he would have to hand it over; his duty and his conscious demanded it. But he wanted more evidence to defend her *before* that happened; *if* such evidence existed. His own investigation had turned up very little so far. But Stone was continuing to search.

He talked with Vernon but the man had little knowledge of Coady prior to his, ah, marriage.

In a shadowed corner of the Dominion Saloon, two men sat staring at each other across a table.

"I'm sorry I can't tell you more about Coady. She must have been here at least a few months before I arrived."

"I understand."

"Now I want to know about Isobel. Why is she still here?"

Stone sighed, raised his glass and drank deeply of the

watered whiskey before replying. "I can't force her to leave, Vernon. Would you want me to fling her over my shoulder, carry her onto a ship and tie her there until the damned boat sails out of the territory?"

"If that's what it takes."

Stone scoffed at that. "Be reasonable, man. If you don't want her, Isobel is a free woman. You can't dictate to her."

"I sure as hell can," he snorted. "I'm her husband."

"No, you're not."

It took that reminder to force Vernon to once again face his confusion. "You're right. I'm not. But it isn't good for her to be here. This is a wild place, MacGregor. She's not safe and I doubt she realizes the dangers all around her. Isobel has been coddled and protected all her life. She's an innocent."

Stone thought it a little ludicrous to refer to a pregnant woman as *innocent*. But he supposed a lady could be naive about other things in life. "I know you care for her more than you want to admit. You came here to see that Isobel survived the typhoid, after all." But had there been no epidemic, Stone suspected Vernon would have found another excuse to come.

"She could have been dead by the time I heard about the sickness and managed to get here," Vernon grumbled sourly.

Stone was secretly smiling as he watched Vernon suffer pangs of guilt. "And now you want to protect her from all the rough characters in town."

Vernon's eyes narrowed. "Is that so difficult to understand?"

Stone shook his head. *Now there was a question!* "Not at all. I can understand a man needing to protect the woman he loves."

"Of course I love her!" he shot back. "That's why I want her out of this godforsaken place."

"It isn't all that bad, Vernon."

"It is for her. Isobel doesn't belong here. I can't let

143

her spend her life living in a tent, freezing in winter, working until her fingers bleed. I won't watch her grow old that way, MacGregor. She deserves so much more.''

Stone smiled openly. "The words of a truly smitten man.''

Vernon scowled and looked away. "It doesn't mean anything.''

Oh, but it did. It certainly did. It made Stone want to say more about the woman who had been Vernon's wife for months, legally or otherwise. But he had admonished Coady for her desire to tamper with this couple's relationship, so he could hardly partake of a little tampering himself. It was none of his affair, after all. Still, in view of the depth of feelings Vernon had displayed this evening, Stone felt himself swaying just a little. "Have you seen her?''

Vernon reached for the bottle of whiskey and proceeded to refill their glasses. "From a distance. I don't want her to know I'm here.''

"I suppose," he said thoughtfully. "Wouldn't do for Isobel to see you. It might get her hopes up.''

Vernon's gaze collided with Stone's.

"Well, she might think you have come to take her back.''

"Humph.'' He raised his glass to his lips.

"She looks particularly lovely, Vernon," Stone murmured. "Perhaps you should come back and visit again in another month or two.''

Coady grew impatient waiting for a monster in human form to march into her life and tear away all she had worked for, all she loved. They could do it, she knew. If Stone MacGregor had uncovered her lie, *if* he had, others could as well. The Mounties would run her out of the territory if someone pointed them in the direction of the truth.

She could not have that.

Marriage By Design

September was nearing the end of its days and Coady knew, even if the worst came of it, she must discover what it was that had turned Stone MacGregor against her.

She could stand the tension no longer.

And she desperately missed him.

Chapter Eleven

His workload was immense.

Confidence men, cardsharps, thieves and murderers seemed to be arriving in droves, accompanied by still more stampeders craving gold. He worked long hours, frequently falling into his bed in the early hours of the morning. But Stone did not resent the amount of work that needed doing; he savored it. Uncovering the misdeeds of swine and brutes was what he did best. But the constant activity, the need to focus his instincts, did not keep him from thinking about Coady.

It was a little bit frightening for Stone when he realized he could so easily overlook Coady's weaknesses. Perhaps that was because he had gained so much respect for her strengths. He had allowed himself to fall in love. He indulged in lustful fantasies when he thought of her slender, feminine form. And, while once again carrying out his duties he had, secretly, been struggling with his conscience.

Seven tormented weeks after receiving the confidential

report he had, true to his professional duty, taken the thing to his superiors.

He had met with Simmons earlier in the evening.

Simmons had been surprised but not in the way most people might have thought. "So, you've uncovered the identity of a young woman who entered the territory illegally?"

"Yes, sir."

Simmons exercised his rank. "Then why are you bothering me with this? Why is she still here?"

The questions Stone had expected had not come. He had been certain Simmons would want to know why he had investigated Coady Blake and the timeframe of everything to do with that investigation. "Well, sir, there are extenuating circumstances. I'm not certain it would be fair to extradite Miss Blake."

A sound very much like a strangled *humpf* issued from Simmons. In his experience, when a man mentioned the word *fair* in connection with anything having to do with the law, there was a very big breach in the case somewhere. "Continue."

"I believe Coady Blake must have used the name Edna Blake when she crossed the Chilkoot."

"Who is Edna Blake?"

"She isn't anyone any longer," Stone told him. "Miss Blake died in Vancouver sixteen months ago while visiting with friends, according to sources here. She was a Canadian citizen and a resident of the Territory up until then. Someone used her credentials to gain free access to the Yukon fourteen months ago."

"And you think that *someone* was Coady?"

"Yes, sir."

"Do you also think Coady had something to do with Miss Blake's demise?"

Stone shook his head. "I *do not*. I would find it difficult to believe but the fact remains, she had the woman's identification. I have been told Miss Blake died of natural causes. I am awaiting confirmation of that from Vancouver.''

''Hmm,'' breathed Simmons as he looked speculatively at his subordinate. ''I think perhaps we should have a man call around to see Miss Blake tomorrow, don't you? We should at least keep her in custody until we have confirmation she has not done murder.''

''I respectfully request that I be given the opportunity to speak with Coady, sir. I have investigated this case quite thoroughly. And I do not believe it will be necessary to have her incarcerated.''

''Indeed?''

''No, sir,'' he said solemnly. ''Miss Blake, or whatever her name should be, will not go anywhere because she caused that woman no harm.''

''Your instincts are usually to be trusted in most things, MacGregor, but are you certain your judgment is not somewhat clouded in this case?''

''I do not believe so and I am fully aware of my duty, Superintendent.''

''Understood. But there is still the matter of deportation. Coady Blake may not be a murderess, but she is here illegally.''

''Yes, sir. I am aware that under most conditions deportation is warranted.''

But he was not going to let her go.

Dawn was close at hand when Stone let himself into his room at the Dawson Hotel. It was black inside his quarters. With September came increased hours of darkness, along with cooler temperatures.

He moved to the small table that stood beside the bed and felt around for the tin of matches he kept there. Striking the sulphur head against the grainy edge of the box, he cradled the flame close to his palm as he removed the chimney from the oil lamp. The area immediately surrounding him was instantly bathed in soft, yellow light.

He stretched, raising his arms high above his head,

only then noticing a small bite of pain in his upper arm. "Damn," he grunted before easing out of his dark coat. Today he had managed to avoid serious harm in the face of a madman wielding a knife, but he had not managed to save his coat. "Curse," he hissed as he examined the one-inch slice in the sleeve of the garment. That made him angrier than the slice out of his hide.

He did not know how his cohorts managed to keep themselves clothed. His fellow policemen had to purchase their own boots and coats with the single dollar a day they earned. Stone was not a poor man in his own right, nor was he extravagant. But a dollar a day did not seem enough to keep body and soul together. Obviously it was not enough for some, as several men had given up their positions with the Mounties to mine gold for others, earning the princely sum of fifteen dollars a day. He could not blame them, particularly as he examined the rent in his sleeve. Well, he would have to mend it when he had the time and the inclination.

He turned and threw the damaged coat toward a chair in the corner.

"Hey!"

Stone sprang into a protective crouch even as he pulled a derringer from the waistband of his pants.

She reacted to the threat before he could speak a single word. "It's me! Coady."

Recognition hit him like a March wind roaring through the Chilkoot. "For God's—" He lowered his gun. "How the hell did you get in here?"

Coady rose slowly from the chair, leaving the offensive coat that had smacked her in the face quite sharply draped over the seat. "I bribed the desk clerk," she said as she took a step forward from the shadows into the light.

Stone looked her up and down. She looked good. She looked wonderful. She looked healthy and more beautiful than ever. "Might I ask why you are in my quarters?"

"You might," she returned. "Where have you been?"

A lot of places, attempting to protect you, he mused. But he would never say those words to her. No matter what was about to happen between them, he could only help her try and understand his motives. "I am happy to see you looking so well," he returned.

Coady felt a moment of shame. "Oh, yes, thanks to you. I should have thanked you for that first. Actually, I would have thanked you weeks ago but you seem to have been amongst the missing."

Stone sighed and reached for the bottle of cognac on the chest of drawers. "I've been very busy, Coady."

"Duty?"

"Duty." He flashed a glass in her direction but she shook her head.

"Out of town?"

Stone cast her a glance askance and added a goodly portion more to the brandy he had already poured into his glass. "Coady, we have to talk. Why don't we sit?"

The solemnity of his tone suddenly made her afraid. The terrible, nervous feeling she had been living with for weeks had just increased tenfold. He knew. He must know. And she had come to him because she could no longer stand the anticipation. But, now that she was here, Coady knew she could not deal with seeing a look of disgust in Stone's eyes when he accused her of her crime. "I don't think I have time to talk, Stone. I . . . I should not have come."

He turned and watched her walk toward the door. "What is your real name?"

Coady stopped in her tracks. "Coady Blake," she whispered.

"You are related to Edna Blake?"

Her head dropped forward. Her hand fisted around the doorknob. But, after suffering a heavy heartbeat or two, and with a resigned sigh, she turned to face him. "I suppose we had better talk."

Stone's sincere look of compassion was as intense as

the pain around his heart. "I have hopes it will be all right, lass," he said softly.

"Do you know everything?"

"Not everything, I suspect. I need to hear it from you if I am to help you."

"Would you believe me?"

The question was accompanied by a near scoff that surprised him.

"Why would I not believe you?"

"Others have not," she said flatly. "Success for a woman in business invites a variety of adverse reactions."

"Do not count me amongst the rank and file, Coady. Come," he motioned toward the settee and two wing chairs in front of the fireplace. "We might as well be comfortable."

She cast him a lopsided shadow of a grin. "I may never be comfortable again, policeman."

He flinched at that, making a great show for her benefit.

"I'm about to be hung and you are playing the clown." But she sat, taking the settee, while Stone lowered his bulk into a chair facing her.

Her comment dissipated the small bit of jocularity he had summoned in hopes he could provide her some ease. "Did you kill her?"

"No."

"Then you will not hang."

Her eyes were fixed on his and she knew Stone believed in what he was saying. But, while she would not hang, she would have to leave the Yukon. She knew that and so did he. "I should be flaming angry with you, Stone MacGregor."

"Why are you not?"

"I don't know." She looked around the room, absently, as if searching for an answer. "Most out of character for me."

"I do not believe that, lass. But I was prepared to have

you rain curses upon my ancestors, at least.''

He was smiling at her, smiling gently, understanding her dilemma. The fact that she was not attacking him in some manner told him much.

''When did you start investigating me?'' she asked, watching his eyes again, looking for the truth she hoped to see there. ''Along with Bloodstone?''

He shook his head. ''Shortly after.''

Her smile as she continued to stare at him grew very sad. ''What gave me away?''

''Your pretty face, lass. I had this haunting feeling we had met before. And then you told me you had crossed the Chilkoot more than once in a relatively short period of time. I was stationed there, Coady. I did remember your face but if I had seen you there more than once, I certainly would have remembered.''

''You could not have observed every single person who passed through that post.''

''It was my command. It was my duty to pay close attention to everything . . . and everyone.''

''You are too damned conscientious by half,'' she accused. ''What happens now,'' she asked, resigned to her fate.

Stone took a liberal drink of cognac and set the glass on a small table near his elbow. He leaned forward, his fingers loosely knit together, his elbows on his spread knees. ''Tell me all of it, Coady. Why did you use another woman's identification?''

''I did not have the six-hundred-dollar tariff needed by newcomers to get into the Yukon. Once I had purchased the provisions as required, I had nothing left. I knew the only way I would be allowed in was to pretend I was already a resident.''

''How did you know Edna?''

''I had enough funds saved to get from Seattle to Vancouver but was then in need of a way to earn money to pay the tariff. My dream was to come to Dawson because I believed I could do well here. I applied for a position as a maid in a Vancouver household. I arrived on their doorstep at the same moment Edna stepped out of a hack. She had come to stay with her friends while seeing doctors there. The poor woman was not well even then.''

''And, when she died, you saw your opportunity.''

Her eyes pleaded for his understanding. ''The gold rush would have been over by the time I could earn the money I needed working as a maid. When Edna died, it seemed an opportunity had simply been handed to me. It seemed simple to take on the identity of a long-time resident. But I have lived with more than a little guilt over what I did. And then there was the almost constant fear of being discovered.''

Stone sat back in his chair and studied her for a long moment. ''But why did you continue to use the name once you were here?''

''If I had used my real name and someone had ever checked, there would be no record of my entering the territory at all. I could hardly continue using Edna's full name, her friends here would have given me away in a moment. I suppose I hoped that continuing to use her surname gave me some sort of legitimacy as a resident.'' She shook her head as if the idea that had seemed so right at the time was now completely scatterbrained. ''At least the Blake name was in the records at Chilkoot. Odd what one will do out of desperation. I knew that failure to pay the tariff would mean deportation if I were caught. I was willing to take the chance.''

Stone nodded his head in understanding. ''I think it is most fortunate that I am the one to have made the discovery.''

Coady's mouth dropped open in utter amazement. ''What does that mean? Does this provide you enough points to secure a promotion?''

He ignored her sarcasm. ''Hardly.'' In fact, it could have meant the end of his career had he not been very careful. ''I am awaiting confirmation from Vancouver authorities that Edna Blake died of natural causes. On my recommendation, the superintendent has agreed there is no need for you to be incarcerated.''

Coady sighed once again, appalled that she had wrongly accused him. It was so obvious he was trying to help her but the entire situation simply made her want to lash out. ''I am sorry, Stone. Thank you for that. I am more angry with myself than anyone else, really.''

''Do you have any idea of why I am trying to help, Coady?''

''You always seem to be helping me.''

That was no answer—it was a disappointment. ''Well, give the matter some thought, will you?''

She nodded her head. ''How soon will I be deported, do you think?''

''You are not going anywhere.''

She stared at him, clearly puzzled, watching as Stone pushed up from his chair and walked toward her. Reaching down, he grasped her elbows and pulled her up in front of him. He was close, very close. She could feel the heat of him as he looked down at her.

''We will talk about deportment later,'' he said softly, lowering his head.

His lips moved close to hers, closer still, until Coady reflexively pulled her head back a little.

''Relax,'' he murmured. His lips brushed across hers— a whisper of a kiss. And then his arms went around her and he pulled her up against his chest. His mouth slanted across hers, sending a silver chill throughout her entire body as he kissed her gently but thoroughly. She became very aware of the effect of her breasts against his hard chest.

When Stone raised his head, he smiled down at her. ''Give that some thought, also, will you?''

Some thought? In that moment she was not at all certain she had a mind. Tipping her head back to better see him, she said, ''It is the strangest thing, Stone. I cannot seem to remember why I came here.''

''To find me,'' he said quietly.

"You seem to think you know something I do not."

"I know how I feel," he said frankly. "But I am not at all certain you do."

"Know how you feel?"

He tipped his head back and laughed at her innocent appeal. "About you, precious goose."

Coady's complexion began to change, a soft, warm coloring seeping high across her cheeks. "Oh, Lord," she breathed.

"Don't tell me you haven't thought of this, lass. There are only two reasons you might have for seeking me out. Either to give me a good and proper sample of your temper, or you think you love me and just had to find out."

She shot him a meaningful mock glare. "You are arrogant."

"I have been accused of the same, yes."

"And since you were not the recipient of a good and proper sample of temper, you have assumed the latter?"

"That is about the size of it, lass."

If there was anything that Coady resented, it was people who assumed she was predictable. "Go to hell, policeman." And she turned away, right out of his arms.

He laughed again and pulled her back. "With you," he said low. "I probably shall."

"Such innocence," he murmured as he drew her down onto the settee. "I'm not the boy you charm with penny candy, lass," he continued softly. "I'm a man. But I suspect my thought processes have not been so very different from your own. That is why I dare to say these things. There is something very uncommon between us and it has been there from the beginning."

"I thought it was aversion," she quipped.

Continuing to watch her eyes, Stone's raised his hand to the back of her neck and gently tipped her head to the side. A ghost of a smile caressed his lips in response to the confusion he saw in her. "It is known as tension, my love. Of the good sort." His fingertips lightly caressed the silky flesh over her cheek. "I think I am going to have to kiss you again," he whispered.

Coady willed herself to breathe. "I don't think that would be a very good idea."

"Wrong, sweet lass. It is an excellent idea." His lips touched hers then, gently, warmly, before drawing back so he could gauge her reaction. She was looking timid and perhaps a little stunned. "Not so bad?" he murmured. But his lips slanted across hers again before Coady could respond.

What he was doing made her heart hammer painfully in her chest. Breathing became a challenge even when he pulled his mouth away from hers for a very brief time. He tasted faintly of whiskey. But she was far more intrigued by the warmth of him and the intoxicating odor of maleness than anything else. She had never been close enough to another human being to detect this subtle maleness; not a meticulously *clean* human being, at any rate. She had never dreamed there could be anything so appealing, so fascinating, as the scent of a man. Her body began to experience things entirely new to her, things she could only name as *terms*; liquid warm, frantic beating, pulsing urges. The urge to be closer to him in body was something shocking and demanding at once as Coady found her will directed by something other than her conscience.

She wrapped one arm around his neck, leaning against him, while her fingers roamed across his chest, feeling the warmth of his flesh even through the stuff of his shirt. The muscles there rippled beneath her fingertips.

Stone endured her small exploration as he ran his tongue along the tight seam between her lips. In the next instant he captured her teasing hand and held it pressed against his breast. He pulled his lips from hers and tilted his head in the other direction. His eyes filled with passion, he looked at her. "Part your lips," he whispered.

She did.

And he returned to her more fiercely than before, hungry for her now. A groan of burning desire issued from deep within his throat and he gently forced his way into her mouth.

Stunned, Coady pulled away, her gaze seeking his, questioning.

"It's all right," he said softly. He raised his hand, giving freedom to hers, gently stroking her cheek. "Come back to me," he breathed.

Uncertainty made her hesitate briefly. But longing for something unknown soon overruled her concerns. Coady leaned toward him again, bringing her lips very close to his.

Stone felt his breath catch in his throat as, tentatively, Coady returned his kiss with a small, daring gesture of her own. He felt her tongue press briefly against his lower lip, as if she were testing the taste of him. And then she ventured forward until her tongue met his. It was the briefest of contacts—hardly representative of the boldness he knew she possessed—leaving him discontented over her hasty retreat.

She showed no shyness now as he deepened their kiss, savoring the sweetness and the warmth of her. In her innocence she was doing more to drive his passion than the most experienced seductress he had ever known. When his breathing became labored, and his erection so painful he feared he would not have the will to keep his control in check, Stone ended the kiss, slowly pulling his lips from hers, smiling as he stared down at her heaving bosom. "You've never been kissed like that before, have you?" he questioned softly.

Certainly not! She had never been kissed! Coady could not even remember ever knowing the tender kiss of a mother showing affection for her child. But to him she said only, "No."

The rise and fall of her breasts fascinated him. He looked up long enough to smile at her, pressed a light kiss against her cheek and then lowered his gaze again as he cupped one generous globe in the palm of his hand.

Coady's back stiffened.

"No," he breathed. "Let me. I swear I'll do no more than this." She had lowered her head, watching his hand as he caressed her there. Stone tipped his head to the side, attempting to see her face. "How does it feel, when I touch you like this?"

"It makes me ache," she confessed softly.

He smiled the moment she raised her eyes and looked at him. "That is good."

Her own smile was somewhat crooked. "*Aching* is not good, Stone. I swear to you."

"This kind is," he said before dropping a light kiss on the expensive damask that protected her breast from his view. "I swear to *you*."

A resurgence of her mettle propelled her next words. "You'd have to prove it to me."

Stone threw back his head and laughed. "You tempt me, minx. You truly do."

Coady did not know how to respond to that.

Placing his hands on her slim waist, Stone raised her to her feet as he also stood. "Come along. I think it's past time I walked you home."

"But we have not finished talking."

"Sweetheart, I can barely breathe and you expect me to talk."

She watched him in confusion as Stone retrieved her gloves. It was when he turned back to face her, when the light from the lamp showered his body that she understood. Her large brown eyes fixed on the enormous bulge in the front of his trousers, she said, "Oh!"

He watched her coloring darken and laughed softly again. "Now you understand?"

"Well, yes, of course," she blurted. "I mean, I'm not a child." She raised concerned eyes to his. "Lordy, Stone. That must hurt."

It was fortunate the bed was directly behind him because Stone plopped down on the edge of the mattress and covered his face with his hands.

Coady became very concerned over this bizarre behavior on his part and, stepping forward, sank gracefully to her knees. "Are you all right?" she murmured as she gripped his forearm. "Stone?" she probed, when he failed to respond. And then she heard a strangled sound and noticed his shoulders were shaking. "You're laughing!" she accused and cuffed his upper arm mightily. "Brute!"

He stood and reached for her. "I'm not laughing at *you.*"

She skittered away. "Oh? And, pray, who else is here to make a fool of herself?"

"You did not make a fool of yourself," he said as he pursued her around the room. "It was me, Coady." He caught her when she managed to corner herself between the commode and the wall. Pulling her into his arms, he stared down at her fondly. "It was me, minx. I haven't been so close to losing control since I was a green lad."

She felt her indignation melt as she looked up into blue eyes which reminded her so much of a clear, Yukon summer sky. "Toads are green," she pointed out. "Lads are innocent."

"Aye," he drawled. "Thank you for that." He dared do no more than drop a brotherly kiss on the tip of her nose; if he kissed her again, there would be no taking her home this night. "Come along. We'd best go."

She did not want to go. She wanted him to prove to her that *aching* was good. But that thought made her feel much like one of the whores across town. So she tucked her small hand in his and followed him from the room.

Reluctantly.

When they stepped out onto Front Street, Stone tucked her arm through his.

"Will this thing between us cause you problems with your superiors?" she asked softly as she walked at his side.

"*This thing*, Coady?"

"You know."

He nodded his head, smiling down at her briefly. "I do know. Do you?"

When she did not respond right away, he prompted her. "Is it so difficult to say?"

"It is, you know. Perhaps because I do not know if I truly believe it."

"Believe, lass," he said low. "This *thing* is known as love."

Coady blushed to the roots of her hair, even as she nodded with apparent casualness to an acquaintance passing by. Love between a man and a woman was something to which she was not accustomed. If there had been love between her mother and father she did not want to think about the horrors marriage could bring. She thought she had been in love with Harrison but she eventually realized she had been drawn to him because he was the first person in her recent memory who cared for her, who loved her in his own fashion.

But with Stone her feelings were very new and very different and very confusing. How could she know if she was truly in love? He seemed far more confident than she. What did he know that she did not? And what would she do if she could not stay with him long enough to find out? "I think perhaps our timing is very bad, policeman."

He looked down at her again, stopping to face her. "How so?"

"I know you said I would not be going anywhere, Stone, but there is only so much you can do. I have done wrong and now I must pay."

He grinned, pressed her palm against his arm and continued walking. "Oh, you will pay, lass."

"Then I will be deported," she said miserably.

"No. You will marry me," he said baldly.

Chapter Twelve

Stone returned to his room but never laid his head upon the pillow. Instead he sat on a cold wooden chair, playing with the delicate gloves she had left behind. He spied them the moment he entered the room, lying on the bed where he had dropped them. The gloves were soft, a delicate blue, and so small he marveled at the fragility of the only hand he knew which could possibly fit inside.

As he ran the fine material across his palm, he recalled something his father had told him from the time he was old enough to understand: ''Nothing should come between a man, his conscience, his God, or his country, son.''

His father had been wrong.

A woman could come before all of those things. One woman could and had.

Before the autumn sun had washed across the earth, Stone knew he believed every word Coady had spoken. He had known in advance of their conversation that the woman he loved could no more be responsible for the demise of Miss Edna Blake then she could be held responsible for the colors in the sky. There remained only her failure to pay the required duties upon entering the country. Many people had been deported for lesser offenses. Her lie he saw as a necessity for her own survival, her own self-preservation. He thought he understood how desperate she must have been. But Stone had never known the anxiety of not knowing where he could rest his head when weary. He had never known the hopelessness of never having enough to eat. Coady could have begged in the streets or prostituted herself just to keep body and soul together but she had not done these things. Stone could hardly fault her determination; Coady's drive was one of the things he admired most about her.

He had already paid the money she owed and her marriage to him should ensure that he could keep Coady in the Yukon.

Two days later, the wedding was held as a civil ceremony at the Golden Slipper.

The decision to marry Stone was not such a difficult one to make. On the whole, she thought there were several reasons why they could make the marriage work. He was honest, kind and had made her laugh on more than one occasion. There was also a physical attraction to Stone that she could not explain.

The witnesses discovered Coady's real name was Preston and were awaiting their first kiss as man and wife while Stone and Coady stared into the depths of each other's eyes. He wondered what she was thinking as he reached up and gently raised her veil, folding the silk Chantilly back over the brim of her hat.

He smiled at her serious expression and then bent toward her, pressing his lips firmly against hers in a kiss that could hardly be termed formal and without desire.

Before Stone removed his lips from his bride's, a number of the Golden Slipper's girls were hooting with glee. And Isobel and Harrison were there to congratulate them.

"Better thee than me, old man," Harrison quipped for Stone's ears alone.

"I just know you're going to be happy," Isobel said brokenly.

Coady looked at the woman, surprised. "You're crying," she whispered in amazement.

"That's what weddings are for," Isobel returned primly. And then laughed, reaching out and hugging her young friend fiercely. "Be happy, Coady."

"I will."

She should be happy. She was now assured that she could remain in her beloved Yukon. The authorities had accepted Stone's explanation of unusual circumstances, the payment of the tariff, and her marriage to a citizen as acceptable reasons to allow her to stay. In a place where a man could be turned out of the country for simply displaying a gun in public, Coady considered herself very fortunate; for surely it was a great sin to withhold monies from the government!

If she still had niggling doubts about truly being in love with Stone, she was willing to ignore them. It was enough to say that he was the most important person in her life; that she cared about him; that *his* life was precious to her. Surely these were some of the ingredients of love?

The supper buffet would have a fed a crowd a hundred strong, or, "Ten hungry stampeders," Coady teased Harrison.

"Are you saying I haven't provided well for you?"

She was instantly regretful. "Oh, no! Harrison, you've been wonderfully generous. Thank you for all of this." He had even gifted her with the beautiful hat and gown she was wearing.

He smiled. "I was teasing, pet. And you are entirely welcome." He touched her cheek in that way he had of somehow keeping his distance but also relaying his affection. "Any regrets?"

"None."

"Are you hungry?"

Coady turned her back on Harrison and faced her new husband as Stone spoke. "Yes. I'm starving."

Stone gave her the plate he had brought for her.

Coady accepted graciously, her eyes devouring the selection of oysters, salmon, smoked ham, and cheeses. "Thank you," she murmured as she selected first a small wedge of cheese.

"Choose a table," Harrison directed. "I'll get a plate for myself and Isobel and we will be along in a moment."

Stone motioned toward a corner table.

Coady walked slowly in front of him.

She was pleased when he pulled out a chair for her and held it. "A girl could get used to this kind of treatment," she said as she sat down.

"A *woman* could and should," he returned quietly before he, too, sat down.

His tone, when he had uttered the word *woman* set goose flesh to rising on Coady's skin. She had never really thought of herself as a woman until she had met him. She had been a working person, a female making the best of the brains and the God-given talents bestowed upon her. Stone's comment made her realize she had gone through life in the manner of a fallow individual, nothing more. But, with him, being a woman suddenly seemed right, very right.

He looked wonderfully handsome in his black frock coat with matching waistcoat and trousers. The collar of his white shirt stood high beneath his chin and his black tie had been expertly knotted. Everything about him was elegant and masculine. But Coady found herself wishing to see him more casually attired, as was his habit. There was something undeniably rugged about Stone dressed in a leisure-shirt and snug-fitting jeans.

"You're not hungry after all?"

Startled, Coady blinked before returning her attention to him. "Wool-gathering again, I'm afraid."

"The food is wonderful," he told her.

"Yes." She was searching her plate, making an Epicurean decision.

"I've rented a larger room for us."

Coady's head snapped up. "You have?"

"The hotel has a small suite I thought would suit. It's only two rooms, a bedroom and a sitting room, but I think we'll be comfortable there."

"But I have my . . ."

Stone frowned, staring at her as she failed to complete the sentence. "Your what? Not your tent, Coady?"

"It has served me well," she pointed out. "If we lived there, we would not have to bear the cost of lodging."

Stone rested his elbows on the table and steepled his fingers high above his plate. "I can afford the price of the suite."

"But it seems such a waste."

"You'd rather I move into your tent?"

"Well, actually . . ."

"Coady, I am not a pauper."

"It simply seems prudent . . ."

He frowned and reached for her hand. "You are not afraid of living in the hotel for some reason?"

"Why does it always come down to you asking more questions?" she countered.

"You are?" he demanded softly, suspiciously. He released her hand and sat back in his chair, watching her, realizing she would not look at him. "Why? You will have a place to live and a place to work, each separate from the other. Why is that so worrisome?"

Coady pushed her plate away, having lost her appetite. "It seems too much of a luxury."

"Luxury? What could possibly be wrong with a little luxury?" He continued to look at her, puzzled, as Coady insisted on examining her hands. "Look at me," he demanded softly after several moments had passed. When she looked up Stone thought he understood. "You *are* afraid. Tell me why."

She could see he was determined to have this out one

way or another and he would query her to death if she
could not appease him. "I may become too accustomed
to luxury."

"You could and you should."

She shook her head. "Once one is accustomed to
something agreeable, it is difficult to live without it."

"That is hardly a positive endorsement for your hopes
for the future. Or is it *our* future in which you have so
little faith?"

"I do not mean to be unappreciative."

"I am not looking for appreciation from you," he said.
He was annoyed by her comment but struggled to keep
any indication of his feelings from being revealed by his
tone. He did not want their wedding day to be marred by
an argument. And he understood her fear of lacking the
necessities of life. Resting his knife and fork on the side
of his plate, Stone stared at her earnestly. "Coady, there
is something I want you to understand. Now that we are
married you need not worry about going hungry or being
without shelter again."

It was a nice thought but . . . "Stone, you earn a dollar
a day."

"True. But I have monies other than that."

Coady blinked. "You do?"

"Believe me when I say we have enough to live comfortably."

That was, indeed, good to hear but it also piqued her
curiosity. "How comfortably?"

"I have enough that we can feel secure."

"Really?" She was dumbfounded. "But not enough
that I should give up my businesses? What is left of them,
that is."

"You can give up your businesses anytime you wish,
lass."

Coady munched thoughtfully on an oyster. If she could
lie back and feel secure it would certainly be for the first
time in her life. It would be so wonderful to have a roof
over her head that she could claim as hers. It would cer-

tainly diminish that horrid fear of ever again having to
live on the street. Then again, Stone had not said *exactly*
how much money he had and she did not want to appear
greedy by asking. She also fully intended to contribute
all she could to their life together. "I think I would like
to keep working, Stone."

He nodded his head, understanding. He had suspected
Coady would not want to give up her independence simply because she was now married. It would take time
before she could truly feel secure, no matter whether he
could tell her he was the richest man on earth; which he
was not. "Whatever you wish to do, love, is fine with
me," he said, reaching for his fork. "But, you will move
into the hotel, correct?"

Love? Coady forgot whatever it was she had in her
mouth but she swallowed it as her complexion warmed
over the endearment. "Yes, I suppose if you feel you can
afford it."

"Good!" he said succinctly and began to peruse his
plate. "I have already had your things moved there."

"Don't you think that was rather high-handed of
you?"

He shook his head. "Not at all. It was the husbandlike
thing to do." He grinned broadly. "As your spouse it's
my duty to make your life easier, my sweet."

Coady opened her mouth to reply but was abruptly
silenced as Harrison interrupted.

"Champagne for all," he said expansively.

As Isobel sat in the chair on Coady's right, Harrison
held a shapely tulip glass toward her. "I think I'd best
not," she said softly as her hand came to rest upon the
small mound of her belly.

"Oh, of course." He turned his attention on the bride.
"My pet?"

"Yes, all right." The whole thing suddenly struck her
as outrageous; the gown, the ceremony, the decor, the
lavish meal. *Champagne. Imagine me, Coady Blake,
drinking champagne.*

167

Chapter Thirteen

The champagne had been most wonderful.

Everything else paled by comparison. So Coady decided as she sat in front of the dressing table, staring at herself in the framed oval mirror. Such opulence! To sit on a padded stool looking into a large mirror as she braided her hair. No small square of mirror tacked onto a tent post, here.

The suite was really rather elegant by Dawson standards. There were fireplaces in both rooms. Another luxury. One that would be greatly appreciated once winter set in. The bedroom had a high chest of drawers and a clothes press in addition to the feminine dressing table at which she sat. And the four-poster bed was wide, the mattress, thick. For this night she chose to set aside any concerns she might have had by ignoring her more pragmatic side. The bubbly helped her do that. She would be very comfortable here, thank you very much.

Pulling a brush through thick, long tresses, Coady stared at herself in the mirror and giggled. It was time

perhaps that she indulged in a little luxury. The good
Lord knew she had lived a Spartan life long enough. And
this wonderful suite was made all the better because it
had not cost her a single ounce of gold.

She giggled again, the continuing effects of the champagne. Perhaps she had had too much? She leaned forward, closely inspecting her eyes, and grinned. She was
in unusually high spirits. "That's why they call it *spirits*," she murmured. "Have a little *spirits* to lift your
spirits, lass!" She giggled again and then abruptly
straightened her back. "Be serious now," she whispered.
"It's time you were getting yourself to bed." Pulling her
hair over her left shoulder, Coady's nimble fingers sec-
tioned the lot into three and began braiding.

Stone sucked slowly on the stem of his pipe as he eyed
the bedroom door. He thought about what she was doing
in there that could possibly be taking so long.

Having removed his coat, waistcoat, and the stiff collar
of his shirt, he had made himself comfortable in one of
the two over-stuffed chairs the sitting room boasted. He
had cautioned himself to wait upon Coady readying herself for him, but he had not counted on the fact that time
would come to a halt. That thought forced him to come
face to face with his own impatience.

Well, he wanted her. What was wrong with that? She
was his wife, after all. And sleeping with her had definitely been one of the attractions that had led him to the
altar. But only one; he loved her all right, plain and simple.

Thinking about what Coady felt, or failed to feel, was
far more difficult.

He supposed he was not the first man in history to wed
a woman who did not recognize love when it hit. And
he did not think he would be the last. It was enough for
now that she held at least some affection for him. Coady
showed him that in myriad ways: the way she smiled, a
special smile that seemed to be just for him; the way she

almost shyly tucked her small hand in his; the manner in which she unconsciously brought her body close to his; the glimmer in her eyes that had nothing to do with tears. All these things told him much about his beautiful wife but Stone would be oh so happy when she trusted enough, when she felt secure enough, to utter the words, *I love you.*

He sighed and tapped the bowl of his pipe into a small dish on the table beside him. Taking out his pen-knife, Stone dug the remaining ashes free and set the pipe aside, as he looked at the small mantel clock. More than half an hour had gone by since Coady had first gone into the bedroom. She must surely be ready for him. He smiled doubtfully as he got to his feet and walked across the room. Were new brides ever really *ready* for their husbands? "Some, perhaps," he muttered as he placed his hand on the glass doorknob and turned it. "But not this one, obviously." He frowned and twisted the knob again.

Locked!

"Coady?"

Inside the room, Coady's gaze darted toward the door and her hands fell still on the partially finished braid. "Yes?"

"The door is locked."

"Yes, I know." She scooted off the padded bench and raced, barefoot, to the portal. "I locked it."

On the other side of the polished wood, Stone was rolling his eyes. "Well, unlock it, sweet."

"I am wearing only a nightdress."

Stone was not entirely sure, but he thought he heard her giggle. Perhaps she had drunk more champagne than he realized. Again he tried for patience. "I'm your husband, lass," he said gently. "Open the door."

Coady giggled, seeing an opportunity for a fine game. "But you only married me to save the police the paperwork of deporting me," she teased.

"Unlock this door, Coady," he said firmly.

170

"Was that the only reason you married me, Stone?"

With a heavy sigh, Stone rested his shoulder against the door, foreseeing a lengthy conversation through the keyhole. "No, Coady, it was not."

"Does that mean you might love me some small bit?"

He smiled gently. "Some small bit perhaps, lass." He heard another muffled noise and scowled. "Are you laughing?"

"We *are* sharing a *suite*," she pointed out needlessly.

Stone put his hand on the doorknob again. "Open the door."

His tone of voice penetrated the thick wood of the door as well as her champagne haze. Concerned now that she had truly angered him with her play, Coady turned the key in the lock and quickly stepped back, looking for all the world like a small girl awaiting some form of castigation.

Stone entered, frowning when he saw her standing in the middle of the room as he let the door swing wide. "Was it truly your intention, madam, to keep me from my wife?" he asked softly.

Coady shook her head. "I didn't think—well, teasing you seemed a good idea at the time."

He smiled. "It isn't wise to keep a hungry man waiting my love."

Coady's arms swung wide in an exaggerated motion until she could manage to lock her fingers together behind her back. "Oh, well, I . . ."

Apprehensive. "Don't you want to discover how *aching* can be good?"

She watched him take a step toward her as she remembered the aching, the tightness inside herself, when he had touched her breast only a few nights ago. And suddenly she felt very sober, indeed. "You don't play fair," she admonished softly. "I wasn't prepared for . . . this." She shook her head, searching for a better explanation. "I mean, I am your wife, but I—"

"You hadn't thought about sharing a bed?" he probed.

"Are you adverse to it then or simply ill informed?"

She followed his hand as Stone reached for the partially unraveled braid that rested over her breast. "I don't know. I'm not certain what to expect."

Innocence. "I will give you all the instructions you will need in this matter," he said as he slowly freed her silken hair of the braid. "Then again, I suspect much of it will come naturally to you. We have all night. I don't want you to be frightened by this. There is no need to be afraid," he added.

Coady took exception to that. "I am never afraid of anything."

"This is so lovely." His fingers combed through her luxurious mass of auburn hair. "Lovely. Don't braid it at night."

Her gaze lowered to where his fingers were toying with a thick curl. "It will be a mass of knots come morning."

He smiled when she looked up at him. "Then I shall have to help you brush it out."

Envisioning him doing just that, Coady thought it would be an extremely intimate thing for him to do. No one had ever brushed her hair! She giggled to mask her discomfort and whirled away, returning to her place at the dressing table.

Stone frowned, following the flow of the voluminous white nightdress that completely concealed any trace of femininity beneath its abundant folds. Clearly, he would have to woo her. But he had been so long without a woman, Stone feared he would not remember how to entice one into his bed. Coady would be different, of course, from others he had known. She was a virgin. Wooing her would take all the strength and control he could muster. If she but looked at him with tenderness, the seduction would be done before it had started. He wanted her with an urgency the likes of which he could not describe. Words were simply not good enough. "Slowly," he whispered as he approached the bench.

Coady looked in the mirror as he came to stand behind her. "Did you say something?"

He smiled and took the brush from her hand. "Allow me."

She closed her eyes, feeling the wonder of the brush drawing slowly through her hair, along her scalp and down her back. "The champagne was wonderful," she said, for lack of a better topic. "I believe I drank too much."

"You seem sober enough to me," he returned quietly.

Well, I suppose, she mused. Facing the prospect of joining him in a huge bed was, for her, a very sobering thing. She should not have told him she was *never* afraid.

"There is one thing I should say here and now, lass," he said quietly. "Don't ever again lock that door against me. We are husband and wife and I mean for us to get to know each other as such. If ever there comes a time when you don't want me making love to you, you simply have to say no. But don't ever lock me out of this room."

Coady looked at him in the mirror and tested the theory. "No."

Hung in a noose of his own making! He laughed, a quick, resigned bark. "I wouldn't expect you to deny what you don't understand," he taunted. "You're usually more inquisitive than that."

She had to admit to that, at least. "I am curious."

"Have you talked with no one about this, Coady?"

The gentleness of his tone encouraged her to answer honestly. "No. There has been no one."

"You could have gone to Isobel."

She shook her head. "I would be humiliated. It seems I should know."

Stone put the brush on the table and reached for Coady's shoulders, turning her until she was facing him. Dropping down onto his heels, he took both of her hands in his and looked into her eyes. "It is not such a strange thing," he murmured. "It is a natural thing. There is

173

nothing to fear. I swear. On the contrary, making love is really quite a pleasure.''

She eyed him cautiously. ''For *men*.''

He laughed lightly. ''Women, too.''

''Truly?''

He smiled, tipping forward onto his knees, moving closer to her. ''You liked what we did a few nights ago,'' he said. Pressing their joined hands on top of her knees, he leaned forward and kissed her, a warm, lingering kiss full of promise. ''So sweet,'' he whispered. He tipped his head to the side, smiling as her gaze followed his motion.

Coady, her gaze locked with his, shivered with the intensity she saw in his dark, blue eyes.

''Cold?''

She shook her head.

''Let me warm you,'' he murmured as if she had not responded. ''Let me guide you.''

Warmed, indeed. Her heart was softened, too, by his earnest tone. ''Will you be my guiding angel?''

''Aye, that I will,'' he breathed. ''Trust me.''

He possessed only the smallest hint of an accent, but his Scottish heritage seemed to come through at times when she could most cherish his lilting tones. *Trust him?* Seduced by his breathless, golden timbre, how could she not?

Stone took her in his arms then, kissing her with all the longing he had been harboring almost from their first meeting. She smelled slightly of wild flowers and, from her hair, a light trace of lemon; little wonder it shone so!

He deepened the kiss, gently forcing her mouth open as he pulled her against his chest. He could feel her breasts pressed against him. He hungered to tear the awful nightdress from her and feast his eyes and his senses on the womanly form that he knew was hidden beneath all those yards of material. His left hand pressed against her back, keeping her close, while his right hand strayed upward from her waist until he had captured a softly rounded breast in his palm.

She moaned into his mouth.

"Aye," he breathed.

He stood then, pulling her up, enfolding her in his arms, pressing the length of her body against his. "Feel how much I need you?" he murmured as he patterned small caresses across her cheek with his lips. "Feel?"

Through her passion-induced daze, Coady acknowledged it was nice to be needed but what she was feeling pressed against her belly was just a little worrisome. She had heard of men *claiming* a woman and knew the meaning could be likened to claiming a prize. But if what she thought was about to happen actually happened, she failed to see how they could possibly manage.

Moments later the fearsome thought of Stone's *claiming* her was banished as he began a gentle assault which had her every nerve lurching, her breathing labored, and her body heated. His hands seemed to be everywhere at once. To her chagrin, warm liquid seemed to be flowing from the center of her body and, as Stone pulled the nightdress from her, she bowed her head in an attempt to hide the awful, heated blush she knew was riding high upon her cheeks.

"What?" he whispered. He placed the tips of his fingers beneath her chin and raised her head until he could look into her eyes. "Tell me," he encouraged.

"Strange things are happening."

He smiled, stooped, and swept her up in his arms. "Well, we shall have to talk about them at length," he said somewhat breathlessly as he walked toward the bed. Her hesitancy had come at just the appropriate moment; he needed to step back, so to speak, in order to prolong these wonderful moments with her. He did not want to rush. He wanted to savor her.

He lowered her to the mattress and was immediately disappointed as Coady scrambled beneath the blankets she had earlier turned back. He stared down at her as he pulled his shirt free from the waist of his pants, acknowledging her reluctance to have him see her naked. "The last word I would have used to describe you is *shy*,'' he told her conversationally.

Coady looked up at him. "Unusual for me," she admitted.

Stone nodded his head, threw his shirt on a nearby chair and sat on the edge of the mattress beside her. He could feel her hip against his buttocks as he bent his leg to remove a boot. He took heart in the fact she did not move away. "I suppose it would be easier for you if you loved me?" He so wanted to hear her *say* the words.

Coady gave that a moment's thought. "I suspect there is no difference for a girl's first time."

He willed his heart not to sink. *Give her time*, he silently admonished as he tugged off the second boot. "I promised pleasure and I plan to keep my word," he said as he stood and, facing her once again began releasing the buttons on the front of his trousers. Her show of shifting over, making room in the bed for him, made him smile. It was all a pretense, a cloak, a guise to hide the fact she could not bring herself to view his nakedness. "I can see we're going to have to quickly become more familiar," he said dryly as he slid beneath the blankets and moved against her back.

Stone eased his arm over her, accurately finding a generous breast, insinuating his fingers between the mattress and the heavy globe until the weight was cupped within the palm of his hand. "Tell me about these *strange things* that are happening to you," he said quietly.

Coady could feel the warmth of his breath against her shoulder. Somehow it seemed a strange way in which to have a conversation, with Stone holding her breast as if his hand had been there a thousand times before. She felt his thumb move and her nipple responded instantly. "Like that," she whispered.

"Ah," he breathed. He moved his hand to her shoulder and pulled, rolling her onto her back. "These are good things." She was staring up at him, looking more curious than afraid now, and he knew the time for talk was over. He was happy for that. Even the most patient of men had their limits.

He lowered his head and captured her lips, hungrily possessing her the moment Coady opened her mouth to him. His right hand was busily caressing her breast as he favored her with the demanding kisses only a passionate man could bestow. The fingers of his left hand burrowed deep into her luxurious hair and, responding to her exacting moan, he deserted her soft lips for the greater softness of her breast.

It seemed as if all the heat in her body flooded toward that place where Stone now directed his attention. Coady closed her eyes, breathing deeply as he took her taut nipple into his mouth and began to suckle. The pleasure from the tension he caused flowed down the length of her body to her very toes. Needing, reaching for more, she raised her shoulder even as she pressed the palm of her hand against Stone's head. "What are you doing to me?" she moaned.

Stone raised up briefly, planting soft, teasing kisses along her delicate jaw. "Exactly what you do to me," he breathed. His hand found its way to her other breast then and he stared at it, circling his thumb around the hardened nipple, enjoying the response he knew was now beyond her control.

Coady felt a fresh flow of liquid heat coarse through her the moment Stone's hungry lips took hold of her breast again. He suckled slowly, while his free hand caressed its mate. She bent her knees, pressing her legs together in an anxious attempt to ease the aching that seemed to be growing at a fearful rate deep inside her core. His hand abandoned her breast then and followed the line of her waist, her hip, caressed along her thigh and back again. The gentle gesture did little to soothe her, however. Contrarily, the aching only became more intense, her breathing more labored. Coady rolled toward him. "Help me," she sighed against his neck.

"Soon," he rasped. He raised his head, watching her

Jill Metcalf

as he pulled on her hip, rolling her onto her side to face him. He pressed his pulsing erection against her belly and smiled when she gasped. But she did not pull away. Instead Coady pressed harder against him, straining against him. "Very soon," he groaned.

Coady very quickly found herself on her back again, staring up at him as Stone moved over her, bracing himself with elbows locked. She sensed his knees flexing, felt the heat of him between her thighs. And then he was pressing against the entrance to the center of her aching and she found herself wishing he would enter, enter quickly and ease this terrible thing which had overtaken her very will.

He eased gently just inside her. "I may hurt you just a little, my sweet," he whispered harshly close to her ear. "Just this once." He gasped for a breath. "I promise."

Coady did not care about hurting. How could she possibly hurt anymore than she was already? She was gasping with need, gripping his shoulders. Moving her head from side to side on the pillow, she reached for a very deep breath as she felt him move deeper within her and halt. *What is he waiting for?* her mind cried silently. "Please," she cried softly as she moved her hands to his hips and raised herself to meet him. She felt a small sharp pain deep inside and froze.

"It's all right, lass," he murmured. "Easy." He pushed forward slowly and then he stopped. "Be still now," he pleaded softly as he kissed each of her closed eyes in turn. "Be still a moment."

A moment, however, was all they could spare. Coady began kissing him feverishly, her lips roaming his face, assuring him the pain had been small and brief. "You promised me, MacGregor. You promised me."

He raised his head over her, staring at her as he began to move. He withdrew and saw her eyes darken with disappointment. And then he was easing home again. Again he withdrew and again he returned, gauging her reaction as the pace of his motions grew ever more rapid.

Coady's eyes closed, her head pressed deep into the pillow and her body tensed, just as his own was about to explode. "Now!" he groaned.

Her head came up hard against his shoulder as every nerve, every inch of her flesh responded to his urgency.

Stone pulled her tight against him, swaying her, pressing home, staying deep within her as he shuddered over her.

She cried his name as she quivered and rocked against him again and again, as the pulsing inside her seemed to pull hungrily at his hot flesh.

When at last her body went limp, Stone eased her down, supporting himself over her, as he turned a gentle smile into something very perceptive. "All right?"

Her eyes remained closed but the hint of a satisfied smile drifted across her lips. "Mmm."

He started to rise up but she blindly, accurately, grasped his upper arms. "Don't."

"I am too heavy."

"No," she breathed. "Stay."

He was happy to stay. "For a while," he whispered, and settled a little of his weight on her.

Moments later, when their breathing had quieted, Coady slowly opened her eyes to see him watching her. "You were right," she said softly. "Aching is good."

He nodded his head.

"I don't know why I was nervous. It was silly, really."

He brushed at a wisp of hair against her forehead with the tips of his fingers. "Not so silly. Some women have a deathly fear of this, I'm told."

"Foolish women," she returned, smiling.

She had so many smiles; teasing, wicked, coy, understanding. But this smile was new. This smile bespoke of something revolutionary. This smile was entirely endearing. Never had he felt so close to her as in this moment when he looked upon her radiant face. Heated passion alone had not brought him this close to her. "Am I safe in assuming I didn't hurt you?"

Coady looked shocked. "No. You did not hurt me."

"Good."

"I did think at one point I might break into a thousand pieces," she teased.

He frowned.

"A million fragments of Coady floating toward the sky."

He laughed and hugged her close for a time. After a moment he raised his head and, looking down at her, said reluctantly, "I think you had better let me go now."

She shook her head. And then her eyes rounded as she felt him stir deep inside her. "Oh, dear."

"Precisely," he said wryly. He eased himself from inside her and rolled to his side, pulling her close against him, wrapping her within the warmth and safety of his arms. He was thinking this was just where she belonged, safe and secure, in his bed, within his embrace, when she interrupted his musings.

"What will you do?"

He looked down to see she had turned her face up to him, her head resting on his arm. The expression he saw on her face seemed to be a mixture of confusion and genuine concern. "What will I do about what?" he countered.

"The state you're in."

He grinned, delighted with the day, the evening, and her. "I won't do anything."

Coady's hand burrowed slowly through the hair on his chest. "Are you not uncomfortable?"

He closed his eyes, caressing her cheek with his thumb as he tried not to think of his discomfort. "It will pass, my sweet," he murmured.

"I wouldn't mind," she whispered.

He opened his eyes again. "Wouldn't mind?"

Her coloring quickly rose to match that of the red velvet furnishings in the hotel lobby. "If you want to do it again . . . I mean . . . I wouldn't be adverse."

He laughed softly and pulled her up on his chest. "Oh, Coady," he breathed, "you are a delight."

His comment was high praise of which she was quite unfamiliar. There were a lot of things to discover with him, she suspected, which were unfamiliar. "Does that mean no?"

His smile was gentle. "Patience, my sweet. I don't want to make you sore. There will be many times for us." He. graced her with a mock frown. "Unless, of course, you choose to say no."

She turned her head and pressed her cheek against his chest to hide the telltale blush that just would not ease. "I can't imagine saying no."

That was a good sign, he thought.

There were several moments of silence between them, each entertaining their own separate thoughts.

Coady enjoyed the feel of his hand circling slowly on her back. The caresses sent tiny shivers down her spine and made her wish they could do more. That thought made her realize something about herself. "I suppose I'm forever changed."

"For certain."

She raised up, propping her elbow on his chest, resting her cheek against the palm of her hand. "Do you think we made a baby tonight, Stone?"

He looked at her, at the lazy eyes that indicated just how tired she was after their long day. "It is possible," he said.

"It would be nice, having a baby," she sighed. "A little one to call my very own."

Stone was wrestling with her comment about the little one. "You've been terribly lonely, haven't you?"

She seemed surprised by his question. "Not entirely." she said lightly. "I do have friends, you know."

"But you haven't had anyone to love. And no one to love you in return."

She did not like his pity. "Harrison loves me," she said primly.

"That is very different from what I'm talking about."

Her stern expression melted into one of confusion. "I know. He thinks of me as a sister."

"I think you must be very tired," he said softly, looking at her drooping eyelids. He eased her down onto the mattress. "Lie here close beside me, sweet, and go to sleep."

"My nightdress," she protested weakly.

He shook his head and wrapped his arm securely around her. "You do not need those things. If it's warmth you are needing, I shall be happy to oblige."

That made her smile. "Good. It will save me considerable amounts of laundry."

Stone chuckled softly as he pressed his cheek against hers and closed his eyes.

Chapter Fourteen

Coady did not sleep particularly well that night.

She was not in the habit of sharing a bed with anyone; never had in fact. But as dawn crept stealthily toward a new day, she had to admit the experience was not unpleasant. Stone was warm beside her, she felt closer to him in those early morning hours than she had ever felt to another living soul. He breathed softly as she watched him and he kept her close against his side, as if he would never let her go. There was something fearfully heartwarming in the way he held her. Coady felt cherished by him. It would be nice being cherished by such a man, she conceded as her gaze roamed freely down the length of his body. He had more strength than that evident in the masses of bulging muscles she was busy inspecting. He seemed to possess an inner strength, she was just now learning. He had a number of qualities any woman could admire. The fact he treated her as a person of merit was enough to endear him to her. Most men saw her as a devil with whom they were sometimes forced to do business. In the past she had held no value as a person to anyone, save to herself; and perhaps in some small way to Harrison and Isobel. And now, with Stone, it seemed different. With him it was all very different. The regard and caring Harrison had always shown her paled next to Stone's attentions.

Last night he had loved her. He had been caring with her, gentle in his possession of her, and she had liked it. At least with him she had liked it. She could not imagine another man making her feel the way Stone had made her feel. Somehow, it had just been right between them.

And, as her hand lightly, curiously, roamed down the flat of his belly, Coady determined that she wanted this rightness to go on as it had begun. One way or another, she would be a good wife to him. And if children were to come of their lovemaking, they would know a good life, a childhood totally different from her own. She was no longer poor and without possessions.

He could remember many a morning of waking to winter cold, to feeling iciness seeping into his body until he sometimes felt like his bones would snap. There had been mornings when he had to trick his conscious mind in order to get moving from beneath the blankets. A man never felt so alone as he did awaking cold and alone in his bedroll in the dreadful silence and stillness of a winter predawn.

This morning was not in any way similar to those horrid experiences from his past.

It had been so long since he had awakened to warmth, to the feel of soft, womanly flesh lying against his side. The slight weight of her head upon his shoulder was like no weight at all, but a sensation to be forever cherished. And having her against his side, feeling this surety that he was no longer a man alone, was something he knew he would never forget. This woman tucked securely against him was no lover for a night or even two; she was his wife.

Her hand rested on his thigh, very close to a morning erection that had sprung to life before he had. He became aware of her fingers moving ever so slightly.

And then he realized he could not detect the soft sounds of her breathing, the slow movements of her breasts against him that would indicate she slept. Opening his eyes, he looked down at the top of Coady's head. She lay so still, lost in deep concentration that had little to do with sleep. He could not see her face but his instincts told him she was surveying his naked body, not only with her hand but with a very focused awareness! His voice, when he spoke, was husky with the remnants of sleep and newly awakened passion she had stirred. "What are you doing?"

"Exploring."

"You see what you've done, don't you?"

She giggled and moved her head on his chest.

His hand roamed over the womanly roundness of her hip. "What do you plan to do about it, lass?"

Coady moved her head onto his upper arm, looking up until her warm gaze met his. "Good morning."

He smiled. "Good morning, yourself."

"What shall I do?"

Stone's brows arched severely. "About . . . ?"

"What I've done to you."

"What made you go exploring?" he teased.

Coady's complexion darkened. "You kicked off the blankets."

"*I* did?"

She nodded her head innocently. "And there you were, lying all naked," and beautiful, she added silently. "I couldn't help myself."

"You seem in mighty high spirits this morning."

It was true; she was in high spirits; giddy in fact. Very different from the way she usually rose to greet the day. Business matters required concentration and soberness and she usually awoke thinking of all the things she must accomplish in the few short hours a single day possessed.

185

But this morning she was certainly not thinking of business. She was not certain if this feeling of difference was due to lust or a deep, abiding love. What more could love do? She was already filled with such happiness and wonder. Coady's brow furrowed a little as she considered the matter. "Surely not all lovers feel this way," she murmured.

"Does it feel right to you?"

She nodded her head thoughtfully.

He could see her struggling to identify all she was feeling, seriously pondering the changes a single night had brought her way. He found himself wishing she would know what he already knew; that love did not always come up and smack a person between the eyes. Sometimes love was more insidious than that. But one could find it in a look, a touch, a pounding of one's heart when that oh-so-right person was near. At least it felt right to her. It was a start. And one day she would be able to say the words he needed to hear.

The look in Stone's eyes softened. "If it feels right, lass, it must be right."

She smiled, nodding her head.

"But on this other matter," he said with mock severity. "For this thing that you have done, I think you must be justly punished," he said low. He took her small hand in his and moved it from his thigh, wrapping her slender fingers around his hard, hot flesh. When he felt her tighten her hold, he growled and moved down in the bed until he could bury his face in the mass of auburn, satin tresses lying across her pillow.

Coady felt his warm breath against her ear and drew her closed fist slowly along his length.

"Jesus," he hissed softly.

She quickly found herself on her back for her trouble, with Stone looming over her.

"You're not sore?"

The passionate huskiness of his tone quickened her

heartrate and sent a hot rush of desire through her body. "No."

"Thank God," he murmured. He swooped down upon her then, his first kiss anything but tentative. It was clear to them both just how much he needed her and there would be no pretense about it.

Coady felt the urgency in his kiss, the hardness of his lips as he slanted them across hers, the driving urgency with which he sought to open her mouth. And she got caught up in the frenzy. "I want you inside me."

He raised his head, staring at her for a moment, disbelieving she really understood what she was saying. He had barely begun to pet her and, yet, as his hand briefly caressed her belly and cautiously probed further, he found, in fact, she was hot and moist, ready to receive him. "I must let you explore more often," he said breathlessly as he gently spread her thighs. He positioned himself over her, locking his elbows as he stared down at her. "Guide me."

Coady raised a questioning frown.

Stone lowered his head, moving his lips close to her ear as if whispering would take away her doubts. "Take me in your hand, love."

She did. And moved her head until her cheek was pressed against his.

"Do it."

Coady felt his hips move forward and guided him until she felt the tip of him pressed against her core. She pushed her head back into the pillow and closed her eyes, savoring the wondrous feeling of being slowly filled with him. It was on the tip of her tongue to call out a loving word for him, but this was lust between them, pure and simple. She shook all thoughts away and concentrated on the feel of Stone moving against her, the strength of his body slamming against hers, the heat that was building inside her with each thrust from his powerful body. And then he buried himself deep inside her. Her eyes opened and he remained there, rotating his hips in a circular motion, holding himself above her, watching her.

"Now," he breathed.

Coady felt a flutter that signaled the shattering experience was upon her and, with her arms at her sides, gripped handfuls of bed sheet as her body strained for the glory he had first shown her only hours ago.

"Now!" Stone scooped his arms around her as her belly slammed against his. He pulled back only slightly before pressing forward, exploding as he rocked with her, as their bodies lurched frantically in spasms which left them drenched in sweat.

Her entire body was weak from exertion but Coady managed to wrap her arms around Stone's neck. She needed to hold onto him, she needed to be close as she had never needed to be close to another human being. She wished, somehow, she could get inside his skin and touch her heart to his so he could know what he had done, so he could feel how she was reaching out to him as she could not seem to manage with words. It was a moment that could have brought tears to her eyes, if she could only allow herself to cry over something beautiful. But beauty of this nature was too new for words.

His chest was heaving, just as hers continued to do; he gasped for breath, as did she; their flesh was slick and warm. Coady took a deep breath, pressing her cheek against his, savoring this moment as if she might have to hold it forever in her memory, as if she might never know the wonder of such a thing again.

But she would! He was her husband and they were married for all time.

"I want it to last," she murmured.

Stone's heart, which had been racing like a panicked horse on the run, suddenly stilled. He raised his head and looked down at her. "Want what to last?"

Coady looked into his eyes, searching for the answer she needed. "This thing between us. This marriage."

He rolled to his side, considering his answer as he

stared at the ceiling in the predawn light and tucked her beneath his arm. "I take my vows very seriously," he said quietly. "I, too, want it to last."

Coady nodded her head.

He smiled as he wound a narrow, silken skein of her hair around his fingers. "Friends don't do what we've just done, lass."

She was not certain what that meant; men made love to perfect strangers, if they had the price of a whore. "It is special, isn't it, Stone? You agree?"

"It is special," he said low.

Coady turned her head and pressed her cheek against his chest. His heart beat with a solid, steady thud, putting her in mind of the man she thought him to be; the man she hoped him to be. She raised her left hand and stared at the plain gold band he had bought for her. They had chosen them together, purchased from a back-alley peddler who did not have the wherewithal to set up a shop of his own. But knowing Stone wore a ring identical to her own was somehow comforting. In a time when few men wore such, the wedding band, to Coady, was a show of commitment.

Her thoughts would have to reside with her throughout her day, however. She had work to do and it was enough, for now, to know they had some things in common. "I should get up," she murmured.

Stone's arms tightened around her. "Stay."

She turned her head, resting her left cheek against his chest, and smiled. "I can't laze around all day."

He raised up, bending his arm and resting the back of his head in the palm of his hand. "I have something for you."

Coady's eyes took on a new light. "You do?"

He grinned and nodded his head, wondering how she could be the passionate woman of his dreams one moment and so childlike the next.

She waited until her patience deserted her; a span of

time that could be measured by a single heartbeat. "What?"

He laughed. "There is a small package in my coat pocket."

She flew from the bed as if he had fired her from a slingshot and left him grinning while she raced, naked, across the room to the chair where he had left his coat.

Stone was well pleased with the way this moment was working to his advantage. While Coady searched the pockets of his coat, he inspected her lovely body at his leisure. She was not a tall woman, the top of her head barely met his shoulder, but her shapely legs and long, narrow waist made her seem tall as he looked at her. She had a flat belly and the rounded hips of a woman who would bear children with ease; he hoped that would be the case because he knew that, having watched her struggle through the typhoid, witnessing her pain was not something he suffered lightly. Her breasts were firm and full and more beautiful than he had imagined. He envisioned their children being held by her, suckling nourishment lovingly given. Stone did not know exactly when this strong desire for offspring had suddenly presented itself, but he supposed it had something to do with Coady. He liked children, certainly, but he had never craved to make any of his own with any urgency until now. Perhaps it had something to do with anticipating the pleasure of seeing a small, auburn-haired tyke in Coady's image.

She found the small box and came bounding back to the bed, kneeling beside him. As she settled back on her heels, she did not seem to have a care at all for her nakedness; he liked that about her. He liked her freedom in so many ways.

"May I open it?"

"Of course," he said, grinning over her excitement. "It is for you."

Coady did not break open the box right away but, rather, seemed to relish the moment. Her slender fingers smoothed the top of the narrow, shallow box before she raised it to her nose and sniffed.

He laughed. ''Open it, little goose.''

She gave the box a gentle shake. ''Will it break?''

''It might, if you're not gentle.''

She examined the front and back of the wooden box, looking for the opening. And then Stone reached out a hand and nudged one end of the top. She caught the idea then and began to slide the top along the length, seeing a red velvet lining appear before she saw the pearls. ''Oh,'' she breathed. ''Oh.''

He thrilled at the absolute wonder in her tone but it saddened him, too. She behaved as if she had never been given a gift before. ''If you don't care for pearls . . .''

''No,'' she said quickly, dropping the box onto the mattress as she reverently pulled the string of pearls from the velvet lining. ''They are wonderful, Stone. Beautiful.''

''Here.'' He reached for the pearls.

Coady gave the necklace over and quickly captured her hair, pulling the entire mass away from the back of her neck as she bent forward toward him. His fingers were warm and sure against her flesh and she wondered briefly if she were now, and forever more, destined to be aroused by the most simple touch from him.

''There,'' he announced.

She straightened, her fingers going to the cool, smooth pearls which rested near the valley between her breasts. She looked down, admiring the pure coloring that was closer to pink than white. ''I've never owned anything as beautiful,'' she murmured. She looked at him then, smiling softly before she tipped forward and kissed his cheek. ''Thank you.''

He reached out and captured her hand where it rested between her breasts. ''For your reaction alone, my sweet, you are entirely welcome.''

Her brow creased suddenly as she looked at him. ''But, Stone, you shouldn't spend good money on me.''

"And for whom, love, would you have me spend my money?"

Coady was very obviously taken aback by the question. "Well, I meant . . ."

"Should a man not purchase gifts for his wife?"

"Well, I suppose, but if we save our—"

Stone squeezed her hand. "Listen to me well, Coady. Purchasing baubles for you that catch my eye makes me happy. But if I were to buy a thousand such trinkets it would not see us destitute and starving. I understand your greatest fear, my sweet, but please be assured that your personal history will not repeat itself."

"Going without is difficult to forget," she said quietly. "It's like being haunted by a not-too-friendly ghost."

He smiled and stroked her cheek, gently, lovingly. "Let me chase that terrible ghost away, my darling. Trust me. You will never be without shelter and food again. I will wrap you in the warmest furs and see that your table has the best of food."

She smiled. "I will probably get fat."

He laughed and nuzzled her ear. "*Fat* with child, I hope."

She turned within the shelter of his arms and pressed her lips against his neck. "I think I would like that."

Stone turned Coady onto her back and hovered over her, his lips very close to hers. "Then let's be about it, lass," he whispered.

Coady had hidden beneath the bedclothes when two burly men had delivered the bath and several buckets of steaming water. And moments later, she felt her entire body blush when Stone dropped to his knees beside the large copper tub and reached for a cloth and soap. "I am capable of bathing," she pointed out, although there was no real conviction in her tone. She was pleasantly weary from having spent the morning in bed with him and thought, if left to her own devices, she just might drown.

"I'm quite certain of that."

She watched him wet the cloth and lather the soap and a mischievous glint suddenly sprang to her eyes. "Do you really mean to wash me?"

He grinned and stood, cloth in hand. "Madam, I mean to join you."

She squealed and laughed and scooted forward, bending her knees almost to her chin as Stone sat in the water behind her.

"Come here," he ordered lightly, pulling her back against his chest.

"I cannot believe I'm doing this!"

"I can leave, if you would rather."

She quieted to a demeanor approximating seriousness. "I did not say that," she countered softly.

"Good."

Her head rested against his shoulder, almost beneath his chin. Coady closed her eyes, enjoying the feel of the warm, soapy water sluicing down her body as Stone worked the cloth.

It was then, through the quiet of nothing more than the gently lapping of water, that she heard it. "Listen," she whispered. "Do you hear?"

Stone's hands fell still and he listened, waiting. After a moment, he shook his head. "I don't hear—"

"There," she whispered again. After a moment she called, "Pipit! Pipit!" in a sweet voice. And then she laughed.

Stone had not counted on receiving so much pure pleasure, simply from hearing her laugh.

"I've only seen them in the meadows," she explained. "He must have come here just to sing to us today."

"A bird?"

"Of course, a bird," she returned. "They bob their little white-edged tails very rapidly." She demonstrated and splashed water over the edge of the tub.

This time, he laughed as he soaped the cloth again. "You are happy."

She sighed and dropped her arms across her middle. "I am. I feel very young and alive this morning."

"It's obvious, to me at least, that marriage agrees with you."

"Well, the marriage is young," she teased. "I suspect you might yet set out to try me."

Stone began running the cloth slowly down her body. "Really?"

"You are a wily man, you know?"

"How so?"

"It isn't everyone who could convince me to leave my business in the hands of another for a day."

"Isobel is completely capable."

"But I do have responsibilities."

"And I have something better to offer."

She laughed throatily. "You are vain."

"You wish to counter my assumption?" he teased.

Coady shook her head as he cupped her breasts in the palms of his soapy hands. "No."

"You like what we do and you are not afraid to show me."

"Is that good?"

"That is very good, my sweet," he murmured close to her ear. Seeing her excited and wanting him, almost drove him mad. Just thinking about her being hot and passionate could stir him to desperate need. Like this very minute. But he would not make love to her again, not for a few hours at least. They needed rest and he was starving. He had ordered a small feast to be delivered to their room within the hour. Reminding himself of that helped cool his lust.

The warm water and Stone's slow, methodical attentions added to her weariness. Her sleepy mind acknowledged the gentle nudge of his erection against the small of her back. But Coady knew Stone was too tired to do anything about it; they would eat and sleep for a time, he had said. And when they awakened refreshed, they would dress for an evening on the town. This was their honeymoon; another gift to her.

Coady was basking in his favors, memorizing his softly spoken words, every tender kiss, every nerve-jangling caress. She wanted the events of the day to last a lifetime in her memory.

"Tell me about your life," she said quietly. "Tell me about your family and where you grew up.

"My parents came from Scotland and settled in Toronto when I was a very young lad. I'm the eldest of four."

Her head pressed back against his shoulder. "Let me guess. All boys."

"Wrong. I have one brother and two sisters."

She learned Toronto was in Canada, somewhere north of Boston. "It must be nice having siblings."

"It was horrid."

She laughed. "But you loved them," she returned knowingly. Coady was fairly sure of certain things about him and being a caring man was one of them. She counted herself fortunate in that regard to have married him.

"Aye. I love them."

"What else?"

"My father was a banker and I became a banker, too."

"Really?" Startling news.

"For three years," he said lightly. "I hated it."

"Working with all that lovely money?" she teased.

"Serving wealthy individuals who did not have the manners or the conscience God gave snails."

She tipped her head, turning until she could see his eyes.

Stone responded easily to her questioning frown. "Poor, hardworking folk have no need of banks. The wealthy whine about nothing as if their lives were fraught with constant trials."

"I have not noticed that."

"The nouveau riche understand real problems, because

195

they remember what it is like to be poor. Many old money folk would not know a true-life calamity if it ran up and smacked them in the head.'' Of course he was not placing himself in this category; he had dealt with his share of problems over the years.

She wondered where she might fit in his thoughts on these matters? She had her own deposits at the Canadian Bank of Commerce on Front Street. ''So, you did not like banking. What did you do?''

''I . . . traveled some,'' he said. ''And worked at various tasks.''

Coady stared at the gaudy picture of a deformed bird on the wall opposite, wondering if the artist had been mentally warped or simply unskilled. ''And then you joined the mounted police.''

''A stroke of Fate for which I will ever be grateful because my work brought me to you.''

She drew in a long, slow breath. ''Stone,'' she murmured somewhat in awe. ''What a lovely thing to say.''

He pressed a kiss against the delicate shell of her ear. ''I have other lovely things to say to you, miss,'' he murmured.

Chapter Fifteen

Habitual routines were quickly forgotten.

Coady realized very quickly the following morning that she would have to allow additional time for her routine of preparing for her workday.

Stone interfered at every turn, kissing and petting her, teasing and actually sabotaging the laces of her corset instead of tying the things.

"You said a husband *helps* his wife."

Her accusatory tone did nothing to cool his attentions. "I *am* helping."

She laughed. "You are not!"

They were standing in the middle of the bedroom and he pulled her up against his naked body. "I don't want you to go."

The devil of it was, she did not want to go either. "You said you would walk me."

"I will."

"I have to go *today*, Stone."

"Hmm." He pulled his lips away from her ear and

frowned down at her. "As opposed to next week?"

"Correct."

"All right." He gave her a playful pat on the rump and tore himself away. "You'd best dress yourself then or we'll never make it." The fact was, he must soon return to duty, as well. He had been given only a few days leave.

Coady followed him with her gaze, the sparkle of contentment doing nothing to dim her vision. His nakedness was familiar to her now but nonetheless pleasing. In fact, Coady felt she could spend days and hours just looking at him, if she could afford the time. And being with Stone made her understand what people meant when they said they were feeling lighthearted. It was a giddy, youthful thing, being with him, and yet there was seriousness in what they did together, too. It was all very complex, really.

Coady busied herself untying the knot Stone had so neatly created in her corset laces. "I thought I saw Vernon Shield the other day," she said conversationally. "But, I suppose not."

Standing beside the bed, Stone stepped into his trousers. "It could have been Vernon."

Coady's hands stilled as she looked across the room at him. "You mean Vernon has been in Dawson?"

Stone nodded his head and reached for a clean shirt from the clothes press.

"And he didn't see Isobel?"

"Oh, I think he saw Isobel," he said, turning to face her. "She was his primary reason for coming."

"She didn't mention—"

"Vernon doesn't want Isobel to see him."

"That's foolish."

"Is it?" Stone pushed his arms into the shirt. "He may have driven her away but Vernon doesn't want to let Isobel go. By skulking around he can still see her, at least."

She frowned.

He smiled. "Think about it."

Her corset secure, Coady smoothed her stockings up her shapely legs before shrugging into her blouse and reaching for her serviceable brown skirt. "You are suggesting he loves her?" she murmured, buttoning her skirt as her gaze roamed the room, searching out her spats and shoes. "Why would he refuse to marry her, if he loves her? It makes little sense."

From the chair near the bed where he was pulling on his boots, Stone admired the full roundness of her rump as Coady peeked beneath the bed. "It makes sense if he loves her too much."

"Too much?" she muttered toward the floor. Having failed in her search, Coady got to her feet, muttering, "Not there." She padded toward the clothes press. "Is there such a thing as too much love?"

Ready for the street, Stone lounged back in his chair. "Only if a man feels he should be giving his woman more."

"Hah!" she called triumphantly. The spats had been on the floor of the wardrobe, just where they should have been. Her brow furrowed as she wandered to the side of the bed and sat down, facing him. "You mean Vernon sent Isobel away because he couldn't give her the things he felt he should give her?"

"That is precisely what I mean." Stone retrieved her buttonhook from the table near the chair and joined her on the bed.

Coady turned on the bed and placed her legs across his knees, ceding to his offer of help with her spats, at least. "How do you know this?"

Stone directed his attention to hooking small buttons and pulling them through the leather buttonholes. "He told me some of this when we were at their claim and I've talked to him since. When he came to Dawson just to get a glimpse of Isobel, that's when I understood just how much he loved her."

"And you didn't tell me?" she asked accusingly.

Jill Metcalf

"I am telling you now that I understand completely."

"This is terrible. I think Isobel would rather be with Vernon than have *possessions*, if that is what he has in mind."

Stone sent her a curious look, considering the source of the statement. "Is that what you think?"

Coady met his gaze with a surprised one of her own. "Of course. If a woman had to choose between possessing *things* and possessing the man she loved, she would choose the man."

"My God," he said softly. "You continually surprise me."

Coady did not know what he meant by that; she was still thinking about Isobel and Vernon. "What are we going to do?"

Stone finished the last button and lowered her feet to the floor. "About what?"

"Isobel and Vernon."

"*We* are going to do nothing," he said, getting to his feet and fetching his coat. "I am hoping nature will look after the *doing*." He grinned in the face of her frown. "The last time I saw Vernon, I suggested he return to see Isobel again in a few months. It appears he may be visiting more frequently than I thought. And, if he is the man I think he is, the prospect of fatherhood could very well dissolve his stubbornness and alter his thinking on the matter of keeping Isobel with him."

She smiled as she breezed past him toward the other room. "You *are* a wily man."

But could Isobel forgive Vernon's rejection? Would she take him back for the sake of her child? These were questions that nagged at Coady's mind as Stone walked her to her place of business that morning.

Isobel was behind the desk, penning a letter, by the time Coady arrived.

"I'm no longer in the business of writing letters for the men," Coady said as she swept inside.

Isobel raised her head and frowned. "This is a letter of my own."

Coady grinned foolishly. "Oh."

"No bashful groom at your side?" the older woman teased.

Coady blushed to the roots of her hair. "The bashful groom is not at all *bashful*, as I'm sure you have guessed. He plotted with you in advance so he could keep me prisoner for an entire day."

Isobel looked properly horrified. "It must have been dreadful."

"Awful," said Coady, pulling off her gloves. "Terrible."

Isobel started to laugh, rocking back on her chair. "I am sure!"

Coady had been right in not allowing Stone to enter the tent with her. She had suspected it would be difficult enough, facing Isobel on her own. Considering they had not gone out of their hotel for supper after all, or for a single moment the previous day, in fact, it stood to reason that she and Stone must be Dawson's latest scandal. And, based on the way Isobel was eyeing her, Coady was quite certain now.

Since Isobel was a frequent visitor, Coady had added a second chair to her shop, placing it in front of the table she so often used as a desk. She sat down and stared at the woman who had fast become her friend. "I don't care what people think."

If Isobel had been surprised by the offhand comment, she did not show it. "You should not."

Crossing her legs, Coady smoothed her skirts over her knee. "I think I will be very happy that I became his wife."

Isobel frowned. "You married him. Why would you think you wouldn't be happy?"

"Before we married I questioned my own intent. I mean, I questioned whether I was marrying Stone so that I could stay here or because I really cared about him."

"And . . . ?"

Coady grinned, slanting a smile at Isobel. "I love the Yukon, but I think I care about Stone more."

Isobel sank back in her chair, smiling softly. "He must have been pleased to hear that."

Coady's smile slipped a notch. "I haven't actually told him how I feel."

"Well, don't you think it's about time?"

It probably was, but it seemed easier somehow to say the words to another woman. "Did you tell Vernon how you feel?" she countered.

Isobel's smile dissolved and her gaze dropped toward the floor.

"Did you?"

She shook her head.

"It isn't easy, is it?"

"Even thinking about it is like baring your heart. A man could take that heart and touch it gently or he could squeeze the life from it."

"I don't believe Vernon really wanted to squeeze the life from you, Isobel."

"Well, he did."

"Perhaps he acted rashly. Perhaps there is a sincere, loving reason why he did what he did.

Isobel was too much of a lady to respond to that remark in the manner in which it deserved.

"Perhaps we both need to screw up our courage," Coady added, "and tell our men exactly how we feel. They won't know otherwise."

Isobel raised angry eyes. "You are forgetting—I no longer have a man."

"But if he knew how much you loved him . . ."

"Please, let's change the subject."

"Isobel . . ."

"Coady, stop."

Knowing she had pushed too far, Coady ceded to her friend's wishes. "I'm sorry," she murmured. But, as she looked around the room, she had not given up hope. She would raise this matter with Isobel again. "Where has everything gone?"

Isobel sat up straight and proud in her chair. "I did quite a business while you were . . . *resting*. A delightful couple came to the shop, Coady. They rented every single tent and stove."

Coady's eyes rounded in disbelief. "All?"

Isobel's head bobbed enthusiastically. "All. The gentleman, Jay Snowden is his name, has found a very rich mine up near the Twelvemile Creek and they're setting up camp there. They came into Dawson for supplies and to hire men to help work the mine. They had the most delightful disagreement right here. Jay doesn't want Mary—Mary is his wife—to live in the camp but Mary kept insisting they could not afford to have her living here in a hotel until such time as the mine starts to pay. It was such a loving little tiff they were having. They even asked my advice," she added importantly. "Well, Jay came up with the idea of taking on partners who could help them get started financially for a share of the gold brought out of the mine. But Mary wants her husband to keep the all the profits for himself because he works too hard just to hand good money over to others."

Coady's eyes narrowed. "You didn't give them money, Isobel?"

Her friend laughed shortly. "Good heavens, no! Such a thing never entered my mind. I need the gold Vernon gave me just to exist."

"I'm distrustful sometimes, I suppose."

"Well, so am I," Isobel confessed. "We have to be cautious with all the unpleasant characters drawn to the area right now. But the Snowdens are quite honest and sincere, I think. Just a delightful couple starting life together and being cautious in how they go about it."

Coady smiled; Isobel seemed to be spreading her wings a little. "And you have made new friends."

Quite honestly, Isobel had even briefly considered inviting Mary Snowden to stay with her while Jay was at the Twelvemile Creek mine. But she could not take such gross advantage of Coady's hospitality. Her young friend was being generous as it was. "Well, I believe I might see a good deal more of Jay and Mary. They have invited me to join them for supper this evening."

Coady thought that was wonderful and she told Isobel as much.

There were inconveniences to being a policeman. There was the almost constant danger, the long and wretched hours and, the greatest sin in Coady's eyes, of course, the miserable pay. Still, Stone was not prepared to give it up. The work provided him with satisfaction. It made him feel he was making a contribution to the good of society. It made him feel as if he was perhaps giving a little something back in return for the good life that he had been fortunate enough to live. And there was Coady now. With her at his side, Stone thought no man's existence could possibly get much better.

He did worry for her, however, should anything happen to him. Coady was independent and capable of caring for herself, it was true. But he did not want her baking bread for the rest of her life, to simply eke out an existence. And, supposing they were to have a child sooner rather than later?

Stone's first priority was to ensure Coady and any children that may come along would be secure. To that end he had his last will and testament drawn up and spoke to his banker. The third step was a request for a meeting with his superior officer.

Raymond Simmons met Stone the following morning. "You said there was some urgency."

"Yes, sir," Stone replied. Now that they were face to face, Stone was not certain how to clearly state his case. "It's about my wife, sir."

"I can't do much about that, son," said Simmons. "You were rather quick in marrying, after all."

Stone frowned. "No, sir. You don't understand. I'm not regretting marrying her."

"Well, what seems to be the problem?"

Stone pushed his hands deep into his pockets. "I have been assigned duty that will keep me away from Dawson over the winter, sir."

"Yes."

"I wonder if I might be reassigned, Superintendent? Something that will not keep me away from town too long?"

Simmons was nodding his head, grinning knowingly. "Can't leave her alone, huh?"

Stone chose to interpret the question in a less lascivious manner then he was certain it was intended. "My wife is young, sir."

Simmons snorted. "That was not what I meant, man, and you know it." He decided it prudent to dismiss the discussion, at any rate. "As a matter of fact, MacGregor, I had planned to change your assignment. This one may take you out of town a time or two but I don't doubt you will resolve the matter quickly."

"Sir?"

"Ben Keystone thinks he has caught the scent of a confidence scheme, MacGregor. If his suspicions are correct, I'm going to need several men I can dedicate to the case. But you are the most effective man I've got in situations like these."

"Yes, sir."

Simmons detected a note of remaining reluctance in Stone's voice. "I understand, son, it is difficult leaving a new bride. I have a wife of my own, you will recall. The first month we were married, I resented every time I had to don my uniform and walk out the door. Mrs. Simmons wasn't at all thrilled with me being a Mountie, as it was. Said it was too dangerous. Well, I've survived so far and so has our marriage. Yours will, too."

"As soon as we know what we're dealing with, and get the problem resolved, I will do my best to see that as many assignments as possible do not take you away.''

''I appreciate that, sir.'' In the meantime it appeared he would have to leave his bride for a short time. The very thought was pure torture.

Ah, but thoughts of his return were an entirely different matter.

Chapter Sixteen

He was waiting for her when she arrived home that night.

Coady breezed into the room, hoping to see him there. It had seemed such a long day. A normal day for her meant total absorption in her work. But today she had been more *absorbed* with thoughts of Stone. On a normal day, she would fall into bed exhausted from her labors. This day, however, she felt as if she could dance the night away. On the other hand, making love a dozen times or so was more appealing.

It was hard to believe her life had taken such a turn. She had completely forgotten that only days ago, she had quivered in trepidation over marrying a man she knew little about. Her present existence offered more intrigue than at any other time in her life. Her senses were heightened. Everything seemed fresh and young and new. She had drifted through her day with the stirrings of excitement and anticipation racing in her veins. She felt so alive!

In spite of her euphoria, Coady did not want Stone to become the absolute center of her universe. She had seen

women shattered by allowing that to happen. Women
who forgot, or did not know they could function and
survive on their own; women who allowed themselves to
turn their backs on independence. Women who became
puppets to men who proved, in the long run, to be scoun-
drels. Not that she thought Stone a scoundrel. On the
contrary, she knew him as a decent man almost from the
beginning. But other things could happen . . . the marriage may not work over the long term. Her husband was
engaged in very dangerous business, and horror of horrors, she could find herself alone as quickly as she found
herself wed if something should happen to him. She
would never allow herself to be destroyed by placing her
heart, body, soul and *fortune* in the hands of someone
who could wrench the very life from her. She had been
penniless before, but never again.

Still, she wanted time with Stone. She wanted their
marriage to work. She wanted a life with him. Coady had
simply been practicing the rules of self-preservation for
so long, she could not let go. The past was fraught with
difficult lessons hard learned. The results were evident in
Coady's very nature. She had long ago adopted a creed
of fearing the future, planning for every eventuality, and
fiercely protecting every good thing that came her way.
That is why, should the need arise, as long as she remained self-reliant and had her businesses, Coady knew
she could deal with any eventuality.

He was sitting in one of the overstuffed chairs before the
hearth and had started a small fire to ward off the evening
chill. When Coady rushed into the suite, smiling, Stone
merely held out his hand to her.

"Hello," she said quietly as she approached.

"Hello, lass," he returned warmly, pulling her onto
his lap.

Coady hooked her arm around his neck. "What did
you do today?"

"Missed you," he said without hesitation.

She laughed softly. "Do you think that might become an occupation?"

He grinned lasciviously. "With you it might."

"I think I would like that."

"Ho!" he laughed. "And leave you to support this family?"

"I could do it," she returned, somewhat wounded.

"I know you could, my love," he said warmly before brushing his lips across hers. "I do not doubt it for a moment. But my intent is to make your life easier, not designate you the MacGregor drudge."

"I have worked most of my life."

He knew that about her. In the wee small hours of the morning, Coady had told him more about her life before coming to the Yukon, for there was more than her mother's death and her own determination not to die cold, hungry and wretched in some hovel. As she lay within the shelter of his arms and revealed her past, Stone could clearly envision most of what she had survived. And it said much for the strength of the woman he had married that she had never once folded and given up. She had faced every hardship life could throw her way and become all the more determined for it. She was unlike any woman he had ever known. Coady MacGregor was her *own* woman and she had all of his admiration and then some.

Lying there in the darkness with her that night, listening to the deepening of each breath as she drifted to sleep, Stone had wondered if ever Coady could learn to lean on him just a little. He pondered the dilemma of gaining enough of her trust that she could allow him to pamper her. He wondered if she would ever have enough faith in his love to entrust her life to him. He had no desire to bend her to his will, to make of her a pawn, a plaything to which he could turn and point out as some prize possession. He merely wanted her to have a good life. He wanted to see her smile, to hear her laughter often. He wanted her free to raise their children, if she was of a similar mind. He wanted her content and growing old with him.

Considering the beginning of her life, Coady deserved nothing less.

Coady looked down at their joined hands, watching his thumb scrape gently back and forth across the backs of her knuckles. "Did you hear me, Stone?" she questioned quietly.

He raised his head, smiled, and planted a quick, sweet kiss on her chin. "I heard."

"It does not say much for me as a woman to have lost your interest on only the third day of our marriage."

"My interest has not waned, lass. On the contrary, I was thinking of you."

She leaned her shoulder more firmly against her chest. "Dare I ask?"

He shook his head. It was too soon to broach the subject of her trust. She would need time to learn that, with him, she could be safe and secure and continue to retain that cloak of independence that she so seemed to need. "I met with Simmons today," he said.

Coady straightened away from him, frowning. "You have a new assignment."

He nodded his head.

"They are sending you away?"

"I will not be gone long, nor will I be far away."

Her slender fingers dug into the fabric of his shirt. "Not so soon. Does the man have no heart?"

"Lawbreakers have no heart, love. They go on with their deeds regardless of the rest of the world."

"We have had so little time together."

He gripped her fingers a little more firmly. "Once this is resolved, Simmons has promised to give me assignments that will keep me close to home." He grinned at her. "And you."

"I wish you would consider leaving that wretched position, Stone."

"Have I asked you to give up your businesses?"

That made her feel somewhat small of mind and attitude. "No. But my businesses do not put me in danger."

"Does it worry you?" he asked slyly, "that I am often in danger?"

He was not sly enough, however. Coady saw through his ruse. "Of course it does," she returned, getting to her feet. "I hate to see so much as a coyote wounded. And I cannot stand by the wharf when they are drowning rats."

He laughed and pulled her back down onto his lap. "You win, madam. I do not possess the wit to spar with you."

"You may spar, sir, but you cannot win."

"Ho!" he laughed again, tipping her back over his arm. "There is perhaps one way in which I might win." He lowered his head, slanting his lips across hers, teasing her with kisses that promised so much more.

Coady had a number of other thoughts she wished to broach in that moment, but she became distracted by his kisses. "You make my mind go blank," she murmured as he began caressing her through her clothes.

He laughed. "That's the general idea, my sweet," he said. "As much as I appreciate your fine mind, I appreciate your body more at this particular moment."

"Only at this moment?" she teased.

Stone looked directly into her eyes as his nimble fingers began to release the small buttons on her blouse. "I missed you *and* your body today."

Coady raised her hand and stroked the fine blond hair at his temple. "Did you?"

"Mmm."

"It's been the same for me."

He grinned. "That's what I like to hear."

"When must you leave?"

The question almost, but not quite, put a damper on the moment. "Tomorrow morning, love."

"We have only tonight?" Her brow furrowed. "Do

you think it's unnatural that I want the lovemaking so much?''

"No."

"It seems a lady shouldn't."

"What makes you think that?" He separated the material of her blouse, bent his head, and placed a lingering kiss just above the lace of her corset.

Coady's head went back and her eyelids drifted closed. "I do not know," she murmured. "Perhaps it is the newness of it all."

Stone raised his head and looked at her, stared at the delicate shields of pink covering the rich brown of her eyes. Her skin was the most pure he had ever seen, her features finely formed, her cheekbones delicately defined, her nose straight, her lips pink and bowed and her chin beautifully rounded. "I think if you search inside yourself, lass," he murmured as he continued to stare, "you might find the answer you are seeking."

Coady was too involved in other pursuits at the moment to search for anything other than the pleasure she knew he could bring her. Wrapping her other arm loosely around Stone's neck, she bowed her head, inviting him to kiss her again.

"Well, come ahead," he whispered.

She stared into the teasing depths of his eyes and met his challenge. Lowering her head, Coady pressed her lips against his while tightening her hold around his neck. Her heart began to beat with a familiar tattoo as she breathed in the clean, male scent of him.

Brief moments of her tentative attentions fuelled Stone's greed for more. His hands went to the back of her skirt where he freed the buttons there, and as Coady's tongue entered his mouth, he pushed the blouse from her shoulders. In a matter of minutes, her clothes were draped only loosely on her body. "Stand for a moment," he breathed.

Coady did as he asked, watching him as he followed her up and caught his intentions. "Here?"

"Here," he said huskily as they began to attack each other's clothes.

First to be naked with his help, standing in a pool of discarded feminine clothing, Coady freed the buttons on his trousers and pushed the material over his hips and down his legs as Stone attended the matter of his shirt himself.

She was kneeling in front of him when she ordered him to sit.

He sat and watched with fascination as she slowly removed his boots and socks. "I love all this attention," he quipped.

Coady flung the last sock over her shoulder, not caring where the thing landed as she stared at him, gracing him with a daring, passionate smile. "Do you, now?"

"Mmm."

Her attention dropped to his lap, to where his swollen, pulsing flesh rested against his flat belly. Moving between his knees, she reached out and wrapped her slim fingers around him.

Stone drew in a deep breath, watching, as Coady's attention seemed fixed with fascination on that part of him over which she, for the moment, had complete control.

Her left hand rested on his thigh, warming his flesh as the tips of the fingers of her right hand began to stroke his length.

"What shall I do?" she whispered as her fingertips roamed down to the base of his erection.

"Whatever you wish, sweet."

Her gaze met his briefly before her attention again focused on the task at hand. "Is it permissible to kiss you?"

"Oh, Lord, yes," he hissed. He held his breath as her head moved forward and closed his eyes in an attempt to focus all of his senses on the welcome warmth of her lips on him. "Oh, my love," he breathed. He reached forward, placing his hands on her shoulders and bringing her up. "Come." Guiding her until Coady straddled his thighs, resting her knees on the seat of the wide, over-stuffed chair, Stone placed his hands momentarily on her buttocks, encouraging her to move forward. He touched the tip of his hot, rigid flesh near the warm moist core of her, caressing her in this fashion as he stared up into her eyes. Her flesh was flushed with passion, her breathing quick and shallow. "Take me slowly," he whispered, positioning himself.

Coady moved down, impaling herself by small degrees, taking a deep breath and holding the air captured in her lungs as if the act of breathing somehow took away from every other sensation she was experiencing. When she felt filled by him, she moved her knees farther along the seat of the chair.

"Comfortable?" he asked in a low voice.

She nodded her head, staring down at him with seductive eyes barely open. She watched his hands go to her breasts and waited, most impatiently, for his lips to follow.

She did not have long to wait.

He laved the taut nipple of first one breast and then the other, sending bolts of sensation through her body to her very core. The heat became intense and she moaned softly, closing her eyes as her hands moved to the back of his head, encouraging Stone to continue.

"You like this."

She could not answer.

"Just think," he said softly, moving his head back, allowing his hands to roam the firm, golden globes at will. "We might one day watch a tiny, auburn-haired little girl suckling here."

"Or a golden-haired baby boy," she returned throatily. She thought the way they were going, she was likely already nurturing his seed.

"You would like that, wouldn't you, Coady?"

"I would, but not right now," she whispered as she moved her hands from the back of his head to his face.

214

"I have other things on my mind, sir," she breathed.

He grinned, directing his gaze to her face as his hand roamed between their bodies. "Aye, lass," he drawled. "As do I."

Coady almost jumped from his lap when his fingertips began to caress her most sensitive place. Her hands dropped to his shoulders, gripping him for support.

"I am going to help you."

His breathless whisper drove her closer, drawing her forward until her forehead was pressed against the side of his neck, the tips of her breasts flirting wantonly with the thick pelt of hair on his chest.

She felt the fire building deep inside her, experienced the familiar spiraling of nerve endings as he stroked her. "Stone?"

He did not speak. A labored breath caught in his throat, his heart hammered in his chest, as he felt her pulsing around his aching flesh. Her body jerked on his and he attended her more fiercely. "Now, love," he breathed as a second spasm sent her moving hard against him.

She moaned and his arm went around her. She groaned, throwing her head back, and Stone hugged her fiercely against his chest. Coady's slender body rocked against him as he fought desperately to hold himself in check. When she grew still, and caressed his neck more softly, she began to move on him.

Stone placed his hands gently on her hips, encouraging her movements, thrusting his pelvis upward and away to complement her instinctive motions. Mere seconds passed before his hands tightened and he was holding her still, pressing deep within her. His head fell to the padded headrest, his eyes tightly closed, as he gave in to the fierce pulsing of his need and exploded deep inside her body.

Coady welcomed all he had to give. For some reason she felt this union more deeply than any that had gone before. When his body was spent, when the throes of passion stilled, she pulled him toward her until his cheek rested between her breasts. Gently, she stroked his temple with her fingers. "How can this be?" she murmured. "How did you come to be in my life? Somewhere, sometime, I must have done something to reap such a wondrous reward." Her lips pressed briefly against his temple. "I simply do not know what that something could be."

He *knew*. "I say again, Coady," he whispered, "look inside yourself for the answer."

It puzzled her when he said that. She had looked inside herself. She had found genuine affection for him there, she had found pleasure at having him for her husband and she had found a sense of security she had never known before. There was something to be said for being *two* as opposed to *one*. He was strong in body and in spirit; she had sensed that in him from the very moment she first met him. It would be easy to rely upon him, to rest her weary mind at the end of a particularly troublesome day, to let him be the buffer against her concerns, to allow him to sheath her in the shelter of his own brand of protection. She also knew it was this last feeling, security, which caused her the most hesitation; it could be a fleeting thing and not one she was brave enough to rely upon; not yet, possibly not ever. She could hardly tell Stone all of this, however, because her instincts warned her he might be looking for much more; something closer to a confession of love. *That* she could not give. But neither did she want to hurt him. "We may not have married for the right reasons," she said tentatively, "but we have been given this."

He had married for the *right reasons*; several of them.

Stone felt himself slipping from inside her and mourned the loss. Raising his head, he kissed her fiercely, as if he could somehow prevent the parting. When the kiss was done, they sighed, smiling at each other wearily.

"You are quite something, Mrs. MacGregor."

"You are not so bad yourself," she returned cheekily.

He caught her to him, moving his arms around her as

Coady settled against his chest. "We have certainly made a mess," he murmured as his gaze roamed the carpeted floor; their clothes were strewn halfway across the room.

"I don't care."

He smiled. Content. He wished he did not have to leave her. Even for a few hours.

"Isobel has made new friends," she murmured wearily.

"That is nice."

Already familiar with a few nuances, Coady detected distraction in his tone. Raising her head with effort, she looked at him. "What are you thinking about?"

He reached up and finger-combed her hair back from her temple. "I was thinking I do not want to leave you."

"Too late," she chirped as her gaze darted briefly between their bodies. "You have."

He laughed, enjoying her boldness, wishing the outside world and serious matters did not have a hand in the way they conducted their lives. Growing serious, he said reluctantly, "I meant, imp, I do not wish to leave you on the morrow."

Coady frowned. "I wish the same."

"We'll eat, then I must go out for a short time."

"This evening?"

Clearly, she was disappointed. He would savor that during the evening ahead. Striving for a light tone, he squeezed her hand and responded to her question. "Only for a short time. You would wish me to be completely appraised of the situation before I ride into it, would you not?"

Yes, but not by sacrificing their time together. Then again . . . "Exactly how dangerous is this assignment?"

He grinned. "Does that mean you fear for my hide?"

"Stone."

He feigned a weary sigh. "Very well . . . not dangerous."

"I do not believe you."

"It is true. I cannot talk about the case, love, but I see no real danger in this one."

She seemed reassured. "Thank you."

He smiled at the relief shining in her eyes and wondered if she realized how much she had just given away. "While you are asleep I will creep into the bed beside you. You will hardly know I've been gone."

"Will you waken me with kisses?"

"Dozens."

"I will be more rested than you," she warned.

"Is that a challenge?"

"Perhaps."

A few hours later as Coady climbed into bed, suffering her first disappointment over Stone's arms not being there to hold her, she realized she had forgotten to tell him of her latest good fortune. Then again she wondered if boasting over the rental of her entire inventory of stoves and tents could be painful for him to hear. The boast would be just another indication of her success and she worried that his man's ego would have difficulty dealing with that in a wife. On second thought, she supposed not, since he had known of her successes before their marriage. Still, Coady determined she would refrain from bragging about her own successes whenever Stone was within hearing distance.

She was not certain whether dawn was approaching or the room simply seemed brighter because Stone was in it. He woke her several hours later with tender kisses and warm caresses. "Did you meet anyone important?" she murmured sleepily as his lips trailed along the path of her throat.

"Important? I don't believe so, lass" he whispered. He had missed being shot in the neck. Barely. By a hairsbreadth. But it was the *miss* that was important.

"Are you at least confident about tomorrow?" she questioned as she turned and pressed her body along the length of his nakedness.

As confident as a man could be walking into a situation that was anything but clear. To her he said only, "Yes, love."

And so it began.

Chapter Seventeen

"Good morning."

Harrison looked up from his breakfast. "Well, the first ray of sunshine I've seen today." He stood and pulled a chair back from the table for her. "How are you, my pet?"

"Wonderful."

He laughed. "Does that relate to your talents or your disposition?"

She smiled mischievously. "Both."

"My, we are risqué this morning."

Coady felt her complexion darken.

Relenting, Harrison leaned forward and pressed his hand over hers on the tabletop. "You look happy, Coady. Marriage must agree with you."

She shrugged, trying her best to be casual when, in fact, she wanted to blurt a thousand secrets to this special friend. "As husbands go, I believe Stone may be more amenable than most."

"Amenable?"

"Agreeable."

He nodded his head. "I see. Meaning he is pleasing?"

Coady paused a brief moment. "I suppose."

"You suppose?" he barked another short laugh. "By that look in your eye, my girl, I'd guess he is a damned good stud!"

"Harrison!" she gasped. And then promptly ruined her outrage by blushing more fiercely than before.

He grinned, nodding his head as he picked up his fork. It was not fair to tease her in such a bawdy fashion. She was, after all, a new bride. "Will you have something?"

Coady nodded her head. "Coffee, please."

He motioned with his own cup to Megan Brown, who managed the cafe on his behalf. "Nothing to eat?" he questioned as an additional cup of coffee materialized and his own was refilled.

She shook her head. "No. Thank you."

"That's all, Megan, thanks." He waited until the woman had crossed the room and he had swallowed a bit of griddle cake before asking, "So, where is this paragon d'amour? He's not escorting you about town this morning?"

"He's gone."

Harrison was visibly startled. "Gone! Is the honeymoon over and he fled the town or did the poor fellow die with a smile on his face?"

"Neither," she returned primly. "Stone has received a new assignment. He should only be gone for a few days."

"What sort of assignment?"

"I cannot tell you that, Harrison," she said easily. "He cannot even tell me."

"I would not trust you either," he quipped before slipping another bite into his mouth.

Coady propped her elbows on the table and rested her chin in the palms of her hands. "I suggested that he give up this miserable position, but he would have none of it. It hardly seems worth the danger, working for a dollar a day. I do very well and Stone says he has some money. We could get by.''

MacGregor had possessed a tidy fortune on deposit in the bank only weeks ago when Harrison had investigated the man.

Coady sipped her coffee. ''I came to talk to you about Isobel, in any event.''

''Isobel?''

''She needs something to keep her occupied, Harrison. At least until the baby comes. All my inventory is rented out right now.''

''Everything?''

She was pleased at his amazement. ''Every last thing, thanks to Isobel. She is shrewd in her own way. She let out the last of the tents and stoves to one man and collected three months rent in advance. I won't have to go chasing up the Twelvemile Creek to collect more money until the New Year.''

''There must be something going on up there I haven't heard about.''

''Have you heard of Jay Snowden?''

Harrison shook his head.

''Well.'' She slid forward in her chair, intense, as if she were about to impart some earth-shattering news. ''Jay Snowden and his dear wife, Mary, have found a wealthy claim. A huge strike, apparently. They are starting a camp well along the Twelvemile and came to town for a few days—actually, I believe Mary is still here— to gather supplies and hire men.''

Harrison continued to look thoughtful. ''Something that big is usually the talk of the town, Coady. I haven't heard a word about the Snowdens or a mother lode being found.''

''Oh, dear. Maybe I've spoken out of turn. Perhaps they have managed to keep it quiet.''

He laughed shortly. ''My pet, that sort of news cannot be kept quiet. Impossible.''

She shrugged her slender shoulders. ''I suppose it does

not matter. The real point to my story is, I have nothing left for Isobel to do, really. I have closed down two lines of business and the rental business is out of inventory for a time. I thought you might agree to her helping us open the bakery since that cook you sent for seems to be taking his own good time in getting here.''

"Does Isobel have any talent for baking?''

"If she doesn't, I will teach her.''

"Go ahead then. You two do whatever you please with the place. The last of the workmen should be out of the building by the end of this week.''

"We will consult you, of course, before we spend any money.''

He smiled gently. "I trust you, pet. You know that.''

Coady could feel a sense of purpose taking over, exciting her. "Thank you, my friend. This is just what Isobel needs. The work will help keep her from fretting.''

"Fretting? Over her child?''

"Over Vernon.''

"Ah.'' He nodded his head. "The added activity, while you await the return of your beloved spouse, will not do you any harm, either.''

She agreed, smiling as she got to her feet while pulling on her gloves. "I must run.''

"Coady,'' he said, almost reluctantly. "Could you also teach Isobel how to launder shirts?''

She faced him, frowning. "Launder shirts?''

"Yes, well, she agreed to take on the task of looking after my shirts but the poor woman is not at all accomplished at the chore.''

"*I* always launder your shirts, Harrison.''

He detected a note of proprietary disappointment in her tone and got to his feet, standing before her. "You are married now, my darling,'' he said, taking her hand and squeezing gently. "Your husband might expect you to look after *his* affairs, not those of another man.''

"I can do both.''

"I might know little of being a husband, Coady, but I

223

do know lovers must be attentive to one another's needs. See to your husband, my pet. I must look after myself in my own way."

"I like to help my friends."

"And you shall continue to do so. But washing my small clothes is hardly the thing for a new bride."

"Pooh!" she said, although she smiled and tipped up to kiss his cheek before she went on her way.

Isobel was chattering to a petite woman with brassy blonde hair when Coady arrived at her place of business that morning. She did, however, receive a warm welcome from her friend.

"Ah! Coady," said Isobel. "Come meet Mary Snowden."

Coady faced Isobel's new friend and extended her hand.

Mary Snowden was five feet tall, if she was lucky, with blue eyes that appeared weary. She wore simple clothes, although not outdated. Coady guessed Mary to be perhaps twenty years of age but she noticed there was a hardness around the newcomer's mouth that bespoke of greater years and hinted at cruelty. Perhaps it was the way in which Mary held her lips, all tight and unrelenting.

Coady ignored her first impression. "Hello, Mary," she said. "I'm very pleased to meet you."

Mary took the offered hand and presented a shy smile. "A pleasure, I'm sure."

"Mary's husband has gone back up to Twelvemile Creek to set up their camp," Isobel explained. "Mary is feeling a bit at loose ends without him."

"Oh, well," said Coady. "We can fix that. There is always a lot to do around here. You can help Isobel and myself, if you like." Coady was not at all certain what had prompted her to invite Mary to join in but supposed she had done it for Isobel's sake. The woman needed friends to engage her in a variety of interests when the working day was done. When you were used to companionship, nights could be lonely. Coady had already discovered that.

Isobel was staring at Coady curiously. "What are we going to be doing that requires help?"

Coady's eyes grew bright with excitement. "A new venture. I have told you I will be partners with Harrison in a bakery. We have been planning it for weeks and the shop construction will be complete in a few days." She directed her next comments to Isobel. "I thought you might enjoy working in the bakery. Harrison has agreed. He will pay you a good wage and it will give you something to do until the baby comes along."

Isobel was undoubtedly dismayed. "Coady, I cannot bake. I made sourdough biscuits for Vernon once and he threw one of the things at a passing wolf. The poor animal dropped in his tracks."

Coady laughed. "It did not!"

"Well, you get my point."

"If I can learn to make bread and biscuits, Isobel Sh—Daniels, so can you." Coady cursed under her breath over the *faux pas*; Isobel had been using her maiden name since returning to Dawson, for heaven's sake! "I shall teach you," she added in a quick recovery.

"I'm afraid I will not be of much assistance either," said Mary. "My family always had the best of cooks, you see. There was no requirement for me to learn such menial things."

Oh, Lord, thought Coady. *A silk stocking of the first water!* "Well, you might keep us company then, if you prefer." There was little doubt on that score; the woman would *prefer*.

Mary nodded her head.

"You know I'll be happy to help in any way," Isobel said. "And I would like to learn. I would appreciate an opportunity to support myself and my child."

Ah, a realistic woman, thought Coady.

"Shall we go inspect the new premises?" Coady

asked, feeling her enthusiasm return. "We have to make a list of things we will need to get started." She picked up several sheets of paper and a pencil from her table. "Are we ready?"

Coady looked at Isobel, who was nodding her head eagerly. Mary Snowden, however, offered only a weak smile.

There was little the women could do that day since the workmen had yet to complete the shelving behind the serving counter which ran the width of the shop. Harrison had planned the place so that none of the baked goods would be readily available to eager customers who just might walk off with a portion of the inventory if Coady was not watching. And, suspecting the bakery would be popular, he expected the place to be crowded with men eager for the taste of good bread. Coady had already proven how much demand there was for her baked goods.

After a good look around the new premises, Isobel skipped off to a shop across the way as Coady checked her list of needed supplies.

"Isobel tells me you have recently married," Mary Snowden said from her safe place near the front door. She'd had a time keeping her skirts from being soiled with dust and wood shavings.

"Yes," Coady responded absently. "A few days ago."

"It's a pity you could not marry for love," Mary sighed. "It's really so wonderful."

Coady raised her head and faced the woman. "Pardon?"

"Jay and I were very much in love when we wed. We still are, of course," she said brightly.

Coady wondered where the woman's *enthusiasm* had come from all of a sudden.

"I'm sorry it was not that way for you," Marry added.

"What makes you think I did not marry for love?" Coady asked cautiously.

"I've been told, of course."

By whom? Isobel? That was the suggestion but Coady would not believe it.

"Isobel said you would have been given a blue ticket by the police if you hadn't married this man."

Coady tried to reason her way around what she felt was viciousness on this woman's part, telling herself that Isobel would not gossip about her in this way. But, somehow, she could not get past the hurt of being betrayed.

Mary was warming to the conversation, confident of each blow she was extending. Isobel was her chosen friend. Coady Blake just might get in the way of that. "I don't believe I've ever met a criminal before. Not a *woman* criminal, in any event." She giggled just a little, as if the idea of a woman being a criminal was completely delicious. "Did you do something *very* bad?"

Isobel breezed back into the shop, squeezing past Mary to get to Coady. "I bought some cotton to start making a few doilies for the countertop. Is there anything else we need to do here or shall we go over to the mercantile and order our supplies?"

Coady stared up into her friend's smiling face. She did not want to believe this kind-hearted woman would maliciously discuss private matters out of turn. She did not want to believe, but the hurt Coady was feeling seemed to overpower reasonable thought. "You take the list to the mercantile if you wish," she said dully. "I think I'll go back to the hotel."

Isobel frowned and placed her hand on Coady's arm. "Are you sick?"

She was feeling quite ill, actually. "I have a headache," was all Coady said. She wanted to be alone. She wanted to think. And, if she could not get past this sense she had been betrayed, she just might spend the afternoon feeling good and sorry for herself. Without another word, she turned away from Isobel Daniels and left the shop.

* * *

The autumn sun was bright, although it was losing its warmth, and the air brisk and clean. It was the kind of day Coady liked best, no steamy humidity which she considered oppressive, no freezing winds or deep snow. Autumn was an invigorating time of year and she would normally have a spring in her step, which indicated to anyone who cared to look, that she was a woman who treasured life, who met each day with energy and vigor and a sense of purpose. Not so this afternoon.

Coady crossed Dawson's wide Front Street with slow steps, her head down, her thoughts preoccupied. She fought the overwhelming urge to be angry with Isobel. She did not want to think her friend would tell tales maliciously. Isobel was not that sort. Perhaps Mary Snowden had twisted Isobel's words to make the telling seem mean. That was more likely the case; Isobel might have spoken out of kindness. But it was more difficult trying to determine *why* Isobel would bother to tell a near stranger about Coady and Stone's reasons for marrying.

Coady had just decided she would give Isobel the benefit of the doubt, until such time as they could discuss the matter, when she happened to look between the two buildings she was passing. There, hiding in the shadows, was a man. Instead of quickly removing herself from within reach of the fellow, whose purpose for being there was questionable at best, she stopped and took a good long look. "Vernon?" she asked softly.

He stepped forward, but not completely out of the shadows, as he pulled his floppy-brimmed hat from his head. "Miss Blake."

"Whatever are you doing in there?"

Vernon's gaze darted briefly across the street before he gave his complete attention to the hat he was holding between his hands.

Coady looked over her shoulder and saw Isobel walking along the opposite side of the street, talking with Mary Snowden. "Oh," she said, feeling a sudden burst of compassion for the quiet man. "You have come to see her."

"I just like to know that she's doing all right," he explained.

"Isobel is fine," she said. "Why don't you run and catch up with her?"

Vernon shook his head. "No. I can see she's fine."

Coady took a step closer, wishing Vernon would raise his head so she could see his eyes. "Do you also see she is expecting your child?"

He nodded his head. "I've known for a bit now."

"What do you plan to do about that?"

He did look up then, his gaze colliding with hers. "Nothing."

"She needs you."

He shook his head again. "She doesn't need me, Miss Blake. I'm the last one she needs."

He squeezed past her then, removing himself from the alley and marching off down the street in the direction opposite to that Isobel had taken.

Coady frowned at the man's retreating back.

Stone was a little put off that his new assignment was to be delayed by a least a day until Ben Keystone could be available to accompany him. He expected to find the suite empty upon his return late that afternoon. His first indication he was not alone was the woman's short cloak he tripped over near the door. He bent and picked up the garment, frowning at a nearby chair as he imagined that had been the intended landing place for the cape. He dropped it over the high, wooden back. "Coady!"

Lying on her back on the bed, staring at the ceiling, Coady closed her eyes. "Here!"

He entered the room while in the process of shrugging out of his short navy coat. "I'm surprised to see you here at this hour of the day."

"Half a day was all I could take."

He frowned, dropping his coat on a chair he passed on

his way to the bed. Sitting on the side of the mattress he looked at her closed eyes. "Bad?"

She opened her eyes and turned her head until their gazes met. "Not as bad as learning Zachary Bloodstone was a fraud. And not as bad as facing deportation. But bad enough."

He smiled and reached for her hand, holding it firmly against his thigh. "Tell me."

"I met Mary Snowden this morning."

"Ah. Mary Snowden must be significant," he said casually. "How?"

She told him.

"Vicious little snippet by the sound of her," Stone said as he pulled off his boots. "Shift over," he said gently and, when she did, he lay down beside her, propping his head on one hand while the other arm dropped lightly across her middle. "You are hurt?"

Coady did not need to answer, the look she gave him told exactly how she was feeling.

"You've actually given this woman's words credence?"

"You don't think Isobel would be malicious either, do you?"

"I do not. Not the Isobel we know. She might have spoken without thinking, perhaps. People often say things they later regret."

She sighed. "Lord, that is true."

"I think you should talk with Isobel."

"I have already decided to do that."

He smiled and dropped a kiss on the tip of her nose. "That's my girl."

"It is frightening how a few words spoken by someone I care about can hurt so much."

"You reacted the way anyone would react. But don't forget your friend did not speak the words you heard. Taken out of context, words can be manipulative, among other things."

"But why? What could be Mary's purpose in doing such a thing?"

He shrugged, looking at the slender hand resting below his. He began stroking the backs of her fingers. "Perhaps Mary feels she needs Isobel more than you do? Perhaps she wants Isobel's friendship all to herself?"

"Well, I am not going to let her break up my friendship."

He grinned. "I'm not surprised by that."

She smiled for the first time since he had entered the room. "You think you know me pretty well, don't you?"

His gaze met hers. His smile matched hers. "I'm learning."

"By the way, what are you doing here? I expected you to be gone a few days."

"A small delay but a frustrating one. I want to get on with the task and get it resolved so that I can be back here with you."

She smiled at that, nodding her head. "I think a proper kiss and a hug would make me feel better," she said boldly.

Oh, she does have her soft spots, he thought, *my hard-nosed little businesswoman*. She was feeling battered and bruised and it was gratifying to know she would turn to him for comfort. He pulled her gently into his arms and kissed her tenderly, a kiss meant to ease her pain, to heal her with the power of his love. She needed love and he knew it. But when would Coady know?

Stone ended the kiss slowly, raising his head to smile down at her. "Better?"

Coady nodded her head.

When he moved onto his back she followed, turning onto her side and settling her head on his shoulder. It was cozy being here with him like this. Odd, perhaps, to be lying on the bed with him fully clothed and not responding to each other with passion. Coady saw the moment as something more intimate than lust, however. It was quiet and peaceful in their small room. The sun's rays spread a bright path across the carpet and, lying next to him by the light of day, Coady felt more secure and at rest. "I saw Vernon today."

Stone was taking his turn staring at the ceiling. "He cannot seem to stay away."

Coady raised her head until she could see his face. "Have you talked with him recently?"

Stone turned his attention upon her and nodded his head.

"It appears he comes here often."

"Apparently."

"He was hiding between buildings when I saw him. Isobel was walking just across the street but he wouldn't go and speak with her."

"I doubt he ever will, lass," he said gently.

She bolted up, turning on the bed to face him in one simple flowing motion. "But if he comes here to see she is all right, he must care for her."

"Oh, he cares. He cares deeply."

Her frown deepened. "Then why did he refuse to marry her? Why won't he talk with her?"

"Vernon feels he can't offer Isobel the life she deserves," he said simply.

Coady's hand shot into the air and fell back to her lap just as quickly. "You have said that before but I find it ridiculous!" she said with obvious impatience. "How can men be so . . . ?"

Stone arched one brow. "Yes?"

She thought better of completing her sentence. "Isobel is miserable without Vernon. She obviously loves him. And a woman in love does not care about anything other than being with her man."

"Is that so? And how would you be knowing that?"

"Every woman knows that."

Stone allowed himself to indulge in a small ray of hope, considering Coady had not looked at him while she had spoken. "So, if you loved me, just for the sake of argument," he said quietly. "You would not care where we lived or how we lived?"

Coady thought about that. "Well, for the sake of argument . . . no."

She was a tough one, that was a fact. But Stone's heart began beating just a little faster because he felt they were on the right track. *"A woman in love does not care about anything other than being with her man,"* he quoted. "That is what you said, is it not?"

Reluctantly, she responded. "Yes. That's what I said."

He continued to stare at the ceiling, concentrating on the conversation, waiting for even the slightest change in her tone. "Do you believe that?"

"Well, I said it."

"But do you believe it, lass?"

"Yes," she said softly, as if her own words were teaching her a whole new lesson.

Stone decided he was going to brave it out. "If I offered you a trip around the world would you take it?"

She had already caught onto his game, of course. "I would not like taking a trip if I were all alone."

"If I offered you a castle for your home, would you take it?"

"I would not want to live in a castle if I were all alone."

"What do you care most about, Coady?"

"Being with you," she said in a small voice.

Stone rolled onto his side and pulled her tightly into an embrace. "Louder."

"I care most about being with you."

"And why do you care most about being with me?" he asked, his words a soft whisper against the shell of her ear.

"Because I love you," she whispered back.

He raised his head and looked down at her then. "I couldn't hear you, my love."

She smiled, swallowing a giggle that threatened to have her come undone with joy. "You are a brute."

He nodded his head. "I still need to hear the words."

"I love you!" she said loudly, laughing as she wrapped her arms around his neck. "It's true. I've been too afraid to admit it, let alone say it."

Stone pressed his palm against her cheek and moved her head back until they could look into each other's eyes. "You must never be afraid of your heart's desires, sweet," he said softly. "Never. You deserve everything you want from life and, if it is within my power, I intend to see that you get it. I love you, Coady. I think I started loving you that first day when you were so hoping to sell me a frilly garter."

"But you still had Bloodstone investigated," she pointed out.

"I didn't know then that I was falling in love. I was doing what I have been trained to do. I felt truly terrible when you had to face those couples and tell them they were not married."

"Is that why you insisted on traveling with me?"

He nodded his head and his thumb caressed her chin. "I volunteered for the duty."

"And you have been there ever since to catch me when I stumble."

"I will always be with you, my love," he breathed as he lowered his lips toward her. "Always."

Chapter Eighteen

The days were becoming very chilly, the nights cold and, before the end of October, Isobel knew she would have to give up the tent Coady had so generously given and find herself a room in one of the hotels. Evenings inside the tent were already unpleasant but she dressed warmly, reluctant to use the gold Vernon had given her until she had no choice.

She would soon be earning a wage of her own, though, and need not fear being completely penniless by spring. The bakery would open before the weekend and Harrison Trelaine had come along with a generous offer in exchange for her assistance in managing the shop. Isobel was filled with a sense of pride every time she thought of earning her own way for the first time in her life.

It would be difficult, once the baby came along, but she knew she could keep them both in moderate comfort. At least they would not go without necessities. She and her baby would survive. Coady had taught her a woman could overcome almost anything, if she set her mind to survival.

Isobel hugged a blanket around her shoulders and threw another small log into the wood stove. She thought of her friend as she lowered herself onto the straight-backed chair before the fire. Coady was, no doubt, tucked up in a warm bed with her husband's arms around her. Isobel longed for that kind of warmth, longed for the feel of Vernon's arms around her. But that would never be, never again. And she could not resent the happiness in Coady's life simply because she was miserable. Well, not miserable, perhaps; she was making a life for herself, after all. But she dearly wished she could be sharing that life with the man she loved.

She heard a quick knock against the tent post before the canvas entrance was pulled back allowing Mary Snowden to enter. Isobel's natural smile returned to its rightful place. "Whatever are you doing here?"

"Does that mean I'm not welcome?" Mary asked sharply as she walked toward the stove.

"Of course not. I'm happy to see you. But it's late for you to be about the streets alone." She stood then, offering her chair to her guest.

Mary sat down and smoothed her skirts, looking around the tent Isobel called home, not bothering to hide her distaste. "I do not know how you tolerate this miserable cold, Isobel," she said. "I swear I do not."

"It isn't that bad."

Mary grunted in a most unladylike fashion as she reached beneath her cloak. "I was miserable with loneliness and knew you would be sitting here freezing." She grinned wickedly. "I have procured something to warm us," she added conspiratorially.

Isobel frowned at the dark green bottle. "I do not take spirits, Mary."

"Nonsense. A little wine is good for you. And a good hostess does not allow a guest to drink alone. Fetch us some glasses."

"I really shouldn't . . ."

"If you mean to be unfriendly, Isobel, then I shall leave."

Isobel thought about rebelling against the younger woman's imperious threat. Mary was very much like her mother, Victoria, in many ways. She was adamant about most things, hard and cool and demanding. Mary Snowden and Victoria Daniels acted as if life, and most people, owed them just about anything their hearts desired.

Isobel was quite the opposite, really. Years of tutelage had programmed her to obey most orders and directions from almost any source without question. And she certainly had not intended to insult her new friend. "Well, perhaps just a little."

Isobel possessed one glass and one cup. She brought these to Mary.

Mary eyed the items distastefully, but filled the glass and then the cup, giving the latter to Isobel after settling the wine bottle on the plank floor near her feet with great fanfare.

Raising her glass high, she smiled. "To our friendship."

Isobel smiled and nodded her head. "Friendship." The wine was quite pleasant actually, sweet, like drinking dessert. She found the first taste was deserving of another. "Very good," she said as she lowered the cup and sat on the end of her narrow bed.

"Of course. I wouldn't bring anything but the best this dreary town had to offer."

The play of shadow against the meager light from the fire and the lamp near the bed etched harshness into Mary's features that Isobel had never seen before. It made the woman appear cruel. Mary's dark scowl did not help matters either. "You really hate it here?"

The woman's mouth drew into a tight line. "Lord, yes. You do not?"

Isobel shook her head once, stopping immediately

when the motion made her slightly dizzy. "I do not hate it at all."

"The Yukon hasn't done much for you," Mary returned snidely as she watched Isobel's eyelids drift downward.

Isobel was surprised at how quickly the small potbellied stove had warmed the room. She realized the warmth had made her drowsy and popped her eyes open, smiling sheepishly at her visitor as she shrugged the blanket from her shoulders. In the next instant, she became aware of slumping, sagging in the middle like a puppet with several severed strings. She straightened her spine, reverting to years of teaching, hearing her mother's nagging voice echoing the merits of a fine lady's posture. "A lady can be distinguished by her bearing," Isobel mumbled with total recall of Victoria's strident tones.

Her eyes began to drift closed again.

Mary lowered her untouched wine to a place beside the bottle and got to her feet. "Look what this horrid place has done for you," she said conversationally as she walked toward the bed. "You have ruined your hands by working, you have lost your husband, and you are now quite alone and pregnant."

Isobel fought to open her eyes but failed. In the next moment, she was falling onto her side on the bed.

"Stupid woman," Mary muttered. She grabbed hold of Isobel's feet and swung her legs around until the older woman was lying on her back. Mary looked down with contempt at her sleeping "friend." "Fool," she breathed.

Turning on a heel she marched to the tent opening, raising the flap and peering outside into the darkness. "Jay?"

Moments later, Jay Snowden dashed inside the tent. "You're certain she's asleep?"

"Well, she fell over right enough."

Jay hated Mary reverting to the harsh Cockney tones of her birthplace. "Mind your tongue," he would say, reminding her of the expensive elocution lessons he had paid for with hard-earned money.

He walked to the bed and pulled one of Isobel's eyelids back. "You're right, she's gone already." He turned and faced his spouse. "You'd better get yourself back to your room."

Faced with leaving him alone with the older woman, Mary suddenly turned doubtful. "You're not going to make love to her?"

Jay slanted her a frown of disgust. "You think I find that appealing?" he questioned, pointing toward Isobel's swollen belly. "But you know I've got to make it look real, my darling. This woman must awaken in the morning thinking she has fornicated with me."

It was the one way they could make Isobel their puppet. Mary understood that; they had practiced the scheme often enough. Still, every time Jay was with whatever woman they had chosen as necessary to their confidence game, Mary endured terrible jealousy.

Jay watched doubt steal across her face and sighed silently; it was always the same. Walking toward her, he took Mary's cold hand in both of his. "I enlisted another investor today."

That brightened the moment. "You did?"

He nodded his head. "With Isobel's money and a bit more we will soon have enough to get out of this godforsaken place."

"Oh, Jay. That will be wonderful. Let's go somewhere warm this time."

"Of course, my love," he said. "But first we have a little more work to do." He leaned forward and lightly kissed her lips. "Off with you, now."

Casting the prone form of Isobel Daniels a hateful glance, Mary turned and left the tent.

Jay Snowden was a man of twenty-five years, short of stature but long on arrogance. He was as dark-complexioned as the devil and took the living the world owed him anyway he could get it. And it was a good living at that. Jay was amenable to taking the path of least resistance. Any easy mark was to his liking. Isobel was not easy, however. Women with morals seldom were. But he had long ago learned how to deal with such women. A little blackmail usually produced healthy payments to offset the threat of scandal.

He bent over Isobel and quickly, efficiently made the pregnant woman naked. As he was ridding himself of his own clothes, he stared down at her swollen body. It was true, what he had told Mary; he was not at all moved to passion by that big belly. It was pity, actually. He might have enjoyed Isobel otherwise. She was quite pretty, with her fine features and delicate build. Her breasts were large and tempting. He looked at the thatch of hair at the junction of her thighs. Unlike Mary, Isobel was a natural blonde. Still, he could not stand around all night admiring his victim. He had much to do to make his tale believable when the Daniels woman awoke from her drug-induced sleep.

Chapter Ninteen

Gold had found its way into the MacGregors' hands.

Coady had practically melted into Stone's arms the first night he brought her a small sack filled with a dozen ounces of gold dust. But, when he made lingering, passionate love to her, she forgot their newfound riches for several hours. She even forgot to ask how he had come by such wealth.

The following morning, however, she learned he was gambling. "But why are you spending nights gambling? I thought you were to go on assignment away from Dawson."

He grinned, placing his arm around her waist and pulling her up hard against him. "I know you are not that eager to be rid of me, my sweet. Not after last night."

"I'm not eager to be rid of you at all," she confessed. "I am simply confused."

"Let me just say we have altered our tactics in dealing with this case. For my part, I am just as happy because it means I can spend more time with you."

Except in the evenings. Evenings he was out and about gambling more than she would have liked. It was not the most stable of pastimes and over that first week Stone would sometimes arrive home empty-handed. On other occasions there would be a small sack of gold he would cheerfully drop into the palm of her hand. Coady would rush to the bank with each coin he gave her. The sum in their account began to grow quite respectably.

Now Coady curled up in bed with Stone. Earlier in the day she had rediscovered a sense of insecurity within herself. It was frightening to know she and Stone could lose everything they were saving through a single, badly turned card. "I think we should wait a bit longer before we put money into a house," she told him.

He removed his lips from her breast and raised his head to look at her through the shadows cast by the fire-light. "Why? I thought you were eager to start building."

It was three o'clock in the morning and Stone had just returned to the suite. As was his habit, he was more inclined to make love to her than talk.

Coady ran her fingertips absently along his forearm. "I am, but what if you should lose badly one night? Your luck could turn and—"

"Ah," he recognized her old haunting insecurity again. "Coady, I will never gamble with our future. Never, lass. What I am doing is a means of gaining information. It helps me in my investigation. The money I gamble can be lost, if that is the case, without our feeling a pinch. I gave over the winnings, because I thought it might amuse you. I did not mean for the occasional loss to cause you concern."

She sighed. "I'm sorry. The threat of loss—"

"I believe I understand, but you must trust me. Because I have not experienced utter poverty does not mean I cannot conceive of how terrible it must have been for you. I am mindful of your fears, Coady. All I want to do is help you put them to rest."

She smiled softly, chagrined by her own weakness. "I

think you are a good man, Stone MacGregor,'' she whispered.

He nuzzled her neck, kissing the soft spot just below her ear. He had other weighty matters on his mind and being with her gave him ease when he was weary of puzzling through his current assignment. He pulled away from her and marched across the room, quickly throwing another log on the dwindling fire. He wanted to ask her about the Snowdens and how well she knew them. He already knew Coady had met Mary on several occasions. He wondered why she had not told him Jay Snowden had rented every tent she possessed. He wondered why she had not told him of the considerable profits she had made the first week Snowden had been in town. He worried for her, keeping such company. He also worried for Isobel, who was a frequent companion to Mary Snowden.

When he returned to the bed he pulled her up in the center of the mattress until they were facing each other, sitting with their legs folded between them, holding hands.

The concentrated expression he showed her made Coady suddenly afraid. "This must be dire,'' she said, trying for a light tone and failing miserably.

"How well do you know Jay and Mary Snowden?''

"The Snowdens? What brought them to mind?''

"I need to know, Coady.'' He reached up and touched her cheek, briefly tracing her frown with the pad of his thumb. It was the type of caress in which he frequently indulged.

"I do not know them well. I know Jay not at all. And Mary is a person I would prefer not to know.''

"You have not liked her from the beginning, have you?''

Coady shrugged. "She does not seem very genuine. I think she sets herself a cut above everyone else.''

"But Isobel likes her.''

"Isobel, clearly, is desperate for friends,'' she returned dryly.

He smiled. "Perhaps."

"So, you are investigating the Snowdens," she chirped.

"Perhaps."

"I will not tell anyone, Stone."

"I did not expect you would. Otherwise I would not have asked you about them."

"Are they dangerous, somehow?" she asked in a small voice. "Isobel seems to be fond of Mary and spends a good portion of every day with the woman. Should we worry for her?"

"We do not know exactly who they are or what they are as yet. I doubt, somehow, that they are dangerous. At least from what we have learned so far."

"So this is why you are out gambling every night?"

He nodded his head.

"Do men actually talk of anything other than cards when they are sitting around a poker table?"

He laughed shortly. "You would be surprised at what men discuss while playing cards."

With a gleeful glint in her eye, she tipped toward him. "Tell me."

"Not on your life!"

"You are certain you are not seeing another woman?" she asked with feigned severity.

Stunned, he blinked in surprise. "Why would you think that?"

"Perhaps I am being foolish," she admitted.

"There is no other woman, Coady. There could not be another woman."

Her gaze was fixed with his, her heart thudding crazily. "Why not?"

He shook his head. "No other woman could possibly attract me the way you do, my love. No other woman could possibly give me as much pleasure simply by gracing me with a sweet smile. No one could ever stir my heart the way you do when you look at me with wanting."

"I do not ever look at you with wanting."

The disbelief in her tone made him laugh. "You **may** not want to admit it but you do, you know."

Coady blushed to the roots of her hair and he pulled her tight against his chest.

"I'm glad you want me. It is the same for me," he added with obvious pleasure. "I am faithfully yours now and forever. Please believe that."

Coady was completely in awe of his sincerity. "And I will be faithfully yours now and forever," she returned softly.

The dancing flames of the fire provided the only light, softly bathing the occupants of the bed in a flickering cast of yellow, keeping the shadows confined to the corners of the room. Stone lay on his back with Coady tucked beneath his arm. The fingers of his right hand causally stroked her breast as he stared at the ceiling.

Coady was curled up against him, her hand slowly stroking the fine hair of his chest. Her eyes were closed as she drifted in a sleepy haze. She felt exhausted but radiant as she basked in the afterglow of their lovemaking. She needed sleep. She did not doubt that they both needed sleep. But she wanted to preserve the moment more and sleep would deprive her of that. "I could never have dreamed of such happiness," she said softly.

Stone looked down at the top of her head. She lay so trustingly against him. "I should hope it is not a dream, my love."

"Why me, Stone?"

He was confused by the question.

When he did not respond immediately, Coady turned, draping herself half across his chest. When their gazes met, she smiled softly. "I know there are not a lot of eligible women in the Territory but surely there were many you knew back home."

"Some," he said, curious over her thinking.

"But none you loved?"

"Not the way I love you."

245

"That is what I mean . . . why me?"

He laughed. "Why does the sun rise? Why are there stars in the sky? I could answer those questions more easily." He stroked her back. He touched her hair. He gazed into her warm, brown eyes. "I love you because you are you, lass. I love you for all the wonderful qualities I see in you. If I were a man of flowery words, I could come up with a thousand attributes that attract me to you."

She lowered her head to his chest. "In other words, you do not know," she teased. "I know why I fell in love with you."

Stone's eyebrows arched in wonder. "Really? And what might that be?"

"You drove me to distraction with all your questions. That made me think about you almost constantly. You crept into my life, in a way. In short order, I could not think of you *not* being there."

"Ah! There is something to be said for my chosen profession after all."

Thinking of what his chosen profession had done to her own, she said dryly, "We will not go into that." Raising her head, she looked at him again. "We were talking of the Snowdens before."

He recalled. That seemed an eternity ago and far, far away. "We were."

"Is there something you wish to tell me?"

"There is little I can say in the midst of an investigation. Not because I do not trust you, Coady, but because the less you know the less you are at risk."

"They *are* dangerous," she murmured.

"Animals can be dangerous if cornered. I don't know how far these people will go to protect themselves."

"Jay Snowden rented almost everything I had."

"Yes, I know. He is setting up quite a little camp along the Twelvemile."

"There is nothing strange about that. There are many camps, everywhere."

"It is strange if there is no gold."

"Do you know for certain there is no gold there?"

"Not yet."

Coady rolled onto her back and hooked her arm around his. "There is nothing illegal about setting up a camp," she said quietly. "But, if there is no gold, why would he do it?"

Stone remained stoically silent. He had no doubt she would work it out. His sweet little wife was a very clever woman.

"Something Isobel said . . ." She thought for a moment, trying to recall. "I asked her if she had given them money." There was a momentary pause as she turned her head and looked at him. "They are looking for investors, are they not? The Snowdens are selling shares in a mother lode that does not exist."

Instead of answering her directly, Stone simply dropped a kiss upon her forehead.

"They need a camp, and an active-looking one at that," she continued. "They will plant some gold dust, possibly even nuggets, and convince everyone they have a wealthy find. Once they have all the money they think they can get, they will simply disappear." She looked at him, grinning proudly. "Now I know more than I should."

"All of this is absolute speculation," he reminded her.

"But my theory is feasible."

Reluctantly, he nodded his head; she was enjoying this entirely too much.

"In fact, my theory is the one you are working with, correct?"

Again she received an affirmative nod of his head.

"Perhaps we should go into business together . . . the MacGregor Detective Agency."

He cast her a dubious frown.

"The problem is, the scheme is entirely too obvious."

"True."

"It is too old a trick," she added thoughtfully. "People will not fall for it."

"People fall for this old trick every day, my love. Everyone wants to get rich quick."

"I am worried for Isobel. Mary Snowden is persistent in seeking Isobel out and I do not understand why. Why Isobel?"

"Now there is a question. But if you warn Isobel off, she may think you are jealous of her relationship with Mary. You cannot say much at this stage and we do not have any proof that Isobel is in harm's way." Stone gave the matter more thought. "I believe we should convince her to take a room here in the hotel, close to us. Besides, it is getting too cold for her to remain in the tent."

Coady agreed. "I believe I can convince her of that much, at least."

Chapter Twenty

Blinding brightness entered the tent with the dawning of a sunny new day.

Isobel awakened from sleep slowly, reluctantly, unsure whether it was the light or the pounding in her head that pulled her relentlessly toward consciousness.

Lying very still, her eyes closed, she fought complete consciousness. There was heat radiating toward her from a nearby source. Certain she was back on the Bonanza in Vernon's bed she rolled slowly toward the warmth, moaning softly with delight when she found herself pressed against the hulking body of her husband. Blindly, she reached out a hand and wrapped her fingers around his upper arm. But, instead of feeling thick, bulging muscle beneath warm flesh and thick hair, Isobel realized she had hold of something far more puny.

She opened one eye and stared at the profile of a sleeping man she did not immediately recognize.

With a soft gasp she bolted upright in the bed as all the while her gaze remained transfixed on the man. She

249

hastily clutched the bed sheet to her breasts as recognition dawned. "Jay Snowden!" she cried.

Snowden, who had been feigning sleep, opened his eyes and turned his head toward her. As he stared, delighted by the horror-stricken face of Isobel Daniels, a slow smile crept across his lips. "Good morning, my love," he said huskily.

Isobel's eyes, if it were possible, grew even larger. "My lo—?" She scrambled with the sheet, wrapping the thing around herself as she stumbled from the bed. "What are you doing here?" Her gaze searched every corner of the tent, frantically searching out the hiding place of possible witnesses. "Where is Mary?" she demanded.

Jay ignored the fact she had exposed his nakedness during the process of protecting her own modesty. "I should imagine she is in our room at the hotel."

"But . . ." Again, Isobel's gaze searched the room as if answers could take physical form and pop up to educate her. "She was here. She was here and we were having a glass of wine."

Snowden's grin widened. "Yes, I know. You're very amorous when you've been drinking, Isobel."

There were a hundred "buts" demanding answers as she backed away from the bed. "I'm not amorous."

"Oh, yes, you are," he drawled, rolling onto his side and propping his head on a hand. "You're the most incredible woman I've ever been with."

"You weren't . . . *with* . . . me," she stammered. "We were not . . . together."

Jay arched a dark brow and continued to grin at her.

"What are you saying!" she screeched in panic.

He frowned briefly. "Lower you voice, my sweet. Passersby on the street might take notice."

"I am not *your sweet*," she shot back. "I demand to know what you are doing here. I demand to know what kind of game you are playing."

"Game?" he drawled low. "After the things you said,

the things we did, you dare to call it all a *game*?"

Trapping the sheet beneath her arms, Isobel raised her fingertips to her aching temples and closed her eyes. "I do not remember saying anything to you," she whispered desperately. "I do not remember doing anything with you." She opened her eyes then, raising her head as she stared at him accusingly. "I would not do that to a friend," she said angrily. "I do not believe a word you are saying. You are trying to trick me. I do not know why, but I know I've not done anything with you."

A dark scowl fashioned its way across his face. "So by the light of day, you no longer love me, is that it? You were merely using me—"

"I was not using you!" she screamed. "I do not love you! I have no designs on you. You are my friend's husband."

Snowden pushed himself up, remaining on one hip, locking his elbow to support his weight. "You were in this bed with me and you liked the things we did," he growled. "You were like a wild thing, clawing me, begging me."

She shook her head as tears threatened to embarrass her further. "No."

"I'm telling the truth. Which is apparently more than you wish to face this morning, madam," he added pointedly. "The proof of our love is here," he said, pointing to the side of the bed Isobel had vacated. "I, at least, was mindful of you and your child."

She shook her head again, not wanting to look at the spot to which he was pointing. But some inner driving force demanded she must. Horror made her heart race and her mouth go dry as Isobel stared at the stain on the white cotton. "No," she breathed.

"Why are you doing this, darling?" Jay crooned as he rose from the bed and walked toward her. "Why? It was so wonderful between us," he added as he reached for her.

Isobel scooted back, narrowly saving herself from a

fall as her feet became entangled in the trailing sheet. "Why do not I remember?"

"Wine will do that to a woman sometimes," he told her quietly. "I admonished Mary for bringing the stuff to you."

Isobel just could not accept what he was saying, all he was implying. It was true she had no designs on Jay Snowden. In fact, he was not at all appealing to her in any way. He was her friend's husband and she had enjoyed the couple's company on several occasions but, other than that, she felt completely indifferent toward Jay himself. "Why would Mary leave here without you?" she asked shortly. "I don't remember her leaving." For that matter, she did not remember Jay arriving.

"Mary and I argued over the wine, I'm afraid. She left here in quite a huff."

"And you decided to stay to take advantage of me?" That must have been it! She must have been tipsy and he—

"You asked me to stay, Isobel." His dark-eyed gaze locked with hers. "You pleaded with me to stay." He took a small step toward her. "I wanted to be certain you would not suffer any ill effects of the spirits, so I was easily convinced to remain. But then you kissed me and, when I kissed you back, you rubbed yourself against me, pleading—"

"No!" she cried, covering her face with her hands. "No!"

"I am only a man, after all," he said softly, pulling her into his arms. "I'm only human."

Isobel pulled herself away, standing near the cold stove as she glared at him. "You cheated on your wife, is that what you're saying? Do you not love her? Do you not have any respect for me? If I was—"

"Of course I love Mary," he said easily, quickly tiring of the game. "What we did has nothing to do with her."

"How can you be so calm about this?"

"You are overwrought," he said, smiling patiently. "Sit in the chair while I start a fire."

Her gaze briefly roamed his length, as if seeing his nakedness for the first time. "Would you please clothe yourself."

Jay looked down quickly and then grinned at her. "Of course, dear."

"I am *not* your *dear*!" she shouted before sitting.

Snowden shrugged his shoulders, apparently unmoved by her tirade, and reached for his trousers.

Isobel noticed the cold for the first time as she stared dimly at the stove, trying to remember what on earth had happened during the night. She remembered Mary arriving. She remembered reluctantly accepting a cup of wine. She remembered they had talked for a time. But that was all she could remember.

Dimwitted, silent, Isobel watched Jay build a fire in the wood stove.

"You'll feel better when you're fully awake and warm," he said.

"I don't think I'll ever feel better."

From a crouched position in front of the stove, he looked over his shoulder at her. "I asked you last night if you would have regrets come morning. You told me no."

Isobel, her head pounding and her stomach twisting in a threatening fashion, managed to look Jay Snowden in the eyes. "I don't believe you."

He scowled, closed the stove door with a clang, and got to his feet. "Believe what you want," he said tightly. "I know I have regrets now that you've turned our night of bliss into something sordid."

"We did not have a night of bliss!" she shot back.

He leaned toward her, threatening, his face very close to hers. "You saw the evidence for yourself," he snapped. "I was a fool to listen to you. You don't *love* me. You used me."

Isobel shook her head. "Please leave," she said quietly. She needed to be alone. She needed to get her thoughts in order. Perhaps then she would remember.

"Gladly," said Jay.

Isobel did not look at him while he moved about the tent, gathering his clothes. She was aware of hasty movements, the rustling of material, the dead silence that felt like an anvil had been placed on her shoulders. It seemed as if she held that weight, and her breath, until Jay Snowden left the tent.

The moment she became aware of her aloneness her head fell forward, and, with her hands covering her face, she wept.

She was so utterly certain she could not have slept with Jay. She could not. And yet, why could she not remember?

It was all so confusing. Too many emotions crowded in against each other in an attempt to gain supremacy, blocking rational thought. But there was one thing Isobel knew for certain: She *did not* tell Jay Snowden she loved him.

She knew because there was only one man she loved.

Only one man she could ever love.

Mary Snowden stood in front of the cheval glass and smoothed her hands over her naked torso. She was flat where Isobel was grossly rounded. She was large breasted and possessed shapely legs. She was small of stature, but she suited Jay nicely. The one thing she feared sometimes was that Jay would leave her with a child in her belly. They had been together since her sixteenth birthday. Four years. But he would leave her in a moment if she became pregnant.

Mary already had had to rid herself of one child, and the back-alley butcher who had helped her in her hour of need had damned near killed her. Recovering in hospital days later, another doctor had said there would be no more babies. But she worried, all the same.

Her attention focused on the mirror, Mary watched Jay

enter the room behind her. He closed the door to their room quietly and he was grinning as he walked up behind her.

"It went all right?" she asked softly.

"A day or so and that woman will do anything we want," he told her as he wrapped his arms around her, pressing his chest against her back. "She is completely distressed. By the time she sleeps on this for a night or two, Isobel Daniels will be in a complete frenzy. She was a good choice, my love. You did well." He dropped a kiss on her shoulder. "Don't move," he said as he stepped back and hastily began removing his clothes. The instant Jay was naked he stepped up against her again, pressing his aching erection against her. "You know what I want," he growled low, as his hands brutally squeezed her large breasts.

She knew.

It was always the same after he had spent a night in another woman's bed.

He always came back to her.

Chapter Twenty-one

Coady tested the door of her old home and frowned when it proved to be locked. It was unusual for Isobel not to be up and about. Coady was about to walk around back to the tent Isobel occupied when the object of her concern arrived.

"Good morning," she said with a teasing smile. "You overslept, Isobel? Slugabed."

Isobel's countenance was grim as she unlocked the door to Coady's place and entered the room. "Yes. I overslept," she said quietly. "What do we have to do today?"

Coady's smile instantly dissolved as she followed her friend to the desk in the back corner of the room. "Is something wrong?"

Isobel shook her head and sat down.

Coady frowned with concern as she sat in the chair across the desk and stared at her friend's complexion. She had seen less gray on a seagull and the sparkle of life in Isobel's eyes had disappeared. "Is the baby making you ill?"

Again, Isobel shook her head. "I am fine."

"Forgive me, but you don't look fine. This blanched-gray tone I see on your face doesn't suit you at all."

Isobel sighed. "Are we working in the bakery today or not?" she demanded shortly.

Coady was shocked by her friend's abrupt tone. It was so unlike Isobel to snap at anyone. She was the most even-tempered, pleasant-natured person Coady had ever met. Reaching across the table between them, Coady placed her hands over Isobel's. "I think I shall ask again," she said softly. "What is wrong?"

"Nothing." Isobel pulled her hands free and slumped back in her chair.

"Well something has happened between yesterday afternoon, when I last saw you, and this moment."

"Leave it be, Coady."

Coady's heart reached out, crying over the pain in the other woman's voice. "You can tell me anything, my friend," she said softly. "Is it Vernon?"

Isobel raised a stricken, pained expression for Coady to see. "No!" she cried before tears rushed to her eyes and spilled over her long, fair lashes. "Leave it!"

Coady jumped from her chair and rounded the desk, kneeling beside the weeping woman. "Oh, Isobel," she crooned, placing a consoling hand on her friend's back. "Tell me. Perhaps I can help."

Isobel seemed to find some inner strength in that moment. Knowing she could not speak of the horrible night past, knowing she could not so much as whisper a word of it to anyone, she determined she must act as if nothing had happened. Coady would continue to probe as long as she felt there was a problem. Managing a weak smile, an odd mix of chagrin and sadness, Isobel shook her head. "I'm fine, really," she said, squeezing Coady's hand. "It is the baby, I think. There are times when I'm

257

just weepy for no apparent reason. I hate it, actually. It's so unlike me."

"I should say," Coady muttered. "Completely unlike you. Is there anything I can do? Anything I can get you?"

"I think the best cure for me," Isobel whispered, "is to lose myself in work."

They always chose the same table in the rear corner of the Dominion Saloon. There, their backs were protected and they could watch the comings and goings throughout the large, dimly lit room.

"Snowden is back in town?" Stone asked. "You are certain?"

Ben Keystone bobbed his head over his beer. "Followed him myself," he muttered. "You are not going to like where he has been. I will not even speculate over what he was doing there. It is too odious a thing to fathom."

It was early afternoon and there was little activity in the saloon. But Stone's gaze was in constant motion as usual. "So, where has he been?"

Ben was reluctant to speak about this particular matter. He knew this situation could touch Stone directly through his own wife. "He spent the night in Isobel Daniel's tent."

Stone's complete attention turned on his companion and he did not bother to hide his shock. "What?"

"I think you heard me, sir."

"Snowden with Isobel?"

"I followed him there. Mary Snowden was there for a time last night but she left and her husband stayed."

"Jesus, Mary and Joseph," he hissed.

"Shall I have a talk with Miss Daniels?"

"No," he said quickly, shaking his head. "No. I need to think about this a moment."

Ben waited as Stone took a sip of his coffee and began filling the bowl of his pipe with tobacco. Ben had learned a great deal from this man. It was eerie how Stone's eyes looked about a room as if he were devoting his full attention elsewhere and all the while that active mind of his was sorting through something entirely different. Something that had nothing to do with where he was or what he was looking at.

Stone drew on the stem of his pipe as he held a match over the bowl. Once he was satisfied with the glow of the tobacco, he blew a smoke ring above their heads as he watched the quick, efficient motions of the man tending bar. "What I know of Isobel Daniels goes completely against any notion of her being with Snowden for a night. I cannot envision her with *any* man for a night. She loves Vernon. In fact, I suspect she still feels very married to him."

"Even though they were not ever married," Ben muttered.

Stone cast the younger man an impatient frown. "That is beside the point."

Ben shrugged. "I suppose."

"A woman like Isobel does not cheat on the man she loves. And she is too much of a lady to even contemplate inviting a man she barely knows into her bed. She would die before risking scandal."

"Sure, but caught in the moment, maybe she—"

"No," Stone said quickly, shaking his head. "You will never convince me Isobel was willingly with that little pissant." He turned his attention on Ben. "Think about it, man. You have been following Snowden's activities for weeks now. He gets men enthused about his mine, befriends them for a day or two, gets them drunk, while seemingly drunk himself. The next thing these fellows know, they have a worthless share certificate in their hand, a monstrous hangover, and not a nickel left in their pockets."

"We don't know yet about the mine," Ben reminded him. "Snowden has a surveyor's certificate and everyone

259

I have talked with is convinced the mine is legitimate and wealthy."

"Of course they are," Stone returned. "No one wants to admit he's fallen for the oldest confidence trick in history. I will wager those share certificates look as genuine as my Aunt Hattie's death certificate and she has been dead ten years. But if you believe in Snowden, I have a nice ice-bridge across a glacier I can sell you."

"He is working the mine," Ben pointed out, ignoring his superior's sarcasm. "Word has it he hired a dozen men."

Stone's gaze began roaming the room again. "We are going to see for ourselves about that," he said. "We will ride out there tomorrow, as long as Snowden is still in town, and have a good look around. In the meantime, I need to know if Isobel is all right." His intense gaze locked with Ben's. "You did see her this morning, I hope? You waited to see her?"

Keystone shook his head. "I was following Snowden."

"Damn," Stone muttered, dropping his pipe into a dish. "Wait here." He hurried from the saloon and broke into a run the moment he reached the street. He ran first to Coady's place and, finding the door locked, raced to the tent behind. But Isobel was not there. He looked around the sparsely furnished place, eventually focusing his attention on the disheveled bed. But Stone saw even more than Isobel had seen. He stared at the pillows. Unless Isobel roamed around in her sleep, there had been two heads gracing the bed the previous night. Other evidence brought certainty slamming to his mind; there had been a man in Isobel's bed.

Stone ran from the tent, promising he would kill Snowden for dishonoring one of the finest women he had ever met. He would castrate Jay Snowden before the courts could get their hands on him. Thoughts of the evil little monster touching any woman out of turn made Stone seethe with anger. It was worse that Snowden had touched someone close to Coady, a woman for whom Stone would slay a thousand dragons.

He did not even want to think about *how* Snowden had carried out this particular misdeed because every plausible machination that came to mind was more heinous than the last.

He had learned only that morning there had been another woman to whom Mary and Jay Snowden had devoted considerable attention. *That* woman had been the wife of a very successful miner, one of the few men to truly find a rich strike of gold. The man's name was Henderson Furley and he had reported his wife, Elizabeth, missing two weeks ago.

Elizabeth Furley had yet to be found.

"If we finish scrubbing these shelves and sweep the floor once more, I will consider we have completed a good day's work," Coady said conversationally.

Isobel was putting her heart and soul into madly scrubbing one single spot on a lower shelf. "We can do more," she said dismally. "I don't mind working into the evening to get the place clean."

Coady minded; she wanted to see Stone before he went off on one of his nightly jaunts. "Isobel, why not move into the hotel? You could be near Stone and me and you would certainly be more comfortable."

Actually, Isobel had been thinking just that. If she were in a proper room where she could lock the door, perhaps she would not do anything foolish. Anything more foolish than she had already done.

Isobel nodded her head, concentrating on wearing a circular patch in the wooden shelf.

Both women were startled by the thud against the front door as Stone hit the thing before completely opening the portal.

"What on earth?" Coady dashed around the end of the counter toward the front of the shop. "Stone?" Coady frowned as he hurried across the room toward her.

Stone's gaze went briefly to Isobel. Assured the woman was alive, he realized he had to say something about his hurried entrance. "I know. I'm supposed to open the door before I come through it."

Coady laughed. "Well, whatever is your hurry?"

"I missed you," he said bluntly.

Isobel turned her back on the couple and began scrubbing the spot on the shelf.

Coady's complexion warmed. "I'm flattered, Mr. MacGregor, but I can't believe you *ran* here just to see me."

The glint in his eyes said she should believe. But his attention was focused more toward Isobel. "I thought I might take you ladies to lunch."

Coady frowned. "It is long past the noon hour."

"Oh," he said, now staring openly at Isobel's back. "I suppose that means you have eaten?"

Standing in front of him, Coady looked over her shoulder, following the direction in which Stone was looking. When she turned back to face him, she was sporting a curious smile.

He shook his head as he reached for her hand. "I shall let you two get on with your work."

Coady raised up, accepting a small kiss on her cheek. She thought frantically, searching for something that would keep him near. She missed him during the day and, since he was not sleeping in preparation for his nightly prowling, he might very well keep her company. Certainly Isobel needed some cheering up and Coady was not managing that very well. "I am trying to convince Isobel she should move to the hotel," she said. "It is too cold for her to be staying in the tent now."

"I agree."

Coady looked over her shoulder. "Did you hear that, Isobel?"

The woman nodded her head.

When Coady looked back at Stone, she was frowning, tipping her head in the direction of her friend. Tugging on his hands, she stood on the tips of her toes. "There is something very wrong," she whispered close to his ear.

Stone's gaze locked briefly with Coady's before he released her hands and walked around her. "What do you say, Isobel? Will you come to the hotel?"

Continuing with her work, she said quietly, "I think it is time."

A moment of silence drew into an eternity as Stone waited to see if Isobel would turn and face him. He felt Coady's hand steal into his and he lightly squeezed her fingers. "Would you go to the hotel and see if they have a room to spare, lass?" he said quietly. "I will help Isobel get her things together."

Coady was watching Stone, who had not taken his eyes off Isobel in the past several moments. She could not help but feel her husband knew something she did not. She could also see by Stone's steadfast regard that he was assessing Isobel's behavior. Coady would have to wait until they were alone before she dared question him about whatever he knew.

Stone had managed to get Isobel's attention with his offer of help. She whirled to face him, knowing she could not have him see the bed she had left untouched. "I can manage," she said quickly, even as she admonished herself for leaving the bed in the same condition it had been in the moment Jay Snowden had crawled out of it.

Stone looked down at Coady, squeezing her fingers again as he tried to reassure her he would take excellent care of her friend. "Do you mind checking with the hotel?"

Coady shook her head. "I will be back in a few moments."

Isobel wanted to plead with Coady to stay. Instead, she watched her friend's hurried exit.

"Coady is worried about you," Stone said softly.

Isobel turned her back on him and scrubbed. "What gave you that idea?"

263

"She whispered to me."

"Coady is overly sensitive."

"That spot must be clean by now, Isobel," he said as he walked around the counter to her side. "Would you like to tell me what is wrong?"

"No."

"Why can you not look at me?"

She looked. Briefly.

Stone reached out and placed his hand over hers, stilling Isobel's scrubbing. "I know, Isobel."

It took a moment for the meaning of his comment to sink in. "Oh, God," she moaned silently.

"We have been watching Snowden's activities for weeks. One of my men—"

Isobel moaned again, a near wail as she turned away, leaning heavily against the counter, her eyes closing as if she could shut out the pain of it all.

"Tell me," he said quietly.

Isobel's complexion turned a heated, horrid red. "You are intruding and you are very rude."

"I am your friend. So is Coady. If you have trouble we—"

"I have not got trouble," she shot back. "Your man was wrong. It was Vernon with me last night, if you must know. Not that it is any of your business."

Stone stuffed both hands into his pockets. "I see. So, you are moving to the hotel so Vernon will be more comfortable?"

"No!"

"No?" He gave her a curious look.

"I'm moving there to escape the cold," she said flatly.

"Or for greater protection?" he questioned, not without kindness.

She slanted him an angry look and walked away.

Stone watched her round the far end of the counter and cross the room to stand looking out the large, framed window. He knew she would lie to him until the snow atop the highest mountain peak melted and there was nothing he could do or say to convince her otherwise. She was not seeing him as a friend, she was talking with a Mountie and, whatever threat Snowden had used, Isobel was quite obviously not going to be forthcoming.

At least not with him.

He wondered if Mary and Jay had already bled money from her. Although he doubted that had happened yet. The Snowdens tended to befriend their victims, make them vulnerable in some way and then a day or two later, when they were sure of success, they struck. If he was right, Isobel would hold onto her gold for a day or two. *If* he was right. At this stage, however, he was not as concerned for Isobel's money as he was for Isobel. Snowden was like a wild dog, unpredictable and very dangerous. It worried Stone that the man could possibly be more dangerous than he had proven to be so far. Blackmail, if that was Snowden's game, was one thing. Physically endangering vulnerable women was something else again and it was something over which Stone had been worrying for days. They had one woman missing already and he was *not* going to let Snowden get a second.

But pushing Isobel at this moment was not going to be of benefit. She was clearly disturbed and needed reassurance more than an interrogation from him. He would have her guarded as much as possible and would hope that, when the woman was not as traumatized, she would confide in him. In the meantime, he could only hope to reassure her in some small way.

"As your friend, I have something to ask you," he said as he joined her near the window.

Isobel stood with her arms crossed beneath her breasts, a stance that accentuated her growing belly. She did not acknowledge his approach.

"Are you all right for funds, Isobel?"

She knew he was trying to help. She knew he was her friend. A true friend. Isobel thought she would possibly never again have friends as loving and caring as Coady and Stone. But that did not mean she could confess her shame to either of them. "I have the gold Vernon gave me," she said quietly. And that was *all* she was prepared to say.

Still, as she watched Coady walking along the street on her return journey, Isobel sensed Stone knew more than he was letting on. He certainly knew she had been lying about Vernon spending the night. She did not know precisely how much he knew or thought he knew, but Stone MacGregor, sure as the sun was losing its heat, had not come to take his wife and her friend to lunch. It was some small comfort that a man like Stone Mac-Gregor was so obviously concerned for her. Still, she could not bring herself to confess her folly of the night past. She would, in some manner, find a way to assure Coady and Stone that all was well.

Isobel watched Coady crossing the street. "I do believe I will be more comfortable at the hotel," she said calmly.

"I am quite certain of that. Isobel, if you need . . ."

She turned her head and smiled a wintry smile. "I know who my friends are, Stone. Thank you."

"Just do not forget that."

Isobel nodded her head and returned her gaze to the busy street.

"If I might be permitted to give you one bit of advice?"

There was a frigid pause before she returned a reluctant, "Yes."

"Do not go anywhere alone, Isobel. Please have someone, Coady or myself, or . . . Vernon with you."

Just hearing Vernon's name increased her shame tenfold. But to Stone she said only, "I am not in any danger."

"I will not press you to tell me anything you are not prepared to speak of," he said softly. "But please heed my advice."

"All right."

Stone reached for her hands and pulled her around to face him. "You have no reason to feel shame for the actions of another."

"I shall keep that in mind."

Stone looked quickly toward the street, seeing Coady was only steps away. "They will contact you again," he said hurriedly, his hands squeezing hers. "But you must not be afraid. I will see that you're protected. You must do whatever they ask of you."

"But . . ." She wanted to know how he could be so certain the Snowdens would contact her again. If Jay Snowden had half a brain, he would get his wife out of Dawson before Mary discovered his philandering.

The front door flew open.

"There is a room," Coady said cheerfully. "A few doors along the hall from ours."

Chapter Twenty-two

Stone threw another log on the fire in the sitting room and returned to his large, overstuffed chair. He had bathed and wrapped a towel around his hips easily an hour ago. And now he was waiting, impatiently, for his wife.

They had enlisted Harrison's aid during the afternoon to move Isobel's belongings to the hotel. The large tent had been struck and the bits of furniture she possessed were now stored in Coady's place.

Stone had managed to convince the two women of their need for supper. *He* certainly had needed his supper, but Isobel had eaten little. He worried over that. The woman was nurturing a child; she needed sustenance— they both did. But whatever had happened to Isobel at the hands of Jay Snowden was obviously going to have a long and lasting effect. There had been times during the day when Stone had looked at Isobel's troubled countenance and wished he could take Snowden by the throat and slowly squeeze the life from him. He could not do that, of course. He had devoted a good portion of his adult life to law and order. He reveled in a vision of Snowden suffering at his hands, all the same.

Stone had not had further opportunity to speak with Isobel alone that day. But he had, on the pretense of seeking Harrison out, managed to share a quick conversation with Ben Keystone. He had ordered a street-clothed man to be watching Isobel around the clock. If the Snowdens approached, the officer who happened to be on duty was not to interfere unless he felt Isobel was in jeopardy. It was important Jay Snowden be allowed to complete his scam; only then would they have enough evidence against him to seek a conviction. Stone did not like putting Isobel in the position of having to face the man who had wronged her, but he had little choice. He knew she would be approached again and he knew she would hand over whatever funds she had remaining. He would also see that she was reimbursed for the loss of her gold. If he had to return the funds from his own resources, he would do it.

As to Isobel's suffering over the mysterious nighttime actions of Jay Snowden, Stone was not certain he could help with that. Once Snowden was arrested for a myriad of other wrongs, perhaps the little worm would confess his wrong against Isobel Daniels. But that was doubtful and Stone knew Isobel would not speak of her horror. He was certain, to her way of thinking, if no one knew of the incident, it had not really happened. He also knew the matter would remain in Isobel's thoughts and fester there if no one was able to help her.

He wished he could turn the clock back and save her the anguish of having befriended two of the Yukon's worst.

He was confident, however, that it would all come to a head in the next few days and then perhaps Isobel could put it all behind her and, given time, forget.

The police now had a specialist within their ranks who would easily determine whether the mine up on Twelve-

mile Creek was legitimate. From there, they would seek
out the persons holding share certificates and determine
exactly how each had come to be in possession of the doc-
uments. Stone had little doubt every single holder of a
share would initially be too ashamed to admit his failing.
He could only reassure the victims not to feel bad at all because they had been gulled by two of the very best.

At least Isobel was ensconced in the hotel where she
would be close to Coady and himself. She should feel
safer, having friends nearby. Coady had been helping Isobel get settled ever since they had left the cafe. And that
had been an eternity ago. Or so it seemed. He was hungry
again *and* he was in need of Coady. He was beginning
to think she was like a drug and he was well and truly
addicted—he seemed to have to be with her every moment of every day.

Not that he minded his wife's devotion to her friend
for the evening. He understood. He was certain Coady
would assume he had gone off for the evening by now,
in any event. But he was not going out tonight. He was
determined to spend the entire night with his wife and
duty be damned. He would have to leave her in the morning for a day or two, and being away from her for even
a short time was not something he relished. He did not
even want to think about it. He certainly did not want to
think of spending a cold night, lying on the near-frozen
ground, without Coady snuggled against his body. But
he had this assignment to complete and it was obvious
to all the men involved that they must do so with all
possible haste before Snowden lost his grip on reality
and, in his greed, seriously injured or killed some innocent soul.

He wondered if life for Coady and himself would ever
reflect some sort of normalcy as long as he remained with
the police. He supposed not. But it was a life he loved
and he did not want to give it up. And he would not as
long as Coady could cope with his absences on occasion,
the almost constant danger, and the low pay. He grinned

as he reached for his pipe. It was the wage that irritated her most. About everything else she was, so far, mainly curious.

Curious? Yes.

She had hounded him half the night about the things he had *not* told her about Isobel's trauma and the unscrupulous Mr. Snowden's activities. And he had been honest and forthright, telling her almost as much as he, himself, knew with the exception of one detail. He told her because of her worry for her friend. He told her so that Coady might be wary and protective of Isobel and cautious on her own behalf. He had told her because he loved her and because he could not be with her every moment of every day. He had told her in hopes of keeping her safe and protected from the most sordid and horrid side of Dawson.

He had sent word to Simmons he would not be available for duty tonight. Stone did not want to be interrupted. Coady's love was still new to them and he wanted them both to bask in the glow of her discovery. They would forget everything that had happened during the day, forget everything around them, for this one night.

He had planned carefully for the evening that was left to them. The champagne was cool and the chicken would soon be the same; if Coady did not return soon to their suite, it would be a cold supper for them.

He reached across the small table set for two in front of the warming fire and pinched the flames of the two candles. There was little use letting the things burn to stubs, and staring at the romantic setting, the carefully laid out food and the sparkling glasses awaiting champagne was doing more for his hunger than his libido.

All in all, it was a small statement of his love for her and little enough at that. Stone felt Coady would appreciate his efforts, however. It was the small things in life that seemed to bring her the greatest pleasure. Not for her the airs of women who preferred to live an exorbitant high life. Coady might like to experience the finest res-

Jill Metcalf

taurants but he doubted she would care to make such places a steady part of her life. Besides, in Dawson City, Harrison's cafe was the finest.

She was more at home in her plain skirts and shirt-waists than she would ever be in silks and diamonds. He suspected she would enjoy a more current wardrobe but she was too cautious with a dollar to allow him to buy her more than an ensemble or two.

The suite door opened just as Stone was taking a sip of brandy.

Coady saw him right off and her surprise was obvious. "I thought you would be gone."

He shook his head and put the brandy snifter on the table near his elbow. "Not tonight."

She closed the door. "Does that mean I have you to myself for the evening?"

"Lock it."

She grinned and then she laughed softly as she did as he requested. "I assume that means *yes*?"

"I wasn't thinking only of our safety," he said, smiling as she slowly approached. "I like privacy when I make love to my woman."

Her gaze roamed his near-naked body appreciatively. "What a nice welcome, darling," she drawled.

He threw back his head and laughed.

Coady smiled happily as she planted herself on his lap and wrapped her arms around his neck. She was particularly happy he was staying home tonight. She needed him.

Stone put his arms around her and held her tight. "Are you all right?" he asked softly.

She nodded her head. "I wish I knew what was wrong. I wish I could help her."

Stone understood completely. "You are helping just by being her friend."

Coady pulled back until she could see his face. "I wish she would talk about it."

"Perhaps she cannot, love," he said softly. "In her

272

own way, in her own time, perhaps she will be able to speak of it.''

Stone touched her cheek. "Is she settled?"

"Everything is in order. I think she will be comfortable there."

"She is only a few steps away from us if she needs us," he pointed out. "Now, as much as I am concerned for Isobel, there is nothing more we can do tonight."

Coady sighed. "I know."

"Could I borrow your attention for a short while then?"

She looked into his eyes, saw the suggestion of passion which had, unbeknownst to her, risen a degree or two the moment she entered the room. "What sort of attention did you have in mind, sir?"

"This," he growled as he swept her back over his arm and kissed her thoroughly.

"Goodness," she breathed, when Stone raised his head a moment later.

"Thank you," he said, as he completed the task of freeing her breasts with one hand while supporting her back with the other.

She had not been aware of his fingers unfastening her buttons. "You are amazing."

"Thank you, again."

She laughed softly as he lowered his head toward her naked breast. "And humble, too," she murmured. But then all thoughts of talk vanished from her head and Coady was breathing in, gasping as his tongue worked magic around a nipple that had grown taut with need. "I think I must be rid of my corset, Stone," she whispered.

"I think so, too," he breathed.

He followed her up when she stood, leaving his towel behind on the chair and not caring. "Let me," he said, even as he pushed her blouse over her shoulders and down her arms.

Coady managed to unfasten the buttons of her skirt while Stone attacked the strings of her corset.

"We are learning to work faster at this," he quipped. She giggled.

"You really do not need this damned thing, lass," he muttered, struggling with a lace. "Why not give it up?"

"And walk around half naked? Definitely not."

When she was as naked as he, Stone hefted their small dinner table out of the way, snatched a small pillow from the sofa and threw it to the floor in front of the fire. "Lord, I need you," he said, as he lowered her to the floor.

Coady had thought his possession of her would be swift and urgent but Stone surprised her. This was to be a leisurely loving.

He brought the small bit of brandy remaining and stretched out on his side beside her. The fire warmed them, the dancing yellow light caressed her skin as he held the glass for her to drink. This surprised her, too. He seldom offered her spirits.

"It will ease the tensions of the day," he said softly.

"*You* will ease the tensions of the day," she murmured.

He stared into her eyes, even as he set the glass out of harm's way on the hearth. "Is that what I do?"

She nodded. "And more. I know I am fortunate to have you."

Stone touched her cheek, lovingly stroking her soft skin with the tips of his fingers. "I could turn that about, lass. I, too, am fortunate."

"It is strange how fate brings lovers together."

"Aye," he breathed as he lowered his head and approached her waiting lips.

Coady tipped her head back, savoring the warmth, the moistness of his lips on hers. He could make her tingle clear to her toes with just such a kiss. He made her anxious to be pressed against him, to be possessed by him. She opened her mouth the instant his tongue probed between her lips. Moaning softly, in a way that bespoke growing passion. "Oh, Stone," she breathed, when he tore his lips away.

He devoted his kisses to the soft skin beneath her chin as his hand caressed first one breast and then the other. He circled a taut nipple as his lips moved further down her throat. He raised his head and looked at the breast he cupped in the palm of his hand. "I do love these," he murmured.

"That is good," she said breathlessly. "They are all I have to offer."

He grinned at her then, turning his head to look into her eyes for just a moment. "You are so very wrong, my love," he whispered. "You have much more to offer." His head lowered and he took her nipple between his lips, suckling, drawing the passion from within her.

"Please."

He shook his head as he transferred his attentions to the other breast.

"Do not make me wait," she growled.

He smiled against the warmth of her flesh as his hand caressed along her hip and further. He raised his head and watched her as his fingers caressed that part of her so in need. He knew her well when it came to this by now. Slender fingers caressed the hair on his chest, while her other hand stroked up and down his side. "Touch me," he said.

Coady's hand roamed down over his ribs, his flat belly, until she could wrap her fingers around his heated flesh. She ran the tips of her fingers along its length and absently caressed the tip with her thumb as she became aware of what his own fingers were doing. A tiny, warning pulse had her arching toward his hand, pressing her hot, aching core against his fingers in an attempt to ease the glorious agony which he had brought her.

"All right," he breathed. "All right," he said again as he positioned himself between her legs.

Coady watched him draw near. Through narrowed eyes, with parted lips, she begged him to come to her.

Stone pressed forward, inched forward into her welcoming heat. His breathing was harsh as he looked down at her, locking his elbows as he remained above her, giving her freedom to . . . "Move."

Coady placed her hands on his ribs and rotated her hips against his. Stone had taught her well. He understood the meaning of this particular freedom for her. He would keep his weight free, until the very moment he knew she needed him. And then he would wrap his arms around her.

"It's—"

"Yes," he breathed.

Her head tipped back, her eyes closed and her lips parted on a series of ragged sighs.

He pulled her against his chest with one arm, supporting their weight with the other as Coady's body rocked against him. She clung to him, groaning with the force of her climax. The same instant he lowered her back to the floor, Stone began to move within her. Stroking slowly in and out a time or two until the first shuddering of his large body forced him to press deep inside her.

Coady held him against her, taking all of his weight and gladly. It seemed to go on forever, the spasms, the deep moans of release. And all the while she rejoiced in the life he was sharing with her, deep within her.

Stone remained still over her, pressing his face into the softness of her hair as he fought for breath. He wondered if he would ever stop lusting after her. He doubted it. Just one look at Coady, just the thought of her, prompted a reaction the likes of which he had never known with any other woman.

"I think this is it," she whispered after a moment.

He did not have the strength to raise his head. He barely had the breath needed to speak. "What is it?"

"I think you just gave me your son."

He grinned against her hair. "You think so, do you?"

Coady moved her head, her eyes remaining closed as

her other senses gloried in the feel, the warmth, the scent of him.

"Is it so important it happen quickly?" He eased back, withdrawing from her slowly, and rolled onto his side, propping his head on one hand so he could look at her.

Coady opened her eyes and looked up at him. "I will be happy whenever it happens."

"Me, too, love," he said softly as he rested his arm across her middle. "It will mean I shall have to share you, though. I will need some time to prepare myself for that."

She grinned. "You will have nine months."

He studied her expression for a long moment. "Are you trying to tell me something?"

Coady shook her head. "I am ashamed to admit to you that I am not sure."

Stone took his thoughts back in time. "Now that I think about it," he murmured thoughtfully, "you have not had to turn me away."

Coady continued to look puzzled for a moment but, when she caught his meaning, her large brown eyes took on a brighter hue.

"Perhaps because you were so ill," he speculated. "Perhaps such terrible sickness could cause a delay in your monthly."

She wrinkled her nose. "I would rather think the other."

He smiled. "A bit too soon to tell, I should think, lass. If it is true, we'll know soon enough."

Not soon enough for her. "Will you be happy?"

He nodded his head and squeezed her shoulder. "I will. It is about time I had daughters."

"Sons."

"Perhaps some of each. Before I am too old to bounce them on my knee."

"You are hardly ancient. At twenty-eight you have *some* time left, you know."

"Ho!" He rolled half on top of her, pinning her lightly

with a portion of his weight. "How many children would you like?"

"As many as you are willing to give."

He grinned broadly. "That should not be a problem. The other would be a problem."

She frowned.

"With you I do not seem to have the control needed to *not* give you a child."

"Does that mean you have not fathered children by any other woman?"

His brows arched severely. "That was not my meaning, exactly, but, to answer your question, I have not fathered any children."

She squirmed beneath him, teasing, feeling him grow hot and hard against her hip. "What *exactly* was your meaning?"

A devilish twinkle appeared in his eye. "I think you know."

She giggled. "I think we are both insatiable."

Stone lowered his head, whispering against her cheek at the same time his hand found and captured her breast. "Do you want me again, lass?"

Coady wrapped her arms around him. "I want you always," she breathed.

He carried her to their bed where they made love yet again. And, after they had slept for a time, Stone woke her gently.

Coady moved against him, curling into his warmth like a contented kitten that seeks the heat of the sun in which to nap.

"I have something to tell you," Stone said softly.

Coady refused to open her eyes. "Could we talk in the morning?" she murmured.

Stone propped pillows against the bedstead and pulled himself up, settling back against the softness. "I have to leave before first light."

Her eyes flew open. "Leave?" Coady raised her head from his shoulder. "Leave where? This bed?"

"Town."

She frowned, now fully awake. "Why are you leaving town?"

"I am taking some men along Twelvemile Creek," he said.

Coady pulled herself up and turned to face him. "Snowden's camp?"

He nodded his head. "I will only be gone a day or two."

He might as well have said a year or two.

"I will come with you."

He smiled, briefly touching her cheek. "Not this time, lass."

"I want to be where you are."

"It could be dangerous," he said low.

"All the more reason for me to come," she insisted. "Who else is going to look after you? Certainly not a handful of policemen."

"They are very good at what they do." His smile grew sympathetic. "I do love, you, Coady."

"Good. Then it is settled," she said easily, dropping down to rest her head on his chest. "I will get dressed in just a moment."

"You cannot come with me, love. This is duty."

She pushed herself into a sitting position, facing him. "I really do not care about *duty*," she said impatiently. "How do I sit here waiting patiently when I know you are going to be doing something dangerous? I would rather be with you."

He reached for her and tucked her under his arm. "It is that burning curiosity of yours."

"It is my love for you."

"I know that. And it is because of your love that I will be particularly cautious. I now have a very special reason to come home."

"And you had better come home in one piece," she muttered, "or I will never forgive you."

He laughed and nodded his head. "Promise me you

will take care of yourself and Isobel,'' he added when he sobered. "If Mary Snowden comes around—"

"I shall make an excuse and get Isobel away from here. I can protect myself, Stone. I managed quite nicely for years."

"I know," he said tenderly. "But now you have me."

"Not all of you," she said quietly. "The citizens of the Yukon have a goodly portion, too." So saying, she slipped from the bed and went to the clothes press. Reaching for her warm robe she struggled into the thing, thwarting her own efforts as her agitated movements twisted one sleeve before she could get her arm into it.

"You are jealous," he said in wonder. He rose from the bed, going to her, wanting to help, but Coady mastered the tricky garment before he could touch her.

Coady stood and looked at him, staring into the beautiful blue depths of his eyes for a long moment. Then she sighed, a sign of resignation. "I am not jealous. I worry for you. I simply wish your chosen profession had more to do with something harmless."

"I could give up my gun and pick up knitting needles," he quipped.

She slanted him a sly grin. "There is an idea. We could make a fortune—MacGregor Fashions."

He laughed again. "Goose!"

The room was cold, the late October chill having permeated the wooden exterior of the hotel. Stone walked into the sitting room and dropped onto his heels near the hearth. As he began feeding logs to the small, blackened cavity of the fireplace, he watched her move slowly toward the settee. "I will miss you," he said, giving only half his attention to his task. "Always before, I went off wherever I was assigned with no thought to anyone. I looked upon each task merely as a new adventure. Now, all that has changed." Once he set the flame of a match to the kindling and watched the small sticks of wood catch, he stood, turning to face her.

Coady stared at the small, dancing flame. "Will you

put something on?'' she questioned softly. "I find your nakedness distracts me from my worry."

Stone bit a corner of his lower lip in order to curb a smile. "Yes, love."

He disappeared from her view as Coady continued to stare at the flames of the fire. She had not considered this side of their marriage. It was difficult thinking of him being out of her sight for long. It was worrisome that he was riding off into admitted danger and she would have no clue as to what was going on. She had not thought about becoming a patient little wife, sitting home waiting for her man. But then she had not thought about being so ferociously in love. She wondered how other women managed such a gut-wrenching thing. It seemed it was women's lot to watch their men march off to war, to battle, to danger. Now that Coady knew how that felt, she did not like it.

Stone returned clad in a long velvet robe and sat beside her, taking her hand in his and carrying it to his lap.

Now they were both staring at the fire.

"I do not think I will ever become used to this, Stone," she whispered.

"I suppose if you do," he murmured, "it will mean you have given up caring about me."

"I hate your being rational when I'm not."

He grinned but did not flash his smile her way. "I'm sorry."

"I do not want you to go but I know you must."

"I do not want to go, but I must."

"I feel as if I am making a sacrifice," she muttered. "Damn."

Her whispered expletive caused him to look at her and, to his dismay, he saw tears in her eyes. "Ah." He pulled her across the small distance between them and tucked her beneath his arm. "Not tears, Coady."

"I have not cried since I was a child except with you to see my foolishness." *Twice,* she added, angry with herself. "Two days will be a very long time."

"For me, too."

She tipped her face up to look into his eyes. "I did not know loving could be so painful."

Stone pulled her onto his lap. "But it is also so very sweet, my love."

Chapter Twenty-three

Coady knocked on Isobel's door at seven that morning. Stone had left a little over an hour before and already she was lonely.

With the first sound of knuckles touching wood, Isobel awoke with a start. Shaking her head a bit, she rolled awkwardly from the bed. "Who's there?" she called through the thick wood of the closed portal.

"It's Coady, Isobel."

Isobel's momentary fear abated and she turned the large brass key in the lock. Pulling the door open just a little, she peeked through the opening and blinked sleepily. "You are early."

Coady grinned. "You are late. Once we start baking bread we will have to be at the bakery long before now. And I am starving," she said, as the door opened wider and she stepped inside. "I came to see if you would like to have breakfast with me at the cafe."

Standing in the middle of the small bedroom, Isobel swept her long, blonde curls back over her shoulders. "I am not fully awake yet, Coady. I cannot think of food."

Coady nodded her head and proceeded to sit on the straight-backed chair near the window. "All right. I will give you ten minutes."

Isobel eyed her curiously. "Where is that husband of yours? Why are you not having breakfast with him?"

Coady sighed. "Stone has gone."

Her friend appeared so dejected Isobel became alarmed. "Gone? Gone where? He has not left you?"

"He has for a couple of days."

"Oh," said Isobel, relieved her near panic had been misplaced. "Well, I suspect you will survive a couple of days."

"I am not so certain." Coady watched the other woman sorting through the clothes press and was instantly sorry she had acted with child-like petulance. Isobel was surviving and she had been without Vernon for a period of close to three months. She thought she understood now just how lonely Isobel must be without him. A woman could intertwine her very existence around a man in a very short time. She and Stone had been wed less than two months but Coady suddenly understood how very important he had become to her. She hated facing a day without him in it. She equated Stone's absence to walking down the street and suddenly finding her shadow was missing. How could she survive without her *whole* self intact? The thought made her realize how very different her love for Stone was from anything else she had ever known. Different from the love she had felt for her mother. Stronger and more binding than the love she felt for Harrison. This love for Stone was an awesome thing, a power all its own. A power so overwhelming it almost made her afraid; afraid of losing him.

Afraid of ever losing his love.

But as she watched Isobel select a dark blue skirt and paler blue blouse, Coady realized women survived beyond the loss of their men. Isobel had. She could, too, if it ever happened. Still, the very thought made her cringe.

She decided in the next breath that she should stop feeling sorry for herself, stop advertising how much she hated being without Stone even for a short time and have a care for *Isobel's* aloneness and her recent horror. While she had promised Stone she would not reveal her knowledge of the incident, that did not mean she could not encourage Isobel to talk. "How are you feeling today?"

Isobel was searching through the small chest of drawers, trying to locate her recently unpacked underthings. "I feel all right," she said absently.

Coady frowned. "You were so upset yesterday . . . what on earth is that?"

Somewhat shyly, Isobel turned and faced her friend. "I had to give up wearing corsets weeks ago, so I fashioned this." She held up the modified corset that resembled a breast-band with suspenders more than long stays that could be tightly cinched. She could not get a corset to reach around her expanding middle, but her breasts were heavy and needed support. Her problem had been solved by simply cutting a full-length garment and sewing a length of soft cloth along the cut edge to provide comfort for the tender skin beneath her breasts. "It, ah, serves the purpose."

Coady grinned. "Well, aren't you the clever pup."

Having Coady take her thoughts away from horrid memories of Jay Snowden and her unproductive attempts at remembering all that had happened that night with him gave Isobel's spirits a boost. Reaching into the garment drawer she extracted a second modified garment. Coady giggled when she saw Isobel's *combination;* the one-piece version of a chemise and drawers combined now bore a panel of additional material in front that allowed for a rounded belly. "One must be resourceful."

"I am taking notes," Coady said teasingly. "But my sewing experience has been sadly lacking. Fashioning frilly garters does not a seamstress make. Perhaps when I'm in similar straits you would help me?"

"Of course. You just tell me when."

Coady nodded her head.

"Will it be soon, do you think?"

"Sly woman," Coady murmured. "It is a bit soon to tell."

"You will know." Isobel went about the business of making herself presentable to the outside world. "Where has Stone gone?"

Coady's high spirits dissolved instantly. She considered lying but saw no purpose that would serve. If Isobel should hear differently from anyone about town, their friendship could suffer. "He has gone out along Twelvemile Creek."

Isobel dropped a petticoat over her head and let it fall the length of her body. Her eyes, when she looked at Coady, were cold. "I do not care to know of his whereabouts, after all."

"He and several men have gone there, Isobel, in an attempt to uncover Snowden's activities and put him in jail. You might possibly help them get the man off the street."

"I know nothing that would be of help," she uttered angrily as she reached for her skirt.

Coady sighed. "I know you must know something about him, Isobel. Stone—"

Isobel rounded on her friend. "I particularly dislike people talking about me," she raged. "My business is none of yours."

"Oh, yes it is," Coady said softly, her sympathetic gaze defying Isobel's anger. "We love you. When something or someone causes you hurt or harm, it becomes very much our business."

Isobel dropped down onto the side of her bed, sighing heavily. "No one can help me this time," she whispered brokenly. "I think I have been master of my own demise. The difficulty is, I am not sure."

Coady sat beside the older woman and placed a reassuring arm around Isobel's shoulders. "Why are you not sure?"

Isobel covered her face with her hands. "I cannot remember!" she cried. "I do not remember why Jay Snowden was in my bed, let alone what took place there!"

Coady felt as if her own blood had drained away on the spot. "Oh, my God," she breathed. Stone had not told her that.

"He was there!" Isobel wailed. "I woke up in the morning and that . . . man was there!" Then she simply folded against her friend.

Coady wrapped her arms around the sobbing woman and held tight. "It was a trick, Isobel. It must have been a trick. You would never—"

"But why?"

"Please do not cry so. It is not good."

"I will never be able to face you again. I will never be able to face anyone again," she said and then abruptly hiccuped.

"You will face me because you know I care about you. You would not have confided in me otherwise. And you will face anyone and everyone because you have done nothing wrong."

"Then why do I feel this terrible shame?"

"That will be gone once Stone discovers exactly what Snowden is all about."

Isobel's tears ceased as a new terror invaded her being. "You will not tell anyone."

Coady shook her head. "But if you tell the police everything, the knowledge will help them put that skunk in jail for a longer period of time."

Isobel opened her mouth to protest but thought better of offering a rebuttal. "I believe Stone must know anyway," she sighed wearily. "I told Stone it had been Vernon in my tent that night but I suspect he did not believe me." She then retold the conversation she had had with her friend's husband in the bakery the previous morning. "I know I did not invite the man to . . . stay with me," she added. "But what possible reason would he have for being there?"

Coady grimaced. "Several distasteful possibilities come to mind," she muttered. "But you are not to worry. Stone will look after that weasel and I am certain nothing happened between you two. You would know, Isobel. You would know even if you cannot remember."

Isobel was not convinced of that but she did feel somewhat better for having shared her horror with a friend who was so understanding. "I am sorry I cried," she whispered. "I am just living in horror that the gossips will get hold of this and . . ."

Coady waited a long moment and then prompted, "And?"

"And Vernon will find out."

"Perhaps you should explain to Vernon yourself and then he will know the truth before the gossips twist it out of recognition."

Isobel rose, shaking her head as she walked to the single window. "I could never talk to him about this."

Coady suspected the opposite would be true if Isobel but had the chance. "We will see," she said and popped up from the bed. "Now, are you awake enough to think about food?"

Isobel turned from the window and smiled as she reached for her cloak. "Perhaps."

Coady returned the smile as she walked toward the door. "Come on."

They entered the Dawson Cafe moments later and chose a table close to the rear. Coady sat opposite Isobel, with a view of the entrance.

They had only just taken their seats when Coady noticed a tall, slender man entering the crowded room. He sat a few tables away. He was not a man of memorable note but he had a pleasant face and keen dark eyes. She dismissed him summarily as being no one she had previously met.

She was watching for Harrison, actually. As the women discussed the progression of the bake shop and planned for opening day, they devised an additional list of items to be purchased for which they wanted his agreement.

By the time their food arrived, Coady had taken note of the number of times the dark-eyed man had focused his attention on Isobel. "Do not turn around," she said softly as she directed her attention to cutting a small wedge of fried egg. "I think you have an admirer."

Isobel blinked, her blue eyes reflecting surprise. "What?"

"I think you have an admirer," Coady whispered again. "There is a man over there, behind you, and he keeps looking at you."

Isobel was panic stricken and flustered all at once. "He no doubt thinks I'm someone else."

"Now, why would you say that?"

Isobel detected a note of displeasure in her friend's tone. "Because I'm a pregnant lady. What man could take an interest in—?"

"You are a beautiful woman," Coady said sternly. "Why would he not look?"

Isobel attacked her egg with fury. "It does not matter."

"It *does* matter," Coady insisted. She cut another section of egg, popped it into her mouth and stole another look at the man. This time their gazes collided and locked for an instant. Coady then hurriedly looked away. "For heaven's sake," she muttered.

"Pardon?"

"Nothing," she returned absently. But she was more than curious now. The stranger seemed to be taking too much of an interest in Isobel. "Isobel," she whispered, "do not panic but can you describe the weasel for me?"

Isobel looked up from her plate and frowned. "Why?"

Coady's expression remained as innocent as she could possibly manage. "I think perhaps that is he."

"Oh, lord," she breathed but gave as good a description as she could manage under the circumstances.

Jill Metcalf

"That is the *skunk*," Coady muttered.

"I wish to leave."

"You are safer here." Coady said hurriedly. "And as long as I am with you, he would not dare approach."

Isobel dropped her knife and fork on her plate and her hands into her lap. "I am not as certain as you are about that. He is a very determined man."

"He is a skunk and you know they only prowl at night."

"I just do not understand what he wants with me."

"Your gold is one good possibility."

"Lord, I think I am going to be ill."

"No!" she ordered in a hushed but severe tone. "Do not dare to let him see your fear."

"I suppose you would not be afraid, in my place?" Isobel snapped.

"Terrified."

Isobel was somewhat stunned by the blunt confession and, after a moment of staring at her forthright young friend she began to laugh.

Coady grinned. "That is better."

The two women continued with their meal although both had lost their appetites.

"What is he doing?" Isobel asked after a time.

"He consumed his food in an immoderate rush." She smiled sweetly as she muttered, "Perhaps he will grow gaseous and turn up cold as a wagon tire."

Isobel smiled at the jest but her voice betrayed her anxiety. "I simply wish he would leave."

Coady reached for her coffee cup. "You have your wish, my friend. He is standing."

"If he comes over here, I will—"

"There is nothing to fear," she whispered. "One of Stone's men is within earshot. He told me there would be someone close to you at all times until this is over."

Instead of feeling relieved, Isobel felt the weight of having to have someone shadow her every move. "I wish it were over now."

"Soon. A day or two, perhaps." Even as she spoke the words, Coady was stunned to see Jay Snowden look directly at her, smile and nod a greeting. "He *is* a brazen one."

"What is he doing?"

"Leaving."

Isobel sank back in her chair. "Thank the good Lord," she breathed.

After a half hour had passed and the two women had indulged in a second cup of coffee, they managed to put the distasteful incident behind them. Snowden, after all, had not made a single move to draw Isobel's attention. And it was a comfort knowing one of Stone's men could be found nearby.

Their consultation with Harrison complete, Isobel and Coady turned their attention to the newest project in Dawson: the bakery. The work helped distract them from other distasteful thoughts.

Having arranged for the delivery of flour, sugar, salt and a myriad of other necessities, they walked to the new building.

"Have you given any thought to inviting Vernon back?" Coady asked conversationally as she unlocked the bakery's front door.

"*Invite him back?*" Isobel muttered, following her friend inside. "I think you have forgotten that it was he who asked me to leave."

"If you were prepared to fight for him—"

"I am not about to lower myself and go begging a man who doesn't want me," Isobel said sternly. "What sort of woman do you think I am? I am making a life for myself and I will make a life for this baby, too. I do not need a man."

"But you love him."

There had been a great deal of caring in Coady's hushed tone that effectively smothered a greater portion of Isobel's anger. She sighed. "One does not simply fall out of love,'' she said softly. ''But it is hopeless, Coady. Do not dwell on it, please. Vernon does not care about me and he never will.''

Coady knew Stone would disagree with her interference but she simply could not let Isobel's statement go by without being challenged. Besides, today of all days, Isobel needed to hear something positive. ''Vernon cares.''

The simple statement was so matter-of-fact, Isobel became curious. ''How would you know?''

''I have talked with him,'' she said easily as she hung their cloaks on a wall peg. ''He has come to Dawson a few times, Isobel. He comes to see that you are all right. Those are not the actions of a man who does not care.''

''If he has come here, why have I not seen him?'' she asked shortly.

Coady smiled a sad smile. ''He skulks about in alleys.''

Isobel faced her friend, her mouth drawn in a severe line. ''Is this some sort of game you are playing?''

''I would not play at something as serious as this.''

Coady saw again the same raw pain mirrored in Isobel's eyes as she had seen that day down on the Bonanza when Vernon had cruelly rejected her out of hand. No woman deserved to suffer such anguish and Vernon, had he been near, would have received a good kick with the toe of Coady's shoe. It was not the first time she had felt that way either; Coady had come close to trying to knock some sense into Vernon the first day she had met him. But a display of anger would not bring together what had been broken apart.

That did not mean she was prepared to give up altogether, however.

''Perhaps you would like to—'' Coady's sentence was abruptly interrupted as she approached the bakery counter and was rudely yanked behind the thing.

Before Isobel could scream, Jay Snowden hauled Coady's back against his chest and brandished a barbarous knife, pressing the blade against her slender throat. "Not one sound," he growled. "From either of you."

Coady strained, pressing her head back against his shoulder in an attempt to put some distance between her windpipe and the knife. "We have no gold."

"I could dispute that, *Mrs.* MacGregor, but I do not have the time. I am not interested in gold at the moment."

"If it is me you want," Isobel put in hurriedly, "let her go. I will come with you."

He graced her with a menacing smile. "Alas, my plans have changed, dear Isobel. I no longer have an interest in you either."

"There is a man—"

He pressed the blade against her flesh to effectively cut of Coady's remaining words. "The policeman? That fool remains so far back in the shadows he must think he is to be hiding from the very persons he is supposed to be guarding."

Coady felt her heart turn in her chest. "You seem to know a—"

"A lot? I do ma'am. Yes indeed, I do. I know, for example, that your husband is on his way to my claim, as we speak."

"No. He is—"

"Do not bother to deny it. I have my means of gaining information that is vital. And, just so you know, *Mrs.* MacGregor, the moment the good inspector arrives there, you will become a widow."

Coady let her legs sag and attempted to direct her elbow into the man's gut in the same instant. Snowden, however, was stronger than he looked and tightened his arm abruptly around her middle, forcing the air from her lungs in a whoosh. "If you try anything like that again, I will kill your friend while you watch!" he hissed.

Coady's mind searched frantically for a means of escape, a means of getting away from this monster so that she might warn Stone he was riding into a trap. But she

could not risk Isobel being harmed. And Snowden was
agitated enough to kill, she did not doubt that. She could
feel the frantic pounding of his heart against her back.
"What is it you want?" she asked, in feigned defeat.

He grinned as he looked across the short distance to
where Isobel stood trying desperately to control her shaking. "I could say it is your friend, my dear, but I have
had her. And, due to circumstances beyond my control,
my need of her is not what it once was. No, it is yourself
for whom I have need, *Mrs.* MacGregor."

"You will not like me," she returned fiercely. "I
promise you."

Snowden laughed.

But Isobel's attention was surreptitiously drawn to the
wall behind Snowden. The wall separated the actual bakery from the storefront and in its center was a swinging
door. That door had just moved a small bit. She could
not see who might be back there, but Isobel quickly determined it would be wise to keep Jay Snowden distracted. "How did you get in here, Mr. Snowden?" she
asked conversationally. "The door was locked when we
arrived."

"Let us just say, dear Isobel, that the back of the bakery is somewhat damaged."

"It is amazing you did not draw attention," she said
with a calmness she was not feeling. "There must have
been a good deal of noise if you caused . . . damage, as
you say."

"When miners are celebrating in the streets at night,
there is little that can be heard over the din. Now, enough
chat," he added angrily.

These were Snowden's last words as Vernon Shield
jumped on him from behind, solidly grabbing the knife
hand that had never wavered from Coady's throat.

The two men went down and Coady skittered away.

Isobel squealed and rushed forward.

Coady pushed her back to safety. "Not now!"

The struggle between the two men in the cramped area

was short lived as the knife twisted in Vernon's hand and was pressed between his ribs by Snowden's surprising strength.

"Fool!" he growled as he pushed himself to his feet.

Isobel did scream then, loud and long.

Snowden whirled and jumped, catching Coady's wrist. "Shut up!" He shouted to the room at large.

Coady placekicked a well-aimed booted toe against his shin but he did little more than grunt before slamming her back against the wall.

Vernon lay on the floor, dazed and clutching the handle of the knife that was buried in the side of his chest.

Snowden placed the palm of his hand between Coady's breasts and pushed, effectively pinning her to the wall. Then he bent to the side, gripped the handle of his knife, and pulled it free.

Vernon groaned.

Isobel forgot everything else and rushed to the other end of the serving counter, scurried behind it, and knelt at Vernon's side.

Snowden was busy trying to keep a squirming woman in place. "Stop!" he ordered and gripped her arm. "You are coming with me."

"No!" Coady attempted to throw her weight backward but Snowden was the stronger.

"You are going to get me on a ship," he grunted, pulling her toward the swinging door. "No greenhorn policeman would dare harm the wife of a superior officer."

The last of Snowden's words were lost on the couple who remained in the storefront as the swinging door closed. Vernon attempted to rise but Isobel pushed him back. "No."

"Someone has to help her,"

Isobel got hurriedly to her feet, awkwardly rushing out onto the street. "Help!" she screamed. "Someone, help!"

Chapter Twenty-four

The temperature dropped to a chilly eighteen degrees that night.

Stone missed the warmth of Coady lying next to him.

"Go to sleep," Ben grumbled from the far side of the fire.

Stone grunted as he turned over again in his bedroll. "I could be snuggled up with my pretty little wife," he returned shortly, "instead of lying out here in the cold."

"When duty calls, sir," Ben said wryly, "we must obey."

Stone muttered a rude expletive and rolled onto his back to stare at the stars. "At least it isn't snowing yet." It would not be long before the hills and valleys, like the mountains which surrounded them, would be covered with white. "I want to head up to Forty Mile tomorrow," he told Ben.

Ben knew why. He had been expecting the order.

They had found little at the site of Jay Snowden's so-called gold camp on Twelvemile Creek. With the exception of empty tents—Coady's tents, of course—filled with all the necessaries working men would need. There were no men in sight, however, and less evidence the mine contained much more than pyrite—fool's gold. A cook tent had been outfitted with pots and pans but there was no food in sight. It seemed an elaborate ruse, an expensive proposition that had not made sense to Ben at first. And then they literally stumbled across on old man who thought it the joke of the century he had been hired to guard the camp and paid additional gold on occasion to play a role as Snowden's cook. "Everybody knows if I were to undertake boilin' water I'd drown in the stuff!" he had hooted.

The old man had been good enough at telling tales; tall ones, perhaps, but Stone suspected there were enough facts intermingled with the fallacies to warrant going north along the Yukon River to Forty Mile and possibly beyond that to Fort Constantine.

According to the old-timer, Snowden would hire men by the day to work in the mine. A few found conveniently positioned nuggets about the time Jay was leading a tour of the place for prospective investors. He paid the men well, knowing generous sums would leave them with hopes of earning more of the same another day. This way he could ensure their silence for at least a short time. Long enough to reap monumental rewards. If the old man had been right in his headcount of over two hundred potential investors having toured the place, Stone reckoned Snowden could have realized something close to one million dollars from the scheme. Jay had been smart enough to invite only five or six men to visit the mine at any time, thereby pleading a need for large sums from them in order to get the camp running to maximum potential. By the time the smooth-talking Snowden finished his pitch, the invitees were starry-eyed with visions of large quantities of gold being unearthed.

Ben had already spoken with two men who had invested five thousand dollars and were mightily proud of the share certificates Snowden had signed over to each of them.

Jay Snowden was no small-time operator.

He was also desperate enough and sinister enough to kill, or have killed, whoever got in his way.

It was the old miner who had saved them.

Stone and Ben had walked out of the cook tent and stared right into the bore of a Colt Lightning Magazine Rifle.

"Ain't your lucky day," said the grinning gunman.

"T'ain't yours neither," said the old man as he let off a double-barreled shotgun. The old man spit a stream of tobacco juice on the ground as he ensured the gunman was not going to get up. "Don't know about you fellas, but I hate when they plays dirty." With that he turned on a heel and walked back into the tent.

The two policemen stood stunned for several moments.

"Well, he's a piece of work," Ben muttered.

"I would call him a damned good friend." Stone moved to the side of the dead man and, kneeling, began searching pockets. But his efforts bore no fruit. "No identification."

"Do we really care who he was?" Ben asked sardonically.

"Someone may. Have the men haul him back to Dawson. Perhaps someone there will recognize him. You stay with me."

Stone's last two orders before he and Ben left Snowden's claim were to make arrangements for someone to come out and pick up Coady's tents and to notify his wife he would be gone a little longer than he expected.

Forty Mile was not what it used to be.

Located on the border of Alaska and the Yukon Territory, Forty Mile had been as lively a spot as gold and corruption could induce. Whiskey men made a financial killing as illegal booze wormed its way into the heart of the mining community, eventually causing its near destruction.

When the first Royal Northwest Mounted Police arrived in Forty Mile, in early August 1894, the post was already being deserted by decent men who chose to winter elsewhere. Eventually these same men took up claims in other parts of the territory while those who chose to remain simply avoided the saloons of Forty Mile.

But there would always be men to frequent the saloons and the efforts of the Mounties to eliminate the sale of illegal whiskey and bring discipline to the post, met with considerable resistance from the miners. Twenty policemen were enlisted to accomplish the task.

Stone MacGregor and Ben Keystone avoided any contact with members of the uniformed detachment at Forty Mile. For what they had in mind, anonymity and a little drunkenness would serve their purpose far better than law and order.

The saloon was as seedy as any the men had ever patronized.

"Good selection of prime candidates here," Ben drawled.

Stone nodded his head as his gaze roamed the room. "What say we get a table gathered for poker?"

Ben cringed. He hated losing money. Particularly since it would be his. He reluctantly eased himself from his chair. "I'll spread the word."

Stone watched him go. He had already planned his opening remarks, designed to get the conversation aimed in the direction of Jay Snowden's activities. Whoever decided to join their game would talk eventually. If the selected men had never come in contact with Snowden, they no doubt would know of someone who had. Mining towns were like that; everyone knew everyone else's business.

Stone's thoughts turned toward Coady, as they did during every quiet moment he had. He missed her. Amazing how a man could soften so quickly. Taking away his creature comforts, of which he considered Coady the apex, was like a wound to his heart. Being surrounded by men as he was meant nothing. He was lonely without her. He wondered what his sweet little wife was doing at that moment.

Working herself to near exhaustion to get the damned bakery ready for opening, he supposed.

Snowden squeezed Coady's upper arm so fiercely her fingers were beginning to feel numb.

"I fail to see how you think I can help get you on a ship," she puffed as he half pulled, half pushed her toward the docks.

"Oh I have the means to get on the ship," he snapped, "I just don't want to get shot while I am about it."

"The police will not allow you to leave," she assured him.

He grinned wickedly as they neared the Aurora docks. "Ah, but they will have to go through you to get me, *Mrs.* MacGregor. And I do not think that will happen. The police in town will not know of MacGregor's demise. But they damned well know your loving husband, the inspector, would have the hide of any policeman foolish enough to allow you to be hurt."

Snowden pulled Coady with him behind a high stack of wooden crates as he checked the dock area in the immediate vicinity of the *Bonanza King*. The docks were a hive of frenzied activity as precious goods were offloaded from several ships and passengers prepared to embark on one of the two passenger boats leaving that day for the ten-day journey to Vancouver and Seattle.

Coady concentrated on Snowden's expressions as he watched the goings on. He had given up the bloodied knife in favor of a pistol that she had seen in the waistband of his trousers beneath his coat. The knife was a silent purveyor of death, while a gun was certainly not. Her heart pounded painfully in her chest as Coady searched frantically for a scheme that would free her from this madman. She reasoned that if she could get the revolver and fire a single shot, men would come running to her rescue. The drawback to this, the most civilized plot she could devise on the spot, was that her rescuers would *have to go through her*, as Snowden had said, to get him. And she did not want to be Jay Snowden's shield. The police were the least of her concerns; they would be cautious about causing any harm to a civilian. But who could say whether some gun-toting dockhand might choose to intervene?

Snowden's plans for her once they were away from Dawson City were also worrisome and she assumed the worst, considering that she would be of little use to him after a time. She quickly surmised that the only way she was going to be helped was to help herself. If she managed to get his gun, the surprise alone might give her enough time to run. If only he would release his grip on her for a split second, she would be gone. If he did not, then she would shoot him. Hopefully she would merely wound the skunk. She did not want murder, even of so vile a character as Jay Snowden, on her conscience.

She felt his hand tighten even more on her arm.

"We are taking the Eldorado," he said, pulling her out from behind the row of crates. "Be a good girl and just walk with me."

"And if I do not, will you shoot me?" she dared, planting her feet. "I think not, for then you would have no protection."

Maintaining his grip, Snowden turned and faced her. "Have you considered the danger you will be in if you draw attention to us now?"

"A little attention might be a good thing." So saying, Coady's hand flashed forward and her fingers faultlessly wrapped around the handle of the pistol.

But Snowden did not relax his grip on her arm and he was fast enough to get a firm grip on her wrist.

Coady pulled the trigger.

Snowden blinked and then stared at her with a stunned

301

expression before he began to sink to his knees. His grip on Coady's wrist remained true for several seconds.

Coady watched in horror as he thumped onto his knees, giving little heed to his fingers slipping down to grip hers. The instant she realized what he was about, Coady jerked the gun in an attempt to free his death grip.

A second shot was fired even as men along the dock responded to the first.

A crowd quickly materialized.

Cries for a doctor rent the air as the gathered throng formed a circle around the wounded.

A man and a woman lay bleeding.

After only two days in Forty Mile, Stone and Ben had enough evidence to put Jay Snowden in jail for a very long time.

"We had best warn the local detachment," Stone said as they walked across the street to a rough-hewn cabin. "Now that the word is out, there are enough angry investors in this town alone to form a good-sized lynch party if they find Snowden before we do."

Ben was not as concerned for Snowden's hide. "They could save us a lot of trouble," he theorized. "By the time we sort out all of Snowden's conspiracies and schemes, we'll have built a mountain of paperwork."

Stone did not relish spending days at a desk completing paperwork either, but the chore went with the territory. He opened the door of the cabin that housed the local detachment of the Mounties and provided his name to the first uniformed officer he spied.

"MacGregor?" questioned the man. "Inspector Stone MacGregor?"

Stone nodded his head.

"There was a young policeman here looking for you about an hour ago, Inspector. Said his name was Elmer Guthrie. From the Dawson detachment."

"I know the man," said Stone. "I sent him back to Dawson three days ago."

"Well, he's here, Inspector, and looking for you. At least he was here. Since we did not know you were in town, we couldn't help him."

"Did he say why he was looking for me?"

The young officer shook his head. "Nope. Said it was urgent that he find you, that was all. Looked like he had traveled hard to get here, too."

Stone could only assume it was Simmons calling him back. He turned to Ben, frowning. "We had better head back at first light tomorrow." To the policeman, he said, "We have something to report. Something you should be aware of."

It did not take many moments for Stone and Ben to appraise the local authorities of all they had learned.

"Oh!" called the officer as Stone and Ben turned to leave. "Guthrie said, if we saw you, to say he was going back along the Twelvemile Creek. He thought maybe you had gone back to Snowden's camp."

Stone nodded. "Thanks. Hopefully we can catch him there."

Elmer Guthrie had been to Snowden's camp and was on his way back to Dawson City when Stone and Ben caught up with him.

"Jezzuz, Inspector, I've been looking for you everywhere."

"So I understand. What is the problem, Guthrie?"

"It's about Mrs. MacGregor, sir. Superintendent Simmons sent me."

Stone frowned as he detected the urgency in the lad's tone. "What about Mrs. MacGregor?"

Elmer hesitated, looking as if he thought Stone might consider shooting the messenger in this case.

"Spit it out, man!" Stone demanded. "What about her?"

"Well, sir, ah . . . she's been hurt."

Stone's impatience was gaining momentum. "Hurt?"

303

"Ah, yes, sir. Mrs. MacGregor has been shot."

Stone's complexion turned ashen before he could whirl his mount in the direction of Dawson City.

"Oh damn," breathed Ben as he, too, spurred his horse into action.

Chapter Twenty-five

Stone MacGregor did not spare his horse in his mad dash to reach his injured wife.

Coady had been shot more than four days before his return to Dawson City, by Stone's reckoning. The time it took would have been far less had Ben not convinced his superior officer of the foolhardiness of traveling at death-defying speeds during the dark of night.

"The terrain is rugged, Inspector," Ben had argued. "If your horse goes down you could break your neck. What help will you be to Coady then?"

Keystone had been right, of course.

That did not mean Stone had to like it.

They spent a few hours rolled in blankets, catching a little sleep while their exhausted mounts recovered. There was no time for food or coffee in the morning. In fact, there was little hint of the sun making an appearance when Stone jumped up, saddled his mount and was off at a gallop, leaving Ben to catch up as best he could.

Stone rode through Dawson's Front Street at a full

gallop, not allowing his horse to break stride before the animal's front hooves hit the boardwalk in front of the hotel. Stone's wild ride drew more than a little attention. As he took a leap from his still moving horse, he looked frantically at the gathering populace, praying someone would have an answer to his question. "Anyone know if my wife, Coady, is here or at the hospital?"

"Here!" called a man from the hotel entrance.

"Thanks!" Stone grunted as he rushed past the provider of the cherished information and bound for the stairs that would take him to their suite.

His spirits were somewhat buoyed by the fact that Coady was not in hospital. Surely, if she were badly hurt, she would not be left without care. He had mentally lashed himself a dozen times during the past day because he had not asked Elmer Guthrie one simple question: "How bad is Coady hurt?" He could have saved himself much anguish had he but taken just another moment of time. As it was he envisioned all manner of horrors as he pushed his horse for more speed. He envisioned Coady writhing in pain. He saw her pale and gasping for breath. His imagination presented a terrible view of his lovely wife laid out on the undertaker's table.

And it was his own damned fault!

He had panicked over the news Guthrie had brought him. The thought that he could lose Coady had struck pure terror in his heart. Never had he loved anyone the way he loved his pretty, smiling lass with her auburn hair and large brown eyes. Never would he love anyone the same. Losing her was equivalent to losing his own life. And their life together had only just begun. He could not, would not, think of it being over. There was so much more he wanted to experience with her.

Stone was breathing heavily by the time he pushed open the door of their suite. He was halfway across the sitting room as the door banged back against the wall.

Lying on the settee, Coady bolted upward and then yelped.

Stone stopped in his tracks. "Coady?"

Her smile would have aroused a more clear-thinking husband. "You are back. I'm so—"

Stone ran to settee and knelt by her side. "I was told you had been hurt," he said hurriedly.

"Oh, a little wou—"

"Should you not be in bed?" As he spoke his gaze anxiously traveled the length of her blanket-draped legs. "Where are you hurt, lass?"

Coady's complexion turned a brilliant purple as he reached down and drew the blanket away from her right leg.

Stone stared at the white gauze bandage for several moments before tears of relief sprang to his eyes.

"Stone?" Coady reached out and touched his hand as he rested his fingertips almost reverently below her knee. "Stone?"

He turned and looked at her, his prolonged agony unabashedly pouring forth.

"Oh, Stone," she breathed as she reached for him.

He went eagerly into her arms, wrapping his own around her, pulling her up tight against his chest, breathing in the scent of her freshly washed hair, the sweetness of her flesh. She smelled wonderful, womanly, and most important of all, very much *alive*. "I was afraid you would die before I could get here," he whispered against her ear.

Coady's head snapped back. "Die?"

He raised his head and looked at her, the moisture in his eyes receding as feelings of relief overtook everything else within him.

"I was never near death," she explained. "But a man was sent to find you, Stone. I don't understand."

Stone pulled back so that he could see her eyes more clearly. "He told me only that you had been shot."

Coady's complexion darkened again. "I shot myself," she confessed. "In the foot."

His eyes grew round and large. "You?"

She nodded her head.

"You shot yourself?"

Miffed by his teasing tone, she crossed her arms beneath her breasts. "Well, it hurt."

"I should think."

"And I was mortified."

He frowned at that. "My sweet, accidents do happen with guns. I am only thankful that you were not more seriously hurt."

"You don't understand."

He tipped his head to the side, curious. "You are still upset, lass. Explain to me."

Her eyes reflected anger as she looked up at him; anger, he suspected that was directed at herself.

"It was bad enough that I shot myself. Then, to make matters worse, I fell straight away into a faint," she said shortly.

Stone was beginning to feel very dense. "I do not see—"

"I have never fainted before in my entire lifetime," she said. "People will think you are wed to a weak-kneed ninny."

Stone could not help it, his lips formed into a happy smile. "You are not weak, nor are you a ninny, my love. Far from it."

"Well, others are now not so certain."

"I do not care what anyone thinks, Coady. I care only that you are alive and will soon be well. And you should not feel badly about a faint. I can assure you I have seen men injured far less who have passed out cold."

"Well, Vernon was injured far more seriously than I and he did not swoon."

Stone was visibly confused by this news. "Vernon?"

Coady nodded her head and pointed to the right side

of Stone's ribs. "He had a big knife right here. It is a wonder he did not die."

"Vernon was stabbed?"

"He will be weeks recovering. If not for Isobel's quick thinking—"

"Wait!" he said, holding up a hand to stop her flow of words. "What the devil has been going on here?"

"Oh, there is more I have to tell you," she said. "I murdered Jay Snowden."

"You mur—"

"Well, I did not actually murder him," she added quickly. "But I did kill him."

Stone's mouth had suddenly become very dry. "I think I need a good quaff of cognac," he muttered as he got to his feet.

Coady watched him walk to the corner table and reach for a bottle and a glass. As he was returning, she smiled. "Would you like me to start at the beginning?"

Stone lowered himself to the floor in front of the settee folding his legs Indian-fashion. "I think you had better," he said as he poured a full glass of cognac.

"Well, somehow Snowden, the skunk, knew that you were about to close in on him so he decided to kidnap me."

"He thought that would keep me from arresting him?"

"No. He wanted the police to have to go through me before they could get to him."

With that, Stone shuddered and raised his glass and took a long drink.

"Snowden, the swine, reasoned that none of the police would harm the wife of a senior officer so he planned to keep me with him until he got on a boat and away from here." She shrugged her shoulders. "I do not know what he planned for me once we were away but I surmised it would not be to my liking."

"An understatement," he muttered, shaking his head as if to clear his thoughts.

"Well," she said, warming to her tale. "In the dead

of night Snowden knocked a hole in the back wall of the bakery, planning to catch me there the following morning. But Vernon had been skulking around again and saw what Snowden was doing. He decided not to call the police that night."

"Vernon."

"Of course, darling. Vernon wanted to see *why* any man would simply cut a hole in the wall of a shop that had little or nothing of value in it. So he hid close by until morning."

"God bless, Vernon," Stone sighed.

"Precisely. However, Vernon watched Snowden go into the bakery and followed. By the time he got inside, Snowden had the knife to my throat."

Stone's stomach churned at the thought but when he looked at Coady, he was surprised to see an impish glint in her eyes. "You are relishing this?"

She nodded her head. "It is the most excitement I have seen since coming to the Yukon."

"Aside from 'Marriage by Design' going under."

"That was not exciting, my love, that was torture."

He smiled in the face of her admonishment. "Ah."

"The only part of this I do not like is having committed murder," she confessed.

"I believe you have left out a good portion of your story, lass. How did Vernon come to be stabbed?"

"He jumped on Snowden," she said, and continued to explain the events leading up to Snowden's death and her own mishap. "There!" she said contentedly. "Now you know everything. Oh, except the police arrested Mary Snowden. They have her in custody now."

Stone nodded his head and took another sip of brandy before setting the glass on the floor. "How is Vernon now?"

"He is coming along quite nicely, thanks to Isobel's nursing."

Stone arched a brow in surprise. "This day is full of surprises."

"I know," she chirped. "He is staying in Isobel's room. Do you not think that is wonderful?"

"It will be wonderful if he bends enough to ask her forgiveness."

"I do hope they reconcile," she said seriously. "But, if Vernon does try to get her back, Isobel has a confession that may drive them further apart." Coady looked visibly shaken as she thought of Isobel's secret. "She told me what Snowden had done to her, Stone. He wanted Vernon's gold. Surely Vernon will understand, though. Mary confessed to having drugged Isobel that night."

"If need be, I will talk with Vernon about that." He got to his feet and pulled Coady into a sitting position. "But right now, my love, I am more concerned about you." Once he was seated on the settee, Stone eased her back across his lap, his arm beneath her for added support. "Are you in terrible pain?"

Her brow wrinkled. "I am pained more by my own ineptness. People tend to laugh, Stone, when one confesses having shot oneself in the foot."

Stone, however, did not see the humor in it. "You could have been killed."

She shrugged. "Snowden most likely would have killed me anyway."

There was a somewhat timid knock on the door to which Stone bellowed, "Yes!"

Ben Keystone opened the door just enough to peer inside. "Am I intruding?"

"You are," Stone muttered, "but come in anyway."

"How are you, Coady?" the younger man asked as he entered the room.

"I am fine now that Stone is back," she confessed. "I was not badly hurt."

"Yes, I know." He cast an apprehensive glance at Stone. "I met Isobel outside and she explained. I suspect Elmer Guthrie will now remain a corporal forever."

Stone's gaze collided with Ben's and it was clear the

inspector would be having a word or two with Corporal Guthrie.

Coady was frowning. "I do not understand why Elmer did not tell you I was not seriously hurt."

"I have to confess some of the fault was mine. I did not ask him outright. But Guthrie was so damned backward in giving me news of you, I assumed the worst and rode off."

"Like a man on a rampage," Ben put in.

Coady turned a sympathetic look upon her husband. "Really, Stone?"

His fingertips brushed lightly across her cheek. "I was like a man demented."

Ben stuffed his hands in his pockets and cleared his throat. "I, ah, don't think I am needed around here. I will check in with you later, Inspector."

Stone nodded his head but did not look up. "Make that much later, lad."

Down the hall from the MacGregors' suite, Isobel was hovering over Vernon as he lay in his sick bed.

"More water?" she asked.

Vernon shook his head. "Why didn't you leave?" he asked.

"Where would I go?"

"Home. To your family where you belong."

"I don't belong there, Vernon," she said quietly. "I was very happy that you took me away from them."

"And turned you into a slave."

Isobel was startled by his comment. "I never felt like a slave," she assured him as she sat in the chair beside the bed.

"You worked like one," he said miserably. "I couldn't let you go on like that."

"You couldn't?" Isobel tipped her head to the side. "Don't you know that I was happier working beside you than I have ever been in my life?"

He raised his head and looked at her again. "You were?"

Isobel's eyes rounded as she realized her statement had come as a total shock to him. "Oh, Vernon," she sighed. "Did you send me away because of that?"

"I couldn't bear to watch you die at a young age from overwork. I've seen that happen too often."

"Coady was right, I should have screwed up my courage."

He blinked. "What does that mean?"

She leaned forward and reached for his hand. "It means I should have told you I love you, silly man," she said tenderly. "I should have told you I don't ever want to be anywhere on this Earth if you are not there."

He squeezed her fingers. "I guess my bullheadedness stopped you from telling me about the child?"

Isobel could not deny that claim. "It was so obvious you did not want me, that you did not love me. I didn't want the child to force your hand."

He smiled as his complexion darkened. "The thing is, I do love you, Isobel. I have loved you from the start. I just could not stand to see you working so hard when you were used to so much more. It hurt me. I worried for you and I knew I could probably never offer you much more than we had. When we were told we were not married, I saw that as your chance for salvation."

"My salvation happened the day you took me away from my overbearing mother. And having more didn't bring me happiness, Vernon. Only you can do that."

He pulled on her hand and she moved to sit on the side of the bed. "Will you give an old fool a second chance?" he said low.

Isobel pressed her cheek against his. "Don't you ever do that to me again, Vernon Shield."

Coady smiled, unaware that Ben was hastily departing their company. "I never thought I would see you cry," she murmured.

"They were tears of joy, lass," he said softly.

"You love me so much, Stone?"

"More than life, my love."

She snuggled against him, content and overwhelmed with her own brand of joy. Never had she known such love. Never had she known such feelings of security. Never had she been prepared to rely upon another human being the way she was willing to rely upon him. "I confess the same," she whispered.

Stone dropped a loving kiss upon the top of her head.

She smiled, staring at her bandaged foot. "Stone?"

"Hmm?"

"I do not feel any pain."

"I am glad for that," he murmured as he pressed his lips against her brow.

When he made no move, she laughed. "Well, what do I have to say?"

He raised his head and frowned down at her.

"Have you been away so long I have to point you in the direction of our bedroom?"

His frown became one of concern. "Are you sure, lass? I could hurt you."

She shook her head and touched his cheek with the palm of her hand. "You could never hurt me, Mr. MacGregor. You will never hurt me."

That was the truth of it, for them both.

Without hesitation, Stone settled her securely in his arms and wasted not another moment on talk.

It was some hours later before they lay back in their bed, pleasantly exhausted and content to merely hold each other.

"I am beginning to strongly suspect you have given me your son, Mr. MacGregor," she said.

Stone tipped up, supporting himself on an elbow. "You really think so, lass?"

She nodded her head. "I will consult with the doctor

tomorrow." She smiled radiantly. "Will you be as happy as I?"

Stone scooped her up in his arms. "Oh, yes, love. Yes," he murmured as he planted several sweet, loving kisses along her throat.

"Stone?"

"Hmm?"

"Did you check on the credentials of the man who married us?"

He threw back his head and laughed. "Oh, yes, love. Yes!"

JAGUAR EYES

Casey Claybourne

Daniel Heywood ventures into the wilds of the Amazon, determined to leave his mark on science. Wounded by Indians shortly into his journey, he is rescued by a beautiful woman with the longest legs he's ever seen. As she nurses him back to health, Daniel realizes he has stumbled upon an undiscovered civilization. But he cannot explain the way his heart skips a beat when he looks into the captivating beauty's gold-green eyes. When she returns with him to England, she wonders if she is really the object of his affections—or a subject in his experiment. The answer lies in Daniel's willingness to leave convention behind for a love as lush as the Amazon jungle.

___52284-5 $5.50 US/$6.50 CAN

Dorchester Publishing Co., Inc.
P.O. Box 6640
Wayne, PA 19087-8640

Please add $1.75 for shipping and handling for the first book and $.50 for each book thereafter. NY, NYC, and PA residents, please add appropriate sales tax. No cash, stamps, or C.O.D.s. All orders shipped within 6 weeks via postal service book rate. Canadian orders require $2.00 extra postage and must be paid in U.S. dollars through a U.S. banking facility.

Name_____
Address_____
City_____State_____Zip_____
I have enclosed $_____ in payment for the checked book(s).
Payment <u>must</u> accompany all orders. ❏ Please send a free catalog.

NORAH HESS

After her father's accidental death, it is up to young Fancy Cranson to keep her small family together. But to survive in the pristine woodlands of the Pacific Northwest, she has to use her brains or her body. With no other choice, Fancy vows she'll work herself to the bone before selling herself to any timberman—even one as handsome, virile, and arrogant as Chance Dawson.

From the moment Chance Dawson lays eyes on Fancy, he wants to claim her for himself. But the mighty woodsman has felled forests less stubborn than the beautiful orphan. To win her hand he has to trade his roughhewn ways for tender caresses, and brazen curses for soft words of desire. Only then will he be able to share with her a love that unites them in passionate splendor.

_3783-1 $5.99 US/$6.99 CAN

Dorchester Publishing Co., Inc.
P.O. Box 6640
Wayne, PA 19087-8640

Please add $1.75 for shipping and handling for the first book and $.50 for each book thereafter. NY, NYC, and PA residents, please add appropriate sales tax. No cash, stamps, or C.O.D.s. All orders shipped within 6 weeks via postal service book rate. Canadian orders require $2.00 extra postage and must be paid in U.S. dollars through a U.S. banking facility.

Name_____
Address_____
City_____State_____Zip_____
I have enclosed $_____ in payment for the checked book(s).
Payment <u>must</u> accompany all orders. ❏ Please send a free catalog.